I went back down ... Tim. It was seale ... ered me in. It stil ... smell that follow ... shown me the photos, so I knew exactly how she'd been found. Sitting at her desk, slumped over it, most of her head missing. The window-frame was still stained, but someone had cleaned the glass. The top of the desk was ingrained with copper-coloured blood. I ran my finger over it, morbidly: 'I liked her, Tim. I liked her a lot.'

Also by Bernard Bannerman in Sphere Books

THE LAST WEDNESDAY

CONTROLLING INTEREST

BERNARD BANNERMAN

SPHERE BOOKS LIMITED

A SPHERE BOOK

First published in Great Britain by Sphere Books Ltd 1989

ISBN 0 7474 0383 X

Printed and bound in Great Britain by
Cox & Wyman Ltd, Reading

Sphere Books Ltd
A Division of
Macdonald & Co (Publishers) Ltd
Orbit House
1 New Fetter Lane
London EC4A 1AR
A member of Maxwell Macmillan Pergamon Publishing Corporation

For Pamela *and* Andrew

Chapter One

'Jabulon,' he said.

Jabu-who?' I asked.

'Jabulon,' Russel Orbach repeated like he was telling me the time of day.

'And who, when he's at home, is Jabulon?'

'You asked me – or would have done so if you knew anything about grammar: of whom is Andrew Mather more frightened than his father, and I am telling you – Jabulon.'

We were at Frederick's Restaurant on Camden Passage in Islington, in the downstairs, glassed-in garden room, and I was paying.

Two questions spring immediately to mind. The first is why we were in Frederick's, rather than my usual eatery in North London, M'sieur Frog's. The food at Fred's is twice as expensive, and because the cuisine is nouvelle you only get half as much. The answer is that I was foolish enough to invite Orbach to name the place for our meet and he had the sense to make it cost.

Which leads to the second question. Why was I dining with my arch-bogeyman – if not enemy – Russel Orbach? The answer is somewhat more complicated than to the first question. I have to go a little way back in time to explain. At least as far back as the morning I attended on Ian Mather – Iron Ian as he is known throughout the legal profession in which his stature is about as near to the top as mine is to the bottom – at his office off High Holborn.

I could see why they called him Iron Ian. His manner was as flexible as a rigid steel girder. He sat across a desk bigger than the bed platform in my Earl's Court basement apartment, where between jobs I spend the greater part of my life. It took me several minutes to cross the office after I was ushered in by his secretary's legs. But apart from the leather desk set, the desk was entirely empty of files or documents; only that morning's *Times* lay on it, at an angle so true it must have been set in place with a T-square.

'Did you know?' He asked by way of opening greeting, turning *The Times* around so that I didn't need to read it upside down, and pointing to a two inch column towards the bottom of the front page.

'I heard,' I said.

I'd heard the night before, when Sandy rang to tell me. Once upon a time, Sandy Nicholl and I were partners in a law firm in north London. Nicholl & Co, not Nicholl & Woolf. Once upon another time, she kicked my butt out of the office so hard it took me several years to pick myself up out of the gutter I landed in. I bore no grudges. She was right. I was doing myself more harm than the firm. My specialism was defending drug dealers; I liked to get paid in kind.

In the middle of the Disraeli Chambers' case, we'd re-encountered, not entirely coincidentally, and she'd jolted me with an altogether different kind of shock: we became lovers and so had remained, on and off, since. At the time of her call, we were off, and its subject-matter had quite a lot to do with why.

The article began:

'The body of a woman solicitor was discovered by staff arriving yesterday morning at the Holborn offices of the prestigious London solicitors, Mather's. Katrina Pankhurst, 32, had been shot. Police are investigating.' The article was accompanied by a photograph, ten years old, probably the formal picture taken at the admission ceremony. I'd read another paper already that morning, *The Times*' sister-paper, *The Sun*. They had somehow obtained a more recent, holiday snapshot, and published a picture of Katrina Pankhurst in a bikini.

Katrina. Kat, I used to call her, sometimes to her

annoyance. Hanky Pankhurst on other, less public occasions, when she wasn't in a position to deny it. For a few months, now about seven or eight years ago, Katrina had been employed by Nicholl & Co as a locum for an assistant solicitor on maternity leave. She had done her training at Mather's; in short order married, quit work and separated; after she left us she went back to Mather's. During her stay with us we had, in a desultory fashion, been lovers. Our affair ended the day she returned to Mather's.

I waited for Mather to continue. I had been summonsed the previous afternoon, with a letter hand-delivered by a uniformed flunky carrying a bright red leather bag. He stood at my basement door, hesitating at the vision of me unshaven, bleary-eyed, hungover and still not dressed:

'Mr Woolf?' he asked doubtfully.

I mumbled ambiguously. He might have been a debt collector, though most of those from whom I borrow money don't employ uniforms to get it back. More like animals.

'Mr David Woolf?' he repeated.

I shrugged:

'I guess. Whaddayawant?'

'I have a letter for you, sir, from Mr Mather, from Mr Ian Mather.'

I got the point. God wanted my attention. I held out a hand and, reluctantly, he passed it over. I started to shut the door in his face, but he shook his head:

'I'm to take an answer back, sir.'

I felt like telling him to bottle my bad breath and take that back to his lord and master. But most of the reason my breath was bad was booze, and most of the reason I was drinking was because I didn't have money to eat. I ripped open the envelope to see what Mather wanted. I read that he required to see me, on a professional matter, the following morning at nine o'clock. I was invited to confirm to the bearer that this would be convenient.

Convenient it wasn't. At nine in the morning, I am largely incapable of coherence. Like Tallulah Bankhead, I hardly knew there were two nine o'clocks in the day. The most I can normally manage is to roll off my bed, hang onto the railing to stop myself falling off the balcony, slide down the ship's-pitch steps and try to stay upright until I reach the lavatory. I re-read the letter. I hadn't imagined it. There was definitely a reference to a professional matter. As reluctantly as the messenger had handed me the letter, I conceded that I could keep the appointment.

I promptly went back to bed. It wasn't that I needed more sleep, even in anticipation of an early start the next day. More that I had nothing else to do. My last case had ended abruptly when I'd informed my client that the man his wife was sleeping with was a considerable improvement. I hate sex-snooping almost as much as I hate serving summonses. With divorce available from mail-order catalogues, you'd think no one would care anymore: but they still want to know who. That was a month before, and I hadn't worked since.

I lay in bed with my arms folded behind my head on the pillow. What could Ian Mather want with me? A firm like Mather's has a couple of the larger investigative outfits on retainer, and its pick of all the rest. Its clients were rich enough to afford the biggest and best. Mather himself was believed to be so powerful he could use the police as an alternative, even if no crime was involved. He was a sometime freemason, a member of the governing board of the United Grand Lodge of England and Wales, the central body of freemasonry throughout the English-speaking world.

If that wasn't enough, the firm's principal client was Sterling Latimer: Latimer International, Latimer Communications, Latimer Chemicals and Pharmaceuticals, Latimer Computers, Latimer this, that and anything that people can be seduced to spend money on. Most Latimer subsidiaries were so powerful that they constituted a significant economic influence in their individual areas of operation. When Latimer called, so they said, the marshalls of democracy, the captains of industry and the colonels of military juntae alike came running. Though an American, Latimer had made his

4

first millions in this country, before returning in triumph to buy up most of his native land. What could Ian Mather want with me?

While I waited for him to explain, I withdrew a pack of Camels from the pocket of my cracked leather jacket. Even I knew a leather jacket wasn't conventional wear for a visit to a man like Mather, but it was the only one I had apart from my suit, and that was still waiting to be cleaned after I fell into a puddle outside Lewis' night club on the Old Brompton Road after an otherwise spectacularly uneventful evening a couple of weeks before.

I'm not sure if I really enjoy Camels, but did you ever hear of a private eye smoking Silk Cut or Number Six?

'I'd rather you didn't smoke,' Mather said flatly, expecting to be obeyed.

I shrugged:

'That's OK. It's been nice meeting you. We could do this more often, whaddayathink?' I got up and started the long, slow trek back out of his office, picking my feet one at a time out of the deep pile carpet. Between the cows that produced the leather furniture, and the sheep that grew the wool, Mather was keeping the animal kingdom pretty well occupied, if shorn.

I'd almost reached the door, believing my bluff had been called and silently cursing my stupid pride, when he snapped:

'Wait.'

I didn't turn around. There was a word missing: please.

Instead, he used his intercom to tell his secretary to bring in an ashtray. I didn't tell him I didn't mind using the floor but waited for her to come in, so I could follow her across the room again, watching the way she moved and wondering if it was still possible to get it up at Ian's age. Though he didn't look it, I knew he was in his early seventies. Money's a great way to keep your health: I'd like to look that good at his age. As a matter of fact, I'd like to look that good now.

I sat down again. He was a clever man. He'd let me

win the first round so that I wouldn't be so willing to gamble on the second. He brought his hands together in a spire and asked:

'What is it with your sort, Woolf?'

'What sort's that, Mather?'

'What is it you want, Mr Woolf?'

'You asked me to come to see you. I want you should tell me why. I want you should stop talking to me like I was a junior articled clerk. And I want you should tell me how much you're going to pay me.'

'I take it that last is the most important?'

Now I knew what sort I was. Whenever I meet anyone new, I have an irrational impulse to tell them I'm a Jew. An old Jew I once talked with about it explained that it wasn't pride, but self-defence. If you don't tell them straight out, they're bound to come out with something racist, and that's embarrassing because either you have to put up with it, which makes you feel like a coward, or provoke a hostile scene, which reinforces the image as excitable and aggressive. I should have listened to him and told Mather before we'd even begun.

We glowered at one another for a full minute. I hoped he had someone to charge for it because I was certainly going to make him pay me.

'I know about you, Mr Woolf. When this happened, yesterday, I called for Miss Pankhurst's personal file, and saw your name. She worked for you for a brief period. Your name was familiar, and I remembered it from the Disraeli Chambers' business.'

I remembered it from then too. I'd like to describe it as my biggest case, but the truth is it's the only big one I ever handled. A bunch of left-wing barristers were being offed, one by one and it took me from number three to number five to make the connections needed to bring it to an end. In my moments of fantasy – which means whenever I'm not asleep – I like to think of myself as the lawyers' investigator, the way some surgeons can be described as who doctors would choose to be operated on by.

'What happened?' he asked, apparently idly. Most of

6

the true story never came out. Too many people would have been embarrassed: Russel Orbach, for example.

'What happened is what you read. The rest is privileged.'

He didn't argue. By accident, I'd given the answer that allowed him to open up:

'It's about Miss Pankhurst. . .'

That much I'd worked out for myself. But all I said was:

'It was Mrs, actually. Pankhurst was the name of her first husband, while she was at university.' For that reason, she used to say, it didn't count. 'She got a great deal of mileage out of the name, but the big secret was, it wasn't her own to start with.'

He looked at me blankly. I don't think he got the point. I'm not even sure the name Pankhurst meant anything special to him at all. Women's suffrage was still a bit progressive for his taste. Apart from his own daughter – one of his four children in the firm – there were no women partners, nor of course Jews or blacks.

He cleared his throat:

'I want you, uh, to investigate, Mr Woolf. I want you to investigate her death.'

I paused to take it in. He was a pillar of the establishment, a believer through and through in all things English and Tory-blue. Granted, a member of his staff had died, and not of the heart-failure which comes with the pay-packet in a place as pressurized as Mather's. All the same, his only instinct ought to have been to leave the matter in the hands of the police.

'Why?'

'Why what, Mr Woolf? That is what you do, isn't it? Investigate?'

'Yeah, I guess. Sometimes. But why do you want me to investigate her death? That's what I'm asking.'

He swivelled around in his chair, so that his back was to me, and I heard him sighing as he stared out the bay window. When he turned round again, he looked like he'd aged a decade. The silver hair, each one laid in place by Prince Philip's barber, was now white, and maybe there weren't that many of them after all. He was slumped back in his chair. You could no longer line up the Coldstream Guards by the cut of his suit.

He coughed to clear his throat again:

'My sons, Mr Woolf. My sons are partners in this firm.'

'I know.' All the same, the name of the firm had remained Mather's, the apostrophe before the 's', not after it. It had never been Mather & Co, nor certainly Mather & anyone else. To write it as Mathers was near heresy.

He was having a hard time telling me. I decided to help him out:

'Your sons are partners in this firm, and two of them had affairs with Katrina Pankhurst, right. You're worried how an investigation will impact on them. You're worried what comes out. You don't want me to investigate; you want me to shadow the police investigation, and protect your image.'

The blood had drained from his face when I told him I knew his sons had both, at different times I hasten to add, had affairs with Kat, and I don't think he heard the rest of what I said because all he asked was:

'How did you know?'

I shrugged:

'It's my job, knowing things. That's why I don't think you really want to hire me, Mr Mather. Because I'm not into saving faces; I want to know who killed Kat, far worse than you do; I'd like to see them swing for it, but since we don't have the death penalty anymore, I'll settle for a minimum stretch of a quarter ton. If I start working for you, that's what I'm going to be trying to do, and if one of your sons is involved, that's what's going to happen to them.'

My speech contained a lot of bravado. But I meant some of it. At least the bit about wanting to see whoever killed Kat swing for it. I don't generally believe in the death penalty; people are pretty shitty anyhow, and most of us don't hang for it. But there's a small number of offences in which I have no doubt it's still essential: stealing from me, getting in my way and hurting my friends. I don't have much to steal, I don't go nowhere

8

much, and I don't have so many friends I can afford to lose.

He began to catch up with me:

'I said I knew about you, Mr Woolf, and I do.' He opened a drawer in the desk and withdrew a folder: 'This is your file,' he extracted a computer print-sheet.

'My file? I got a file at Mather's?' I was genuinely astonished.

'We keep files on everyone we can, Mr Woolf,' his lips twitched in what I'm fairly sure was an attempt to smile.

I'd never really understood before what they mean by advanced information technology. I thought maybe it just meant you got information at the touch of a button rather than a touch of a secretary; I'd rather remain old-fashioned, especially when they look like Ian Mather's.

Solicitors keep files, of course; case-files. The only reason a firm would retain a file on another solicitor would be if the solicitor in question was one of the parties to an action, not merely the opponent's representative. But I could see the value of storing information about how lawyers conducted themselves, their procedural weak points, their sharp tactics, their resources and contacts, their strengths and their Achilles' heels.

'What does it tell you, Mr Mather?'

He closed the file before he answered, to emphasize that he'd pre-read and absorbed it.

'It tells me you're a fighter. It tells me you never let go. It tells me you don't settle unless you never even had a case to begin with.' That was the good news. 'It tells me you did better by your clients than you did by yourself. It tells me your respect for the law was hardly greater than theirs. It tells me that if you hadn't left practice, you probably would have been thrown out of the profession.'

'I was,' I said: 'I didn't leave my practice, I was thrown out of it by my partner.'

'Sandra Nicholl.'

'Yup. Sandy. We're good friends now, though. And Kat was a good friend. I saw her about a month ago.'

He nodded, understanding I had now told him how I knew about her and his sons.

'And what else did she tell you, Mr Woolf?'

'Most of what else is worrying you. In particular, she told me about the leaks.'

'Ah,' he expelled air. The worst was over. The thing he found most difficult of all to tell me was something I already knew.

A murder on the premises is bad news for a law-firm. It discourages clients. It's natural. After all, as the barristers at Disraeli Chambers had discovered, clients aren't keen to start off a case with a lawyer who is not expected to live to see it through. It also discourages recruits, which is damaging to a firm like Mather's with a large reputation, a lot of clients, but very few part-ners. They need new, young, salaried blood to put in the hours, charging for which keeps the profit-sharing partners in new carpets, cars and caviar.

But a thorough professional would prefer a murder to a leak any day of the week. Even a client on legal aid – than whom there is no lower – doesn't want a solicitor who can't keep a secret. And Mather's clients' secrets are worth a lot more than those of a tenant confronting eviction or even a drug dealer confronting cold turkey and turnkey. Aside from Latimer – and that's a fairly hefty aside; Kat reckoned more than a million chargeable pounds a year – their clients in-cluded major banks, share-issuing public corporations, patent-owning engineering companies, every branch of the media, and on occasion the government itself.

The idea of Mather's as untrustworthy was about as absurd as suggesting that Prince Charles is a KGB agent. (I think I'm not allowed to say the Queen, even in jest. Mind you, if most of MIs 5 and 6 and the Queen's art adviser have at one time or another been in the pay of the alleged enemy, maybe the idea isn't that absurd after all).

But that was precisely what Katrina was suggesting when we met. It isn't what I'd been expecting to hear when she rang. Then, I thought maybe after all these years she'd finally realized what she'd been passing up, though that isn't what I said when I returned her call.

'Looking for work, huh?'

'Yes, sure,' she laughed: 'I'm really likely to give up a job at Mather's to come scavenge in the gutter with you.'

'What, then?' I waited optimistically, and wasn't too disappointed in her reply.

'Are you free to meet sometime soon?'

'I could make time. Any day between now and next year any good to you?'

'Gee, I don't know, Dave. What about the year after? Next week? Monday evening?'

'Not re-married, I gather.' Only unpartnered, and the very long married, volunteer an evening, and I've already explained that I knew she couldn't be the latter.

'Right. Nor looking to,' she put a damper on my hopes.

She wasn't a great looking woman. A bit overweight. Her hair was a mess and her dress sense was markedly inferior to her ability at law. But she was warm, and good company. We used to get stoned, go out to the late night supermarkets, stock up on sweet goodies to feed the munchies, and come back, usually to her place rather than mine, to settle in front of the fire and gradually undress the night away. I'd always thought, she knew what she liked and she knew how to get it.

We met in the Freemason's Arms on Longacre. Despite the name, they let women in. She was late and I was already a large Southern Comfort – no ice, no soda – ahead. She dumped her bag beside me and apologized:

'Sorry. Conference with counsel.'

A lot of people don't understand the English legal profession, and that includes a lot of lawyers. The profession is split into two. There are solicitors, who the client has to see first; but if a matter involves some extremely difficult legal task like looking up a bit of law, or has to go to court, the solicitor instructs a barrister to advise or represent. They're the ones with the fancy wigs and funny collars. It's a very cosy relationship, which means the punter has to pay for two lawyers when he probably doesn't even need one: the solicitor who rips him off in the office, and the barrister who sells him out in court.

Conferences with counsel happen at the end of the day. The client and the solicitor trek down to the Temple, where most of the barristers in London work, so that the barrister can find out what a case is about before he actually stands up to present or defend it in court, usually the next morning. With two lawyers in attendance, both paid by the hour, conferences invariably take twice as long as they ought.

Kat gestured at my drink:

'Another?'

'When did I ever say no? Besides, you've already told me there's no point staying sober.'

She pulled a face:

'Still as obvious as ever, Woolf.'

'I wouldn't like to disappoint.' I swallowed the last of my drink and handed her the glass, watching her disappear into the after-work throng and re-emerge efficiently, with a refill for me and a gin and tonic for herself.

She had changed. She looked good. She'd lost weight, her hair was expensively coiffeured, and I guess she spent more of that Mather money on clothes than she used to spend of Sandy's and mine. But, then, there was much more of it to spend. Mather's – for all the Scots influence in the firm – paid well: that's how they managed to keep their salaried solicitors without offering too many of them partnerships.

We bantered good-naturedly while she unwound, swapping names and gossip. She asked about Disraeli Chambers and I told her a whole lot more than later I was to tell her boss. I asked if she ever briefed them:

'No way. They're far too left-wing for Mather's.'

'What about Orbach?' He was already an ex-member when I was involved. Indeed, his efforts had been directed towards making many more of them ex-: ex-members and ex-humans. Orbach was a Queen's Counsel, which is a senior barrister and a mark of considerable success, professional and financial. She shook her head:

'You have to be a card-carrying Tory or a freemason – preferably both – to screw a brief out of Mather's.'

'But not to be employed there?' I doubted she would have joined the Tory party: it already had one female star and she didn't like competition. And the freemasons don't have women members.

She shrugged:

'To get to be partner. Anyway, I'm friendly with most of the children so I guess I'm protected.'

'How many are there?' At that time, I knew only that Mather's was, above all else, a family fiefdom, but I didn't know any of the details.

'Four,' she told me, listing them briefly. The oldest was Randolph, then came Martin, then – in age but, on account of her sex, not next in the pecking order of the firm's hierarchy – Allison Mather Hoyt, and finally the spoiled brat of the family, Andrew.

'Are they all in London?' Mather's had three provincial offices: Manchester, Birmingham and Bristol, serving the north, the midlands and the west of England. I'd read an article about the way they had linked the offices up to share resources, using computers and other technological innovations I didn't begin to understand.

The article was in the *Law Society's Gazette*, the journal of the profession's governing organization, on the principal committee of which Ian Mather had also served, and on sub-committees of which some of his children still sat. I read it not because I was interested in technology, but because – like everyone else – I'm fascinated by power and by how the rich spend their money.

She confirmed that all the children were in London:

'So's John Gauldie. He's the second partner. He and Ian have been together for ever.' The firm had been founded by Mather shortly after the Second World War. He had had, as they used to say, a good war; he had served his country proud, and his country was going to serve him proudly back. His father was a Scots industrialist and that for which Mather's was earliest known was the way Ian had put his father's money into resources and facilities long before the rest of the profession reluctantly shrugged off the habits of the last century and caught up with this. In this respect, Mather had learned from the Americans.

Kat had booked a table at the Cafe Pelican on St Martin's Lane. It's a French theme cafe. The waiters wear long-tailed tuxedoes, carry trays of pungent french pastries high above their shoulders, call out to one another with heavy, guttural accents, sport six o'clock shadows and reek of Gauloise. At least one of them had probably once taken a day-trip to Calais.

I wasn't complaining. Kat was paying.

'I figure I can afford it better than you.'

'I ain't arguing, Kat.'

'Don't call me that,' she hissed: 'I've told you before.'

She wasn't the only one who thought it sexist to call women by a diminutive. Sandy used to get angry with me about some of my pet abbreviations. Once, for a whole week, I insisted on calling her Sandra Jane, which is her full name. We reached a sort of truce when she sent a postcard to my home listing all my male friends I call by an abbreviation. The list didn't cover the card, but that's only because I don't have many friends.

'What do you want me to call you? Ms Pankhurst?' Am I the only one who finds Ms completely unpronounceable?

'Try calling me by my name,' she snapped.

'You're beginning to sound like a wife,' I protested mildly: 'I thought you said. . .' I let the sentence drift back into the nowhere it had begun. She caught my meaning:

'I know about you and Sandy,' she said.

It wasn't exactly a state secret, but we'd been out of

14

touch for a long time and, so far as I knew, she and Sandy had never been close. I wasn't pleased she knew; I've never been able to think of an answer to female solidarity as an excuse not to hop into my bed. Since the revised Katrina had arrived in the pub, I was less willing to accept the limits she had set for the evening than I had been on the 'phone.

'How?'

'I heard. I can't remember who from. It doesn't matter. It didn't surprise me. I always expected it.'

'You did?' I was truly shocked. It had been the last thing I expected when Sandy and I had re-encountered, and we'd never got it on when we'd been in partnership.

'Sure. Anyone could've guessed you'd end up together. You were made for each other, like a couple of old trees planted next to one another in a clearing in the forest.'

Kat had a feel for metaphors. I'd forgotten that too, as well as not to call her Kat.

We were into the second bottle, and main course (steak: if I'm not working, I grab it when I can; it might be my last meal for a week) before she began to talk about what was worrying her. It took me more probing than I get from the dentist on my once every five years visit, and that's saying something.

'You gonna tell me why you called, or do I got to drag it out of you like pine needles from a carpet after Christmas.'

'Hey, that's not bad. Can I have it?'

'Be my guest. I'm yours. So? Tell. If it's not my body you're after, what's on your mind?'

'Couldn't it be I just wanted to see an old friend?'

'After these years, you suddenly can't wait to see me? Really.'

But she wasn't listening to my answer. People often do that, like they aren't expecting me to say anything worthwhile.

'You are a friend, aren't you, Dave? I mean, I know it was never that big a deal between us, and I know we haven't been in touch forever, but whenever I think about you, you know, I always think of you like a friend, I'm very fond of you.'

Her eyes were watery. I took her hand:

'I'm your friend, Kat. I'm not saying I wouldn't mind being more, but I'm at least your friend. O.K.?'

She laughed:

'You never give up, do you?'

'What's the line that reminds me of?' I asked.

She knew exactly what I must be thinking of. The reason she and I could communicate so easily, even after such a long break, is because we both believed that few of life's truths couldn't be found somewhere in Hill Street Blues. The show had finished in the States by this time. They kill everything good in America: the Kennedys, Martin Luther King, John Lennon, the Cavett interviews and now Hill Street.

But England was – as England is – years behind, and we were still only half-way through the penultimate series. To help locate it, Robin was at this time still pregnant with Mick's Kid.

'It's in the pilot. La Rue's chatting up Joyce Davenport who he doesn't know is having an affair with Furillo. She says: "Have you quite finished, detective?" And he says, meaningfully: "No, ma'am, I don't finish for a very long time. I just go on and on."'

She was right. It was the line I'd been reminded of:

'And she pours a cup of coffee on his crotch, right?'

Thus did we fully re-establish communication between us.

The story came, when it came, in bits and bobs, like she had upended a jigsaw box and a few pieces were already stuck together to make tiny, but identifiable, parts of the whole. She didn't present it like the skilled lawyer she certainly was. But, then, she wasn't consulting me as a lawyer, only as a friend.

'Did you read, a while ago, oh, maybe a month ago, about the L.C.P. business?'

I shook my head. Unless someone's paying me to do so, I don't read much. Not even the papers. Anyhow, not the ones with a lot of words in. That's why later I

16

didn't turn to *The Times* for an account of her death, but to *The Sun*.

'You must've,' she insisted: 'It was the largest single personal injuries settlement ever in English legal history.'

It struck a faint chord in the back of my befuddled mind. I'd probably heard it on the t.v. news.

'Babies with bits missing?'

'Yuk, but yes.'

I also managed to remember, or work out that LCP meant Latimer Chemicals and Pharmaceuticals.

'Your case?'

'Not mine personally, but the firm's of course.' Of course. It was hardly likely to be Nicholl & Co. On either side. Way out of our league.

'What about it?'

She hesitated one last time, but since she'd booked the evening to tell me, and had to pay for the meal anyway, she went ahead:

'We should have been able to fight it and win. All the evidence was on our side. God knows it ought to have been: most of the expert witnesses worked at some time or another in an institution funded by Latimer, and even if they didn't would want to tap him for research money eventually.'

'I love scientists. They've got the same sort of integrity we lawyers have.'

'I thought you called yourself a private eye these days?'

'Mostly I don't call myself anything. Go on,' I wasn't going to let her back off now. It wasn't that I gave a damn about the subject – personally, I think babies are a pretty bad idea anyhow: they shit and piss and vomit all over the place, and they can't make decent conversation. But I like to know things that others don't, just for its own sake.

'There was just one report which was damning. It was very damning, too. We had it, of course, but the other side got their hands on it and that was it. We had to settle.' I swallowed the impulse to point out that hands was what the other side were missing.

17

'Wouldn't it have to have been discovered anyway?'

Her eyes shone: this was the bit of the job she loved best. Out-manoeuvring the opposition:

'Hell, no. Discovery's for the birds.'

Discovery is the process by which one party to civil litigation has to disclose to the other the documents pertaining to the case which are in his possession. He also has to list those which have been in his possession, even if they no longer are. The only things not discoverable are documents which were prepared with the litigation in mind, such as witness statements, instructions to counsel and correspondence with the client.

In England, discovery is done by lists prepared by lawyers. That way, so the theory goes, the other side can rely on its integrity. The implication of what Kat was saying was that their disclosure in the case would have been less than complete.

She explained how it worked. You only have to discover what is or has been in the possession of a party to the action. In English law, every company is a separate legal person. Latimer had so many subsidiaries, affiliates, even spare companies kept for just such an eventuality as this, that he could show his lawyers a document – for them to evaluate and advise on – in the name of one company, even though what it affected was the affairs of another.

I sniffed:

'It's about as sharp a practice as any of mine.' I didn't like it, either. It was a practice only available to the wealthy. It is procedures like discovery which are intended to place everyone on an equal footing before the law. I didn't need telling the law wasn't equal, but I didn't enjoy being reminded.

'Why're you so surprised, Dave? Didn't you teach me that lawyers are about beating law not upholding it? Mather's aren't different; just better at it. Anyway,' she continued: 'The scientist who did this particular piece of research was no schmuk. He took it to Latimer in the States. I don't know who. One of the Latimer's companies. Coincidentally – I'm sure you're going to find this difficult to believe – he came to the conclusion that his research method may have been unsound just about the same time he was offered some very heavy funding, by Latimer of course.'

'So recanting in open court wouldn't be particularly convincing, right?'

'Right. Meanwhile, and just in case the other side did get hold of it, a copy was sent over here. And that's where the leak came from.'

'Ah, come on, Kat. . .uh. . .rina. How'd'you know it came from Mather's? It could've come from anywhere. It's a classic case for a bleeding heart leak.'

'I agree, which rules out Mather's. But Latimer – in another incarnation – has developed some heavily sophisticated copying equipment, which means you can trace exactly where a copy came from, even several copies down the line. Part of the settlement was, they got back the leaked copy. And Latimer says: it came from Mather's.'

I still wasn't impressed. One leak don't a flood make. Why had Katrina called me out of my cellar to tell me about it?

'Because it's not the first. It's not even the second. I don't know how many leaks there have been from Mather's, but I do know quite a few.'

She told me about them. The first had been a libel action, where the defendant newspaper's principal witness had some long-spent form under another name which nobody knew about – or was supposed not to. Next had been a society divorce, where the husband had a half-million pound estate in the Bahamas his wife hadn't been told about in an admittedly extremely brief marriage but which, again, she found out about just in time to cash it in. The client, and his wife, had both been friends of Randolph and Andrew: Martin and an assistant had to handle the case; the other brothers were too close.

Last of the ones she told me about was a commercial landlord-tenant dispute, which hinged on for how long the landlords could be proved to have known about a construction defect. At the last moment, a discreet connection was made which fixed them with liability dating back several more years than admitted and qualified the damages for inclusion in the telephone directory. In other cases, there were files not in the right place at the right time, and that reappeared shortly before the position of a Mather's client took a sharp downward plunge. And, she assured me, I didn't want to know about stocks and shares: insider dealing.

I heard her out, but something was missing. She wasn't implicated in any of the incidents. She wasn't a partner. She didn't stand to lose financially, nor even if the unthinkable occurred and the matter became public knowledge, would it be her reputation that suffered. I reminded her of an elementary proposition:

'Lawyers are human. They all talk. Granted, they don't usually to the other side, but who knows who's connected to who. They have to talk, you know that. They have to show off to people just how important they are, how privy to privileged information, how trusted. And to do that, once in a while, they have to, well, spill the colour of their beans.'

She pulled a face:

'That's one of the worst mixed metaphors I've ever heard, Dave.' Then she paused for thought: 'Isn't it?'

'I don't know, Katrina. That isn't the point, anyway. The point is: it isn't really enough to be worth a first-class stamp on a letter home, let alone to spend an evening with me. Is it?' There had to be more.

Chapter Two

Without answering, she got up and went to the lavatory. On her way back, she stopped to talk to our waiter and ask for her bill.

'I'd like to go home now. You can come with me if you want.'

I have had more romantic propositions. But beggars can't be choosers. Meekly, I rose and went for a piss while she settled up, just in case I'd misunderstood her offer to pay.

We took a cab back to her flat in Maida Vale. I hate taxis. Not only are they expensive, but the drivers are unbelievably boring. They insist on expressing opinions about everything, and their views are mostly somewhere to the right of Attila the Hun, sometimes even as far to the right as Margaret Thatcher or Ronald Reagan. They're so stupid, they believe they're worth listening to.

There is, however, one time when it is safe to grab a cab. That is late at night, when you're with a person of the opposite sex. Sub-moronic as the average cabbie undoubtedly is, he (and it always is he) can just about make the connection between being left to your own devices and the size of his tip. We sat in the back, a safe distance apart, in silence. I had been idly window-shopping for about ten minutes before I identified the snuffling sound beside me. Kat, gently and effortlessly, was crying.

'Hey, hey,' I slid along the seat and put my arms around her shoulders, drawing her head down onto my shoulder, stroking her hair: 'It's OK, Kat. Whatever it is, it'll be OK.'

She sniffed back her tears and pulled away:

'Careful. You wanna know what that hair cost?' She covered up with humour.

'Funny. They gave it away free the day I was born.'

'Looks like it,' she said. But she took my hand and held onto it so long I decided she might have begun to change her mind about the evening's end-game, though not firmly enough to make me give the driver a tip any larger than I thought I could manage without physical retaliation.

I remembered the very first time I had seen her apartment. She had been working for us for about four weeks, and we had been flirting – the way the single, at a loose end, do – for three weeks and seven days. Popping a head round the door at the end of the day, asking about 'a quick one' (drink). Those quick ones are the worst: they creep up on you unprepared, and the next thing you're too drunk to do anything with it. I think I'll use it as the title of my autobiography: 'Just A Quick One'.

That day, I had been appearing in West London Magistrate's Court, which was too near home for me to contemplate trekking all the way back to the office at the end of the day. But I needed a file for my next case. Kat's home in Maida Vale was about half-way to mine. She agreed to take the file with her, and I would call up for it later. After a couple of solitary joints, I floated over around nine o'clock, and twelve hours later that was the time I left.

We almost always made it at her flat. It was the sole possession with which she had emerged from her second marriage. It was a millstone: it cost more to run than she could afford. Her husband was some kind of City whiz-kid. Ostensibly, his company was engaged in corporate publicity and promotion, like when someone's stock needed a boost before it made a takeover bid, or in order to avoid one. But their fees were often paid in kind, and Tony Galucci had a finger in so many pies I always wondered how he could tell what each one tasted like. (I wish I'd thought of that while she was alive: Kat would have liked the metaphor. It wasn't mixed. Was it?)

They weren't married long: less than a year. Which was – she told me – why she had no claim on him even for sufficient support with which to pay for the apartment. But it was a nice apartment, especially compared to my own. It had lights that came on and off, a lavatory that flushed, hot water, a refrigerator with food in it, at least some of which wasn't mouldy, and I was fairly sure it had been dusted since she moved in.

Also, it had furniture. This, too, was an improvement on my place. In 1974, they changed the laws so that furnished tenants got the same sort of security as unfurnished tenants. My landlord took this defeat gracefully, and when I pointed out that I could feed myself for a month boiling the bugs in the furniture he provided to keep me out of legal protection, he allowed me to junk it, a mere twenty or thirty years after the end of its useful life. Unwilling to risk a change of what passed for his heart, I did so within days: years later, I was still trying to decide what to replace it with. It hasn't changed much since.

I was surprised now to see that she had let her apartment deteriorate, given how much care she had taken to prevent her own deterioration showing. The furniture was the same as when I had last seen it, and the years between had taken their toll. I wasn't convinced she'd dusted it since either. Some of the wallpaper was peeling and the light-bulb had gone in the lavatory, which was bad luck for her when she had a male visitor as drunk as by then was I. It was the apartment of someone who was living on the verge of leaving it.

I found her in the kitchen, sniffing a half-empty bottle of red wine. She passed it to me:

'What do you think?'

I waved it under my nose and hesitated:

'It depends.'

'On what?'

'On whether there's anything else.'

'Depends what you mean by anything.'

23

My puzzled frown told her I didn't understand. She said excitedly: 'We could do some dope or coke.'

I shook my head:

'I stay away these days, Katrina. It reminds me of too many bad times, and it's dangerous to shop for.'

She smiled a superior smile:

'Depends where you get it.'

I didn't ask her to elaborate. I had the impression that though she enjoyed boasting about access to privileged supplies, she wouldn't've told me anyway. I asked:

'Anything else to drink?'

She shook her head sadly. I shrugged – also sad – and took a couple of glasses off the shelf, leading the way into the living-room. I settled on the sofa; she secured herself in an armchair a couple of miles across the room and began talking almost at once.

'Why am I always someone's bit on the side, Dave? Why can't I find someone to stay with?'

'Hey, Kat.' She didn't tell me to lose the language, so I knew she was genuinely depressed, not just making what we sixties' people like to think of as casual, everyday conversation: 'It ain't that bad. You couldn't wait to pass up my offer to settle down with you for the night.'

She stuck her tongue out at me in a last attempt to keep the conversation at a level that didn't require a qualified psychotherapist in attendance.

'It's Martin,' she announced: 'It always has been.'

I worked out the code without difficulty. Martin Mather.

'Even while we were, you know...?' I asked curiously.

She nodded.

Why did I mind?

She said:

'And while I was married. Before, during, after. That's why I had to hold onto the flat. We were supposed to be a secret so he was never keen on my being at his house, but it's not far from here.' She laughed nervously: 'That's why I told Tony I wanted to live in this part of London.'

It takes style to persuade a husband to buy a home for the convenience of a lover.

'Is Martin married?'

She shook her head:

'He never has been; I doubt he ever will be.'

'I'm surprised then. I would have expected a Mather to enjoy something a little less...' I was going to say tacky, but the word tact intervened: 'Well, a bit more classy.'

Now you know my idea of tact, you understand why I'm a private eye, not a diplomat.

'Oh,' she brushed aside the reference to the state of her apartment: 'It's been years now, it was in much better condition then – you remember. And Randolph doesn't care... I think maybe he even likes it. He likes the idea he can move in every kind of circle.'

My comprehension took a nosedive. I asked for a translation into single-speak.

She explained. She'd been involved with Martin since she went to Mather's as an articled clerk, straight out of college. It had always been a clandestine relationship: upright Ian would not approve his boys having it off with the hired help. Martin had his own house, even then:

'Martin has his own money. Ian kept them on a tight purse until they became partners, and he made them wait to become partners until they turned thirty, one by one. But Martin had – has – an investment company on the side. Cross Course, it's called. It's not a big thing, but it turns over a lot of money, and he's made a bundle out of it, though he doesn't really do much anymore. Tony's involved in it, too: that's how I met him. They're partners. And...' She changed her mind and didn't add whatever she had been about to say. I didn't push. At that point, no one was paying me to probe parts of her story she didn't want to disclose.

'You said "during",' I said cautiously.

She nodded. Martin, her lover, had introduced her to Tony, his partner, and even while she was married to him, she hadn't given Martin up. Like I said: style.

'He left you, didn't he? I always thought it was the other way round, that he was carrying on...'

'I let you think that. He was very good about it, though. One day, he just came back and sat in here, drinking, for hours, without talking. Then he said: "It's not working, is it?" And I said: "No." Then he said: "You're seeing someone else, aren't you?" And I said: "Yes." And he went inside and packed a bag and came back in and said: "You can keep the apartment," and that was it. No hysterics. No Latin macho screaming and shouting. I don't know how it would have been if he knew it was Martin at the time...'

'Does he know now?'

'Yes. We've stayed in touch, stayed friendly.' She stopped talking for a moment and I understood why. Her marriage hadn't meant much more than our affair. Nothing did. Her emotions were wrapped up in Martin and everything else was just a way of passing the time. 'One night, he told me he'd worked out it was Martin and I couldn't lie to him so I said it was.'

'What happened between him and Martin?'

She laughed uneasily, again like she was only telling half of it:

'Tony told me he could live with it. He said: "Martin's twice my size, twice as strong and I make twice as much money because of him." I don't know about the money, but otherwise he's right. Martin is very tough. He works out at Cannons three times a week. You don't want to get into a fight with him.'

Me, I don't want to get into a fight with anyone. After Disraeli Chambers – maybe when I was still in the hospital – Sandy said to me, during one of our incessant arguments about whether practising law or detection was worse for my health – that I was as about as violent as a teddy bear, and half as threatening. She wasn't far out. I may be the only private eye in recorded history who is positively a physical coward.

'Did you know he qualified the long way?' They'd changed the rules recently, to limit the profession to university graduates, presumably to justify the levels of its fees. But until then it used to be possible to qualify by means of five years' articles and day-release study. That was 'the long way'. 'He had to. He was thrown out of school when he was sixteen. He lost his temper and there was some kind of fight and someone else ended up in hospital. Ian Mather had to go and collect him and take him away immediately. He drove him straight down to the office, took him upstairs, and told him he could either knuckle down and qualify – the long way – or he could walk out of his life then and there.'

'And Martin qualified,' I prompted.

'Martin can do anything he sets his mind to.'

'So Tony let it go?'

'Yes.' Her eyes shone. I'd discovered something else that turned her on as much as sneaky legal manoeuvres: Martin getting away with it.

'How does Randolph get into this?'

I'd said the wrong thing. She shuddered. She wasn't ready to talk about Randolph yet. She tried to keep on talking about Martin for a while. She told me how they used to slip out of the office during an afternoon, or they'd wrangle an out-of-town conference. Then, when she got married, he'd come see her at the flat while Tony was at work:

'Once, he even made an appointment to meet Tony the other side of town and showed up here instead.' Again, her eyes glistened, and not with tears, though I suspected they weren't far behind. I thought: charming, charming company she kept; but despite myself, I envied the man's nerve.

After Tony left, it was easier: he could come around whenever he felt like it and, so long as she was working for Nicholl & Co (which meant, save the first month, as long as she was sleeping with me), he did so often, though they were still secret lovers and never went out in public together, which was why she still had time and room for yours truly.

'I'm sorry, I just realized how horrible this must all be for you to listen to.'

I shook my head. Initial reaction aside, I didn't mind:

'I learned a long time ago, no one's going to write a book about my sexual prowess.'

I've always believed there's no such thing as the great lover, in isolation. Not unless we're talking style of spilling seed into a tissue. There's two of you together, or nothing. I'm not saying this is right; it's just what I believe that makes me feel better than believing anything else. Now you also know why I'm not a philosopher any more than a diplomat.

'So what happened when you went back to Mather's?'

'Ah,' her eyes clouded over. This was the painful part. She resorted to the easiest, clearest way to tell me: 'I figured I'd got it all worked out. I knew Martin together, you know. I'd never have anything more than a little bit of him. I was like that scene where Robin and Mick have split up, and he's living in Howard Hunter's trailer. It's in the fourth series, I think. It's his birthday, and he's lonely, and he comes back and she's let herself in and is sitting in the dark, with a tiny birthday cake with a solitary candle on it. Mick says; "I haven't changed". Robin says: "I know I'll never have all of you, but I'd rather have a little bit than none at all".'

'And that's how it was with you and Martin?'

'No. That's how I thought it would be. But I forgot something about Martin: the way he always has to be in control, ahead of the game. For all his toughness, he's frightened to let go with other people, to be vulnerable to them. In my case, that meant he always had to want me less that I wanted him. Once I'd lowered my sights, he had to lower his too: from where they started out, that meant he didn't want me at all.'

I shook my head:

'Kat, Kat. You're a lovely lady. Why do you do this to yourself?'

Without realising it, I'd struck the chord marked Randolph. She burst into tears, this time not the quiet, flowing tears that I had heard in the taxicab, but great sobs that wracked her body as she covered her face, like she was clinging onto it to keep it one piece:

'He hurts me, Dave, he hurts me.' I got up from the sofa and went and knelt down in front of her, pushing her legs apart so as to be able to hug her tightest:

'It's OK, it's OK, Kat.' I'm not that original when it comes to reassurance. I've only got the one lie.

She hugged me back so hard I thought I'd break. I could feel her breasts against my face and the next thing I knew she had grabbed the back of my head and was kissing me hard on the lips, hard so it hurt. For a moment, I kissed her back, but if it was what turned her on, it was doing nothing for me and I pushed her away as gently as I could, withdrawing from between her legs and then settling down on one side of them, so I could keep one arm around her and not pull completely away.

She was still crying.

'You don't know, you don't know the things he does.'

She wanted to tell me, but it was the last thing I wanted to hear. I didn't mind knowing that an erstwhile lover had, throughout our time together, been in love with, or even that she had been sleeping with someone else; I did mind hearing that what turned her on was something so alien to my own idea of loving fun it seemed to mean she can't have been turned on with me at all.

'But why, Kat? Why go along with it?' It was the same question I'd asked before, but this time at least I knew what I was asking.

She had calmed down enough for me to return to the sofa, and what was left of the gut-rot wine. I finished it: I figured it was doing a kindness.

'I don't know,' she said dully: 'Maybe it's how I feel about myself.'

'How did it start?' 'It' could mean her and Randolph, or what Randolph did with her.

'I'm not sure. He's not a particularly handsome man. Quite cruel looking, really, which is appropriate. He's been married three times already. More than me even. We started between numbers two and three.' She caught the look of horror as it flickered across my face. 'Oh, yeah, sure, I'm that dumb. I let him go off and marry someone else and come back. Maybe I was punishing myself for Tony; letting him do the same thing to me I'd done. Once, I went down into the dead-file basement and read his divorce papers. It was easy, no one ever goes down there.'

'I thought lawyers always used another firm?'

'The Mathers didn't get rich giving their money to anyone else. Andrew acted for him: Martin wouldn't, and I suspect Randolph didn't dare ask Allison. She doesn't do divorce. She didn't enjoy her own, and she doesn't enjoy anyone else's. Except she did mine: as a friend. But there was nothing in it. Anyway, I was trying to tell you,' she scolded me for an interruption she had seized on with alacrity: 'I read the file. And his wife – this was his second wife – he married a Mary and two Megs: Meg One and Meg Two. The second one went off to live in Purley afterwards. I mean: Purley.'

I understood what she meant. I shuddered sympathetically. Purley was the last gas station before hell.

'She complained in the petition that he'd opened a bottle of champagne between her legs. And he'd scribbled on the photocopy, by way of reply, "but it was a good vintage." The awful thing is, at the time I laughed. Imagine how it must have hurt, but I laughed.'

She paused for breath. I stayed silent: I didn't want to be told off again.

'Sometimes I think Martin set it up. It was soon enough after I came back. Well, it was long enough after that I'd got the message that Martin wasn't going to play with me anymore. And Randolph just came into my room and said, taking for granted I'd agree, "drink after work?" So I did say yes. And you know what was the biggest turn on? He took me to his home. I thought: wow, here's a Mather who's not afraid to have me in his house. Did I tell you about Andrew?' She went on apparently disjunctively.

I shook my head, hoping I wasn't going to hear she had had a full house. I wasn't. She said:

'He's the youngest. He's the prettiest, too. A bit pudgy and pouting but gorgeous, like you just want to curl up to. I've forgotten his name – there's a council leader who was on the television the other night – he looks a lot like him. Not Livingstone,' She hastened to add, lest I got the wrong idea, forgetting Livingstone was no longer the leader of the Greater London Council but a Member of Parliament instead. They'd abolished the GLC to get rid of him; maybe next they'd abolish Parliament. But though commonly called Cuddly Ken in the papers, he was about as pretty as a piranha on the prowl.

She said: 'Another of the left-wingers.' It didn't do anything for me: the idea of a fanciable politician is also alien. 'Everyone spoils him, even Ian. Mr Goody Two Shoes. Stayed at home through university and college of law until he got married. Beautiful wife, ex-model; two beautiful children. They're still married. They have a flat in town, and a house somewhere in South Oxfordshire where he plays the young country squire every weekend. House parties filled with the beautiful people.'

'D'you ever go?'

She hesitated, then shook her head:

'Even though, you know, even though Martin and Randolph go there quite often, I'm not allowed.'

I understood what she meant. The outsider. The child who doesn't get asked to the party so often it becomes a yearning. Not a question of not being asked, but not being allowed. It was the story of my childhood, too.

'And the rest of it: how did that start?' She hadn't answered the second part of my question.

'One night, it was really just playing around at first. He was tickling me, only it was getting rough and I told him to stop and instead he turned me over and started to spank me, like it was a joke and then he'd pulled down my tights and it wasn't a joke and, you know, I could feel how turned on he was, more than he'd ever been before, and...' She blushed: 'I was too. That's not such a big thing, I suppose, you read about it. But it's different when it's you. And he put me on the floor...'

She shuddered: 'Oh, Dave, he hurt me so much,' she didn't want to say the words, so she gestured to let me know what she meant: 'And none of it was a joke anymore or a turn-on,' and she couldn't finish her sentence for sobbing, so I got back up and knelt beside

31

her again, stroking her expensive hair to say it's OK, I don't think any the worse of you for it, but I didn't say it out loud, because I wasn't sure if I meant it and maybe she would sense the uncertainty or insincerity.

She told me a bit more before I left. Other things he'd done with and to her. He, too, had not allowed marriage to interfere with his fun. She felt, she said, like a rubber ball bounced back and forth between the two brothers:

'Only, that was it,' she concluded bitterly: 'I never did get to bounce back, to Martin I mean. Maybe that was why I went along with it, because that was what I expected, but it never happened.'

And, unless it had happened in the last month of her life, it never would. I was suddenly tired. Selfishly, I told her so. I told her I didn't mind going, or staying, but I think she knew I didn't really want to stay. She shook her head:

'At the moment, you know, I want you to stay and keep me comfort, maybe play bodies together. But when I wake up, I'll be embarrassed and ashamed and I won't want you to be there. So just go, Dave. Please go.'

I got up and she got up too. At the door, she hugged me and whispered:

'I wish we'd meant more to each other, Dave.'

'We mean plenty,' I answered loyally: 'Speak to me.'

I felt her nod against my chest, and then she turned and went back into the living-room as I let myself out. That was it.

I left her alone for a few days, then rang her at work. They said she was tied up with clients and would ring me back, which she didn't. So I tried calling her at home, but I only ever got her machine. Finally, I wrote her a postcard – with a first class stamp on even – and she didn't answer that either. Now she's where they don't deliver mail so it's too late to write and tell her it didn't matter, after all, I didn't think any the worse of her.

Which is why I wanted to find her killer and see off the bastard who'd left me on the hook of my guilty conscience.

I said: 'Which is it you're really worried about getting into the papers, Mr Mather? The involvement of your sons, or the possibility of leaks?'

'Do you think there's a connection?' He asked hollowly.

I shrugged: 'I don't know what's connected. But things usually are.' Katrina had asked to see me, and what she'd told me was everything. So everything was where I had to begin: 'What do you think?'

He sighed to say he didn't know, more expressively than words would have done. I was enjoying – if that was the word – a rare view of Ian Mather. A tired old man, resorting to an unsuccessful, underworked, underpaid, unethical and possibly unhygienic unemployed solicitor to solve his problems for him. I asked:

'Why me? There's a hundred different people you could ask to handle your problems, Mr Mather. Why come to me?'

'Are there, Mr Woolf? Consider the type of investigator we use here. They work for other City firms. They are well connected. How long do you think it would remain a secret that I had commissioned an investigation into Mather's – my own firm? That information alone would do untold damage.'

'The police?' I said half-heartedly.

He snorted contemptuously: the problems would be even worse.

'Put one of your own staff onto it, then. A partner?'

'And who should that be, Mr Woolf? To whom should I show greater trust than I am prepared to show to everyone else? There are only ten London partners, and four of them are my children.'

He didn't need to repeat: with two of whom the deceased had at some time or another been having an affair and who were, for that reason, excluded.

'With the exception of John Gauldie, who started this firm with me, all the partners have been with me since they qualified. I could not possibly show one of them so much greater confidence that the others would be bound to feel that I suspected them.' I had a feeling he was overstating the problem: solicitors aren't the sort of people who come quickly to the conclusion that they might be the subject of suspicion.

'Gauldie, then?'

He shook his head:

'Like me, he's no longer a young man, Mr Woolf. He is extremely busy. He supervises all the Latimer work and is in charge of all our litigation. You cannot imagine what that involves.'

I formed a perfect picture of one million beautiful, mint-fresh pound coins neatly stacked up in my Earl's Court basement. I could imagine it alright; easily.

'John...' He hesitated to look for the right words: 'John gives a great deal to this firm. But he has other interests, and he also commits a great deal of his time to them. If I asked him to take this on, it would interfere with his other activities, and I couldn't do that.'

I read a lot into the 'I'. I remembered something else Katrina had mentioned. I, too, hesitated. Notwithstanding my earlier fit of calculated pique, I wanted to investigate her death. Regardless of remuneration – it would be a lot easier doing it for Ian Mather than for the only other available client: myself. I knew that what I was about to ask might also be my last question on the case. But there was no point starting it any way other than how I intended to continue:

'Those other interests of Mr Gauldie. Would that be freemasonry?'

He bristled visibly. Freemasons are a closed society. They used to be called a secret society, but recently, in a vain attempt to diminish popular suspicion, they started referring to themselves instead as a 'society with secrets'. For myself, I couldn't see the difference. Actually, there have only ever been two secrets associated with freemasonry: who is a freemason, and what it does. They even employ secret handshakes and other signs to identify each other.

'Mr Mather,' I said hastily, reassuringly, remembering the answer I had given about Disraeli Chambers that had pleased him: 'Nothing you or anyone else tells me goes any further than you as my client.' I was lying through my eye-teeth: it would go wherever helped me solve the case. I went on: 'I know you want to say that what I asked is none of my business, and perhaps you're right, but I can't do this job unless I'm allowed to decide what's relevant and what's not.'

For the second time since the interview had begun, he swivelled around in his chair so that I could not see him while he thought about it. Clearly, the question I had asked struck another chord that no one was supposed to be able to discern beneath the deafening drumbeat of death. (I'll go anywhere for an alliteration). When he turned round again, his face was ashen:

'You don't understand what it means to me to have to talk about these things to a...stranger.'

I didn't say out loud what I could have reminded him: he'd invited me in. It wasn't necessary, because I also understood that he had made his decision.

'John Gauldie is a mason, yes. So am I. So are two of my sons. So are most of the partners. So are several of the assistants. That is in no wise suspicious. The craft, Mr Woolf, is designed to make better men of us; it is hardly surprising if we keep this firm in the hands of those we know and have such substantial reason to trust. I take it from your interest,' he added dryly, recovering a little of his composure: 'That you are another of those who consider freemasonry to be the root of all evil in this society. We tend to get blamed for almost everything that happens.'

I chuckled:

'Know the feeling. No, to tell you the truth, I know very little about it and care less. I, well, I've read the odd article and seen the odd picture, you know, of your ceremonies...'

He didn't blush. If you've ever seen a picture of a masonic ceremony, you'll understand why I consider that something to his credit. During initiation, for example, a candidate has to cover his head with a hood, put a noose around his neck, expose a nipple, roll up one trouser leg and wear an apron and a slipper on one foot instead of a shoe. And I'm not talking about schoolboys: freemasons include some of the most powerful men in the country – in the City, the armed forces, the church, the police, industry and commerce, politics, the judiciary and the rest of the legal profession, the media, even the world of entertainment.

Something like one in six or seven adult males – for which read, white males – in England is supposed to be a freemason. But that doesn't make it a cross-section of society, even if you ignore the casual omission of persons of the female persuasion and a different colour skin. Although they are said to come from all walks of life – and do: one of the principal objections to freemasonry in the police force is its membership from the criminal fraternity – what they have in common is that they are well-established materially, and plan to get better.

Freemasonry brags about its charitable objects, but only those with something to spare can afford to be charitable. I've always viewed it as a faintly ridiculous, institutionalized version of the establishment – the old boy network – of which I'm no part anyhow, so it doesn't tread on my toes and I don't need to tread on its. All its alleged combinations and conspiracies would happen even without the aprons. You don't need to persuade or corrupt someone who already wants the same things you want.

I didn't spell any of this out to Ian Mather. I'd made my point, and now that he'd conceded it, I didn't know what to do with it. Instead, I reminded him there was one other matter left outstanding:

'We still haven't talked about money.'

'What are your usual fees, Mr Woolf?'

I'd already decided how much to lie:

'Four hundred a day, Mr Mather.'

That, as nothing else had managed to do, brought the colour back into his cheeks:

'I doubt you've ever earned half that, Mr Woolf.'

I grinned what I hoped was disarmingly:

'Fine, my usual fees are what I can get away with, and I figure that's what you're good for.'

For the first time, he allowed himself a full smile:

'We charge on the same basis, Mr Woolf.'

Lawyers didn't need Freud to tell them people only listen to what costs enough to hurt.

I took his answer as agreement and had started to rise when his 'phone rang. I waited as he listened to his secretary, and as he hung up he waved me back into my seat.

'The officer in charge of the case has arrived to see me, Mr Woolf. I think it would be a good idea if you were to remain.'

I was doubtful. Policemen like private eyes the way Hitler had a soft spot for Churchill. I suggested:

'Just say I'm working for you. Don't spell it out.'

He didn't look too happy at the idea of starting our professional relationship by lying about it, but the door had already opened and there was not time to argue. I didn't turn around. Not even another review of his secretary was worth having to watch a member of Her Majesty's Constabulary for a moment longer than absolutely necessary.

It was a mistake. Mather was already introducing us before I could stop him:

'This is Mr Woolf, Inspector. He's working for me.'

That all too familiar weasel-shaped head broke in half in a ripe guffaw:

'Don't be bloody stupid, sir. Mr Woolf doesn't work for you. Mr Woolf doesn't work period. He doesn't know the meaning of the word.'

Chapter Three

It was a long day, so long I could charge twice.

We didn't stay with Mather. Just enough for Dowell to dictate the terms on which I could remain on the case. I told him everything; he told me nothing. Promising confidentiality as glibly and as insincerely as I had done, he extracted the underlying cause of Mather's concern: not so much his sons the lovers, but his lawyers who leaked. Dowell was quick to consent to my keeping this part of the case.

We withdrew from Mather's office and resumed our conversation in the nearest hostelry. I don't know why, but pubs in the City of London open earlier than elsewhere in the capital: it was only a few hundred yards to the city-line.

He bought the first round, finishing his before the barman brought change. He smacked his lips:

'Ah, God, that's good. I'd forgotten.'

One of his few redeeming features was an affection for Southern Comfort – no ice, no soda. I had introduced them; they made a handsome couple. He explained now that his wife wouldn't let him keep it in the house; one night, he'd worked his way from the top and he and it had ended up empty at about the same time. Nor was it a drink to be found in the average police club.

Tim Dowell had a distinct drawback for one of his professional persuasion. Not only had he once picked up a book, he had read it, all the way through. In fact, though he is understandably deeply ashamed of it, he has a law degree. The British·police hierarchy prefers its subordinates to be uneducated and incapable of thinking for themselves. They probably do a lot of recruiting amongst cab drivers.

As the barman brought our refills, I spotted a pair of city slickers leaving a table and told Dowell to grab it, soon enough for me to be able to ask the barman, behind his back, for a receipt to claim the round on expenses. Have you ever asked a barman for a receipt? It's only marginally safer than failing to tip a cabbie.

'What do you know about freemasons, Tim?' I asked as I joined him.

'Enough to steer well away from the subject. Why?'

I shrugged:

'I thought a lot of your people were.'

The outgoing Metropolitan Police Commissioner had been so worried by the extent of freemasonry on the force that he had issued a Code of Guidance politely suggesting policemen reconsider compatibility of the craft with the job. Newman commanded enormous respect in the force: so much so that, within months, a number of masonic policemen, rather than resign membership, had formed a new Lodge all of their own, the Manor of St James.

'I thought you had to belong if you wanted promotion?' I pursued lackadaisically.

Dowell was uncomfortable enough to get up and go to the bar for our third round in not so many more minutes.

When he returned, he was shaking his head, as if puzzled:

'Odd thing, that. Barman asked if I want a receipt as well. Christ, you're a mean sod, Woolf.'

He had also bought a plate of sandwiches, which he placed in the centre of the table.

'You're just jealous you can't claim,' I stretched out my hand for a half-round of processed ham and processed cheese on processed white: Sandy would have a fit.

So did Dowell. He caught my wrist, the sandwich half-way to my mouth, and brought it firmly back to the plate where I released my grip.

'Buy your own,' he snarled.

'I made you bacon and eggs once,' I complained.

'And I saved your life, sunshine,' he reminded me: 'So that makes us even.'

My life was worth to him approximately the cost of the two fried eggs and three rashers of bacon he had greedily gobbled on his first – unsolicited, uninvited, and literally unwarranted – visit to my home.

'You don't want to talk about freemasons, do you, Tim?'

He shook his head, then, reluctantly, explained:

'My old man was one. I joined for his sake. It wasn't a big deal in those days. I stopped going as soon as he died. I don't suppose I went to a half-dozen lodge meetings. But you're right, you know, it helped. At a time when I was under a lot of flack because of my degree, it was the one thing that worked in my favour.'

'How could you go through with it?' I asked disgustedly: 'All that crap with a hood over your head?'

He smiled wearily:

'You know what it's for? To cover up your laughter. No, you're right, it was bloody rubbish. We all make mistakes, Woolf,' he reminded me.

'Most of them at Mather's are masons, right?'

'I don't know about that,' he lied. 'I don't think the Pankhurst woman could be anything to do with it: remember, no women.'

'They fuck, don't they?'

'Do they? I suppose so; to have children, you know. But I don't think they're allowed to enjoy it.'

It was my round again. When I returned, I changed the subject:

'You gonna tell me what happened, or what?'

He didn't put up a protest, just as I hadn't objected in front of Mather when he claimed it would have to be a one-way street. Those were the rules. You said one thing and did another. Put like that, it ain't so different from everything else.

Katrina had been killed between nine and eleven in the evening. She had been shot, through the mouth.

There were no traces on her hand: suicide was not suspected. I grimaced:

'Gangland stuff?' It was the traditional way to leave a note on the corpse warning others not to talk so much.

'Wants to look that way. In my experience, gangsters couldn't give a damn how they get it done nowadays, so long as they get away with it.'

'Since when did you know anything about gangsters?' His role when last I'd known him was somewhat specialized: he co-ordinated – or shadow-boxed – with Special Branch, the political police. One way or another, the crimes he handled always enjoyed an extra dimension. When he didn't rise to my question, I asked: 'What about the weapon.'

'Thirty-two. That's about as useful as knowing the get-away car had four wheels. They give them away free in boxes of cereal.'

'And?'

He told me what little more they yet had. The firm kept a late-book, for fire-safety purposes. Anyone in the building after eight, when the night watchman came on duty, was supposed to ring down, and anyone who came in had to sign. There was a back exit, but no evidence of forced entry. The watchman on duty swore no one could have come in or left without his knowledge.

'They always say that. It's paid sleep.'

Dowell shook his head:

'I believe him. He's fifty-four, not in the best of health, laid off from his last job and he won't get another if he loses this. Besides, he used to be a special.'

Few people realized that the British police still use what are known as Specials, part-time amateurs to supplement the full-time amateurs.

'Right, right, can't possibly have been asleep.'

'You don't believe in anything, do you, Woolf,' he sneered.

'Not true,' I held up my glass and studied the lonely residue of the one holy spirit I religiously worship.

'You get it,' he said: 'You're charging it.'

I didn't like to admit he had so embarrassed me with

41

his earlier observation I hadn't asked for a receipt on the last round. But we'd still only be even.

According to the book, there had been five other staff in the building, and one outsider. A solicitor had been in conference with his client until late, and they backed each other up. His wife was an office-administrator and had waited for him: they were going out to dinner. Another solicitor and his secretary had been working:

'They can prove it. They were incorporating some faxed material into a contract, and faxing it out again overnight.'

I'd heard of fax, but didn't understand why it could prove the point.

'Don't tell me you haven't got all the modern technology in your basement. And you such a highly paid private detective. Ask Sandy.'

'We're not speaking just now.'

I said earlier Kat had something to do with why Sandy and I were in off mode. I hadn't told Sandy where I was going the night I saw Kat. When I did tell her, after the non-event, it was with the casualness of the complete innocent. Sandy, however, wasn't convinced. She accused me of not telling her beforehand so as to keep my options open. Even my most voluble protests could not conceal that she was right.

When she'd rung me on the evening after Kat had been killed, knowing I probably wouldn't have read an afternoon paper nor watched the local news on television, she had been apologetic, guilty about her earlier outburst. I had been too shocked by the news to take the opportunity to bring us back together, and now I was engaged on the case, I doubted I would see her until it was over. She doesn't like my detecting at the best of times; looking for the killer of a lost lover would be even less endearing.

Dowell explained how a fax worked. Each page was time-stamped as it was transmitted. That meant that when the solicitor and his secretary claimed to have received the material during the afternoon, they could prove it; when they said they'd sent it out again overnight, that could be proved too. I still didn't see why they couldn't slip in a killing between Clauses Seven and Eight of the contract, but unless it was chargeable, there'd be no reason.

I took out my calculator and totted up the score:

'One more.'

'Wainwright, Christopher, greaseball. Says he was working late before going out. Reading a file. Everything I hear says he needs the brownie points. He's thirty-four, by which time he ought to be a salaried partner, but I've yet to hear a good word about his work, and I can't imagine anyone saying anything good about his personality.'

'I gather he impressed you. Why's he still there, then?'

'I'm not sure. It's curious. His older brother is a friend of Randolph Mather, and it seems Randolph got him articles with the firm. Maybe he's just managed to hang on.'

'Do the Mathers have to sign in?'

'Theoretically, everyone does. Ian's not usually there that late, and Gauldie – the other senior partner – leaves on the dot of seven every day, even if he's in the middle of an interview. All the partners have an administrative brief: Martin's the one who instituted the late book. But the watchman says the others aren't as regular as Martin would like to believe.'

'Tell me about the Mathers.'

'Three brothers, and the tastiest solicitor you ever saw outside of L.A. Law.' I was glad he'd kept up with Bochco, the man who made Hill Street and moved on to L.A. Law before he blew it with the half-hour and half-hearted Hooperman. It's probably top of the ratings in the States.

'You're a happily married man, Dowell; leave her to me.'

'I love my wife; I love Southern Comfort; I even quite like my job at times. I'd throw them all up for a weekend on a desert island with Allison Mather Hoyt.'

'Can they all account for their movements?'

'More or less. The mother – Ian's wife – has got Alzheimer's Disease.' I raised a quizzical eyebrow and he explained: 'Premature senility. Progressive deterioration of the brain. What they say Reagan's got. Said to be prevalent amongst Jews. As a matter of fact,' he grinned.

I knew what was coming and waved away the inevitable insult.

'Hoyt goes to the nursing home every evening. Stays until about nine o'clock. That night she went home to Highgate and called a couple of friends, long-distance: she's on the test circuit and it checks.' England was moving in the same direction as the States: soon we would all receive itemised accounts to help us decide whether the people we telephone are really worth the cost.

'Ian was at home in Hampstead and the servant can vouch for him. Martin was at his gym: Cannons in the City. He's playing in a local squash tourney. Went on till late with drinks after. Randolph was with some woman. Andrew was at dinner, with his wife, and then went on to the Clairmount.'

'Gambler?'

'Apparently. The owner says he's got quite a tab. Didn't want to tell me to the last pound, but he hinted eight to nine thou.'

Over a final drink he asked:

'How're you going to tackle this one, Dave? This lot ain't Disraeli Chambers.' Something else we had in common was contempt for the comrades of the left-wing bar. The clients they had to content didn't have either the choices or the experience to spot when they were being short-changed.

Where we differed was, I've never thought lawyers generally were anything special. I suppose the reason for the difference is, Dowell never did it.

'It's a big myth, Tim, They're not so sophisticated; they just wear smarter suits than the rest of us.'

'They've got to have something: they're Mather's.'

I shrugged:

'Maybe. But whatever it is, I don't have it anyhow. If I try and play their game, they'll run rings round me; it's brute Woolf or nothing. It's all I know.'

We wandered back to the office off High Holborn at about half the pace we'd left it. Along the way, I swept up some dust:

'Randolph was with some woman: Kat was supposed to be his woman.' I briefed him on Randolph's idea of loving tenderness: 'And, uh, you ought to know my own relationship with her wasn't exclusively professional.'

'That much I assumed; I never knew you to spend ten minutes around a woman without at least trying.'

'Unfair,' I protested: 'I never made a pass at Mrs Nicholas,' my client on Disraeli Chambers. She was in her sixties and married to a vicar.

As we went up the main stairs towards the office where Katrina had been found, the man himself came down. I didn't know it was Randolph to begin with, of course, but as he passed us, he swivelled and turned his eye on me.

'You must be Woolf,' he thrust a hand out at me: 'Randolph Mather.'

Kat's description had been apt. There was something cruel about him, though I couldn't tell if it was in the eyes or his mouth. He was tall and beginning to bald, and a roll of paunch poked over the top of his waist-band, but he was, like his father, impeccably and expensively besuited, and if the shirt and tie weren't silk they were an impressive imitation.

I was pissed enough to remember my manners; I ignored his hand. I didn't say anything. If I said anything, I'd lose my cool. There was just too much hatred waiting to get out. Instead, I just shrugged and brushed past him as if he didn't exist. The look on his face suggested my gesture was more effective than if I'd taken a swing at him.

Sobered by the encounter, we carried on up to the first floor landing where, to my surprise, I found that the incident had been witnessed. A man – who I guessed immediately was Martin Mather – leaned against the wall, his hands in his pockets, grinning cheerfully:

'I trust you know how to make friends as quickly as you do enemies, Mr Woolf. . . Dave?'

'Dave, sure. You're Martin Mather, right?'

I was predisposed to like him: Kat had loved him for most of her adult life. He couldn't be all bad: she'd loved me a little bit, too.

While Randolph's face showed traces of Ian's, Martin could have been the child left in swaddling clothes on the door-step. He neither looked nor dressed like either of them. He was much shorter, greying, and beefy like the muscle-hungry work-out fanatic I already knew him to be. He was wearing slacks, a tweed jacket and a striped shirt; the tie around his neck looked like it had been knotted by a sodden sailor in a force seven storm.

'My father asked me to find you an office and what my father asks, I do.'

'Always?'

He frowned:

'What's that mean?'

'It means I wouldn't like you to think calling me Dave put you above suspicion, is all.'

'Or: maybe you know how to make friends, but why bother?'

'Something like that.'

'Katrina told me you were a screwball.'

Behind me, Dowell coughed.

'We're keeping the Inspector waiting while we play, Dave. . .'

'Not at all, sir, I was merely agreeing with your description of Mr Woolf.'

Mather chuckled:

'Do you think it's worth settling into your office, Dave?'

'What do you think, Martin?'

'I think. . . I can't see Randolph running to Daddy to explain why you were rude to him, can you?'

'So you're aware of, uh, your brother's predilections, then?'

'I'm aware of everything, Dave. That's what I'm good at.'

'But you never did anything to stop it?'

'I wasn't her keeper. What did you do?'

I couldn't think of an answer so I gestured for him to lead on to my office.

Main man Mather's office was on the ground floor, so this was my first venture on high. I saw immediately why they needed a 24-hour security service: walking around the wide first floor corridor was like strolling through the halls of a museum. One entire length was given over to pictures, one or two of which seemed familiar, but different than I remembered them from prints or posters I had owned at various times in my life. It took me a while to work it out: they were the originals.

Another stretch contained a display of medieval armour and weaponry. Martin, turning round, caught my scared scowl at a sword sharp enough to shave with. He said:

'Yes, it is real. Late fifteenth century. That too,' he pointed to a spear that looked as if it still had a powerful point to make: 'John Gauldie is the buff.'

It wasn't the sort of bric-a-brac Nicholl & Co could have kept around the office, but few of Mather's clients came from the same criminal inclination, and if they didn't like the size of the bill, they had an accountant call up to query it instead of, as ours, reaching out for the nearest lethal instrument.

'How about law reports?' I asked naively. They were what most solicitors used to hide the peeling wallpaper.

'There's a library on the second floor. Why? Did you think you might want to look something up?' He added sarcastically.

The value of the wall-furniture diminished as we rose. Obviously, he had decided to please me: I'd been placed in an attic room so small I could sit behind the desk at one end and shut the door at the other without getting up. I nodded:

'It'll do. Key?'

He took it out of his jacket pocket.

'Only one?'

He smiled smugly:

'Sure. Apart from the security desk. And my master.'
I didn't mind; I'd keep most of my material in my head, and the rest of it at home.

'Drop down and see me when you're ready to talk,' he said as he left.

I went back down the stairs to Kat's office with Tim. It was sealed, but he broke it off and ushered me in. It still had the faint, acrid, chemical smell that follows forensics. In the pub, he'd shown me the photos, so I knew exactly how she'd been found. Sitting at her desk, slumped over it, most of her head missing. The window-frame was still stained, but someone had cleaned the glass. The top of the desk was ingrained with copper-coloured blood. I ran my finger over it, morbidly:

'I liked her, Tim. I liked her a lot.'

He shrugged:

'If I say I'm sorry, does it make it any better?'

'You're a hard shit, Dowell.'

'And you're too fucking soft by half. That's why we work out together. We do, don't we, Dave?'

It was oddly reminiscent of Kat asking me: We are friends, aren't we?

I nodded hesitantly:

'Tim, are you telling me everything?'

He held up a hand:

'Scout's honour.'

'You weren't a Scout, too, were you?'

After he left, I wandered back to my room to work out a plan of action (for which read to sleep off the Southern Comfort). Half-way up the stairs, a frowsy, grey-haired, bespectacled, middle-aged woman clutching a folder attached herself to me:

'Mr Woolf? I'm Marion Mortimore. Mr Martin has assigned me to assist you.'

I stopped to study her. I was beginning to go off Mr Martin. I had plans to use Mr Ian's secretary for my humble needs. She swept past me and – a couple of hundred feet higher up, where the air was thin – waited patiently for me at my door.

'I brought you this,' she said, handing me the folder.

I opened it. It was a directory of all the partners and qualified staff, office numbers and locations, tie-lines, home addresses and phones, how to access the central computer, Lexis, fax, and a bunch of other gadgets I'd never heard of.

'I'll attend to all your correspondence Mr Woolf,' she added: 'That is, if you're going to be writing any letters. I shouldn't imagine you will be writing any letters, will you, Mr Woolf?' She asked conspiratorially: 'I mean, private detectives don't, do they?' She said, her eyes sparkling.

'No, I don't suppose I'll be writing any letters. But, uh, I'll probably need help making out my expenses' claim.'

She had begun to hop nervously from one foot to another:

'You are going to find out who killed Katrina, aren't you, Mr Woolf?'

'Well, that's really a job for the police, Miss. . . is it Miss?'

'Mrs, Mr Woolf. Arthur. . . That's my husband. . . Arthur and I have been married for nearly twenty-five years, you see.' There was something else she wanted to tell me, and, eventually, she came out with it: 'I don't trust that Inspector Dowell, Mr Woolf. He has a small head.'

This, I have to concede, was clinically correct. At first sight, I'd wondered how he had achieved minimum height requirements, but it was only his head that was small, not the rest of him. I wasn't entirely sure that the size of his head reflected on his trustworthiness, but I couldn't fault her instinct so I didn't pursue the point.

'Arthur and I, we like jazz, Mr Woolf. Every Monday evening, we go to jazz.' I tried to keep the boggle inside my eyes. The sight of her and my image of Arthur be-bopping in some smokey room above a pub was a little more than my booze-befuddled brain could cope with.

'Sometimes, well just the twice, Katrina came with us, you see, Mr Woolf. I was so fond of her.' Suddenly she was blubbing and I had to get up to offer her my chair, the only one in the room.

'It's OK,' I said lamely, and in conformity with custom: 'It's OK, you know. I was fond of her, too.'

She sniffled back the last of the tears, and got up, suddenly all office-efficiency again:

'Well, that's alright then. Now, I've written my number on the outside of the folder; you only need to dial the last three; press nine for an outside line. And if you press down that button marked exchange, followed by my number, it means your incoming calls will be diverted to me.'

It was clear as mud, but I decided it would be easier to work out for myself, by trial and error, than risk another teach-in. Before she went, I asked if she could obtain another chair, an upright: there wasn't room for anything else. At the door, she turned:

'Oh, and Mr Woolf, would you like to tell me what you drink?'

I did a double-take:

'What makes you think I drink, Mrs Mortimore?' It came out closer to 'tink I dink'; you try it after half a dozen large Southern Comforts.

'Why, Mr Woolf, all private eyes drink. I've read them all.'

Great. Wonderful. Now I was going to have to live up to her fantasies. I decided not to ask who was her favourite, in case she said Spenser. All that food would be the death of me.

'Right. I drink. Whaddayawannaknow for?'

'So that I can arrange for the hospitality room to send up a bottle, Mr Woolf, of course.'

After all, she hadn't been Martin's idea of a joke. I told her, and promised to introduce her at the end of the day, if she stayed around as late as four o'clock when my evening session usually began.

I was spoiled for choice where to begin. Gauldie, three male Mathers or. Recalling Dowell's description, I picked her number out of the internal directory. To my disappointment, her secretary said she was unavailable at present, but promised to get back to me as soon as Ms Hoyt had a spare moment. I tried to convey to her that my time was the firm's money, not that of a mere client, but I was left with the distinct impression that I would not rate top ranking on Allison's message pad.

I still wasn't ready to talk to Randolph. Martin had positively invited an interview, which meant it would be wholly uninformative unless I first acquired a little bit of material to barter with. Andrew was in conference with counsel, and no one knew when he'd be back. Reluctantly, I decided to start at the top.

Gauldie's secretary told me he would be happy to see me in a half-hour's time. I don't know how long she had worked for him, but happy and Gauldie were mutually exclusive. He must once have been exceptionally tall because now, even slightly stooped, he still towered over me as he ushered me into his room. He didn't offer to shake hands, so I guess he already knew I wasn't a mason. He was gaunt, with high cheek-bones, and his hair was prematurely thinning.

'Mr Mather told me you handle all the Latimer litigation, Mr Gauldie?'

'That is correct. I am the senior litigation partner, so all litigation is my final responsibility.'

'Which also means all the leaks there have been,' I pointed out.

He said:

'I am of course finally responsible for that, too, Mr Woolf. But in practice, there is a large volume of litigation and I cannot of course oversee it all.'

'Of course, of course,' I reassured him: 'But it does mean you have access to everything. What I'm wondering is, who else does?'

He pursed his lips:

'Almost all of the partners, Mr Woolf. You see, we take our corporate responsibilities very seriously here. Randolph works closest with me. Then Martin, for example, is in charge of office administration, and training. That gives him access to all the firm's files. Young Andrew is in charge of bills on account. Many of our clients are far too large and well established for us to seek an initial payment on account: it would cause offence. But people do not object to interim accounts for work already undertaken. So it is young Andrew's duty to make sure that all of us – but, of course, especially the assistants and the salaried partners – are up to date in that respect.'

When I was in practice, our main concern was to win the case: at Mather's, that was secondary to keeping the cash coming in. He listed other 'corporate' duties, indentifying partners by name. He attributed no special obligations to Allison Mather Hoyt. I asked. He pursed his lips again: perhaps he was practising kissing.

'Mrs Hoyt,' not, note, Ms: 'Mrs Hoyt is a partner, of course. Let us say she has a roving brief to assist others in their responsibilities.'

In his view, she was a partner in – and because of – name only. Aware he'd displayed more animosity than might be considered diplomatic, he hastened to add: 'Of course, you could say that Randolph does no more that assist me.' He couldn't let it go at that: 'That would be a considerable understatement of his contribution to this firm, Mr Woolf. He is a very fine young man, and a fine solicitor.' Now I knew what Gauldie thought of Randolph, I knew what to think of Gauldie.

'And Martin? How do you get along with Martin?'

He sniffed, like the name stank. Ian had told me that two of his sons were freemasons: I knew which one wasn't. As if he could read my mind, Gauldie said:

'Mr Mather said you asked about the craft.'

By now, I knew enough of the lingo to understand he wasn't talking about carpentry or creative accounting.

'It would be a grave error, Mr Woolf, and of course a grave waste of resources, to pursue that line of enquiry. I hope I make myself clear.'

Dowell's immediate response had been: 'enough to steer well away from the subject'.

'Mr Mather has already – shall we say extended? – the bounds of necessity on the subject. You would not, I am sure, wish to embarrass him further.'

Me? Embarrass anyone? May my throat be cut across, my tongue torn out by the root and buried in the sand of the sea at low water mark, or a cable's length from the shore, where the tide regularly ebbs and flows twice in twenty-four hours, as the freemasons say (in the initiation ceremony).

'Mr Gauldie, I don't want to offend you.' May my throat be cut across, etcetera. 'There's only two things I want to find out about: who killed Katrina Pankhurst, and who's been leaking the firm's secrets. I take it you've already told the police everything you know on the first subject. . .' I paused for him to nod: if I'd paused until he nodded, I'd be pausing yet. 'How do you think – for example – the LCP report got out?' Remember the LCP report? Babies with bits. . . Right, you remember.

'I don't know, Mr Woolf.'

'Who worked on that case? Katrina didn't.'

He smiled spookily:

'People do not only talk at the office.'

I was surprised: I would not have excepted him to know she and Randolph were a number.

He didn't. He went on:

'She and Martin were very close friends.'

'But you do all Latimer's work. You and Randolph, right?'

He laughed with warmth enough to freeze-dry:

'We are in charge of it, Mr Woolf. Two people could not do all of it. Both Martin, and Mrs Hoyt, assisted at different times on that issue, although so did many others: it was a massive action. You are aware of the other leaks: Westmoreland House – Martin's case; the de Peyer divorce – Martin and Wainwright; the News libel action – Martin and young Andrew.'

'I think I'm beginning to get your drift,' I said dryly: 'Martin Mather is the common factor.'

Yet again his lips pursed:

'I should hate to think it. I'm only stating what your examination of the files will disclose. The obvious, you might say.'

'But Katrina was clean: she wasn't involved in any of those actions. And for the record, she and Martin weren't "close" as you put it, ever since she returned to work here.'

He shrugged indifferently:

'That would simply suggest that one thing had nothing to do with the other, would it not, Mr Woolf?'

I got up:

'Yeah, sure. I guess I ought to thank you for your help.'

'Mr Woolf, I ought to tell you: I do not agree with Mr Mather's decision to employ you.' I'd never have guessed.

'I will be loyal to it, of course, but I do not agree with it. These are matters for the proper authorities. Only.'

I was being pointed at Martin, so that was where I'd go. I found the office Marion Mortimore shared. She told me he was interviewing prospective staff in a room on the ground floor. Before I left her, I gave her a list of files I wanted to find in my room when I got back up. She promised they would be there: along with the someelse she had promised me.

I waited while Martin finished his interview in progress. I could see in: the door was half glass. The candidate was a young, black man. As I shut the door behind us after he left, I said:

'I take it he won't be getting the job.'

Martin chuckled.

'I wondered when you'd get around to that,' meaning he knew I was Jewish: 'But you're wrong, you know. We have black employees, and Jews, and our quota of women. I always thought it was a good idea employing a Pankhurst; kept the women's lobby at bay. We'll have to think of something else now.'

I ignored the sick humour: he was trespassing on my territory.

'But not in positions of prominence or power. That's what matters.'

'Oh, come on, Dave. We don't get the applicants. People go to their own. Look at the black and Asian firms, or for that matter the Jewish firms. Sandy Nicholl was Jewish, wasn't she?'

'She still is, so far as I know. So?'

'So, you were a pair of Jews. We're a family of Scots. We employ our own kind, too.'

His father had said something similar, but he was referring to freemasons.

'Wainwright? Is that a Scottish name.'

'Ah, well, we all make mistakes.'

'How's he survived?'

'Andrew claims he's useful to him. I don't know why: he's only worked with me once, and that was enough.'

'That's enough? Andrew's say-so?'

'His productivity is acceptable.'

'Measured how? Billing time?'

'Yes, of course, how else? The ones who do the least are always the hardest to fault.'

'And Andrew is in charge of billing, right?'

His eyes narrowed as he took my point, but he nodded. I shrugged: I didn't have anywhere else to take it. I decided to order up some stirred shit instead:

'Gauldie says all the leaks are in your dyke. Care to comment?'

It didn't faze him:

'I can add up. What it means, though, is all the leaks we know about. Doesn't it?'

I inclined my head to one side in acknowledgement: it was a defence sufficient to create a reasonable doubt.

He glanced at his watch.

'You're going to have to forgive me now. I have another interview.' He picked up the file: 'This one's one of yours. Who do you think I should give the job to – him or the black?'

Suddenly, his complacency drew blood. I snapped:

'I'd take the job and shove it up your arse, Mather, 'f I was you.' I slammed out of the room so hard I thought the half-glass would shatter. Typically of my bad luck, it held.

Marion had fulfilled my every whim. For some reason that was beyond me, there were two glasses, but otherwise everything was as ordered. I rang down to the desk and told them I'd be staying late: past eight o'clock, if they cared to tell the night-man when he came on duty. And if Andrew Mather came back after his conference, I'd like to see him.

I filled a glass and settled down to the part of this

job that I like the least: reading and making notes. I read the de Peyer file first, remembering what Kat had said: it was a juicy divorce. It made me wonder what I was doing wrong. The man was upper class, desperately rich and, from the photographs snapped by his wife's snoop, fit, extremely well-hung and attractive to women (plural) so perfect I'd only ever dreamed they existed. Mind you, his wife was no slouch. He, too, had been snooping on her. The barristers in the case must have enjoyed receiving the briefs: uplifting material.

On its own, the leak didn't count for much. Through their short marriage, he had never disclosed a half-million pound estate in the Bahamas. He claimed there was no way she could find out about it: it had hardly been declared on his tax returns. At the last moment, what would have been a successful settlement from his point of view took a nosedive when her solicitor wrote notifying Mather's they intended to inform the court that financial disclosure was incomplete – and that the Inland Revenue were bound also to be interested.

Similarly, the leakage of a witness' past record in the News libel action wouldn't make a headline in its own right. As I started to read the file, I remembered the case. One Maurice Francis, Viscount Stonefrost, had sued for a gossip item which implied he had been dealing dope to a close coterie of nobs, sods and assorted snobs. The witness' name was Ron Fitzpatrick, an allegedly reformed character who had once played a minor part in long-firm fraud under a different first name – John – for which he had suffered a fine and a suspended sentence, both of which were time-expired.

Technically, the conviction would not be admissible, but once Stonefrost knew about it, the balance tilted in favour of a substantial settlement. Stonefrost had taken the money and run: to the Bahamas, I noted under the heading of unnatural coincidences. Within a year, he had worked his way through his bonus, and was found floating in a swimming-pool, with more cocaine than blood in his veins.

It was nearly midnight by the time I reached Westmoreland House, and my mind was in no condition to tackle the technicalities of landlord-tenant law. I'd done a few cases years before, when I was in practice, but there would be little in common between defending the tenant of a rent-controlled leaking apartment against a claim for arrears of rent, and the sort of war waged at the expensive end of the commercial market. I was so bad at that sort of work, I never even claimed against my own landlord for the condition of my damp basement.

Andrew Mather was no show, nor likely to at the witching hour. I put the file aside, and let myself out without waking the watchman: it was the same one Dowell swore would never sleep on the job. I was too late for the tube, so I had no choice but to take a taxi. Though tired, I was too hyped up for sleep: there was only one place to go: there only ever is.

Lewis greeted me as if it was a month since he'd seen me, not a mere couple of days. I felt pretty much the same way. Lewis is: fat, old, a friend, a faggot, a villain and a club-owner, in that order. Since the AIDS' scare, he's slowed down and now lives with Malcolm, who manages the club for him, and who he keeps hold of by a judicious blend of threats and a promise to remember him in his will. If I knew Lewis, the promise would be discharged with the age-old vaudeville line: 'Hi, Malcolm'.

I'd once made the mistake of borrowing money from Lewis, and only just survived the collection call from his gorillas. Later, during Disraeli Chambers, he had endeared himself to me when he had looked for a way to explain that their threats of violence didn't mean he didn't like me, and had been forced back on the immortal cliche: 'It was only business'.

Lewis is something else I forgot to mention. He is extremely canny. As the Disraeli Chambers case drifted towards its demise, I'd badgered him into selling me a gun. Then, in time enough to save my life, he told Dowell what I'd done, only omitting the name of my supplier. In fact I had first met Dowell at his club. Since the case, I'd continued to come round whenever I had nothing else to do, which is most nights. We have an agreement: when I'm out of work, I drink for free; when I'm not, I pay double. He thinks he wins; I think I do; we're both happy.

I didn't have to order. One of the waitresses brought the bottle. Oh, yes, he employs women too: some of the clientele is straight; he's not proud; he'll rip anyone off, regardless of sexual persuasion.

'Lewis,' I asked: 'Are you a freemason?'

He guffawed:

'Me, Dave? Hardly. Not my type of dressing up. Know what I mean?'

'What do you know about them, Lewis?'

He shuddered:

'They're wicked, Dave. You don't want to get involved with them. Remember that eytie?'

I knew who he meant: Calvi, the man they called God's banker, found hanging beneath – significantly – Blackfriars Bridge, a so-called suicide no one believed. Lewis' warning to stay clear of them was the third of the day.

'You working again?' he asked as I helped myself to another drink, trying to sound casual instead of concerned about the cost.

I'm like George Washington. I cannot tell a lie. I equivocated:

'I might have something coming up.'

'What sort of line?' Lewis doesn't pass up any information, no matter how insignificant.

'Law. Mather's. Do you know them?'

'Not going to take you on, are they?' He cackled so hard I thought Malcolm might be about to inherit.

'What's so funny?' I asked indignantly.

'You, at Mather's, know what I mean?' He chortled.

I gathered he had heard of the firm.

'They might, you never know,' I sulked.

'They might appoint me a judge of the Old Bailey, know what I mean?'

'What do you know about them, Lewis?'

'Not a lot. Not exactly my type of brief, are they, know what I mean?' Mather's knew less about criminal law than Lewis.

He frowned. He was thinking. He had to come up with something about Mather's that no one else knew, to save face:

'Once upon a time, long ago, probably before you were born, there was a nasty piece of work called James Mather. Never Jim, mind you: James. He was a Scottie, from Glasgow. Things were different then: a couple of villains fell out, they broke a few bones, swung a bit of lead, know what I mean? Not like today someone ends up supporting a motorway or fish-food for sharks. But him, he was heavy ahead of his times. Shooters, knives, he was greedy and if anyone got in the way it was the last time, know what I mean?'

I pulled a face:

'What's the connection? It doesn't sound like he was a partner in Mather's.'

'I once heard, someone said, I can't even remember who or where, he was related. Anyway, he disappeared about the end of the forties, maybe the early fifties. For a while, it was thought he'd tasted his own medicine, but then I heard he was in America, and starting over. That's all. Sound like anything to do with what you're interested in?'

I shook my head:

'No. I'm interested in things. . .' I hesitated to look for the right phrase: 'Well, commercial.'

Lewis persisted:

'He was commercial, too, you know. He got his start in the black-market. During the war, know what I mean.'

I shook my head again:

'Too old, too distant. This's tied up in the girl who got shot the night before last. Even if I was, she wasn't born then.'

'I read about it. Very nasty. It's unnatural, killing lawyers, know what I mean?'

'You never used to, Lewis.'

'Never used to what?' I'd confused him.

'Use that appalling expression, "know what I mean?".
I liked it better when you got your lines off American
movies instead of British television.'

He could take it. He rocked in his chair with laughter
again and squeezed my knee hard enough to hurt me
and catch himself a cheap thrill:

'You don't change, Dave, you don't change. Know
what I mean?'

Chapter Four

There were two calls on the answering machine when I got home. The first was from Martin Mather:

'I'm sorry about what I said earlier. It was inexcusable. Let me make it up to you. Come to my gym tomorrow night; work out a little, then we can have dinner. What do you say? Tell me in the morning.'

The second was from Sandy:

'Dave, it's me. I was wondering how you were feeling. I really am sorry about Katrina, Dave, I liked her too. Oh, shit I hate these machines. I need to talk to you, Dave, it's time we talked. We can't keep carrying on like this, Dave. We're off more than we're on. Oh, I shouldn't have started. Look, just ring me, please.'

Like I said: it was a long day.

I didn't ring Sandy; it was too late, and I was too tired. Oh, shit, as she would say: I didn't ring Sandy because I couldn't face talking to her. I have a real problem with Sandy. A bit like the old Groucho Marx line, how can I stay with anyone who'd stay with me? I love Sandy, just about as much as Katrina had always assumed, long before I knew it; but it's easier to list the things that are wrong with our relationship than to remember what's right.

My idea of first thing the next day, when I got in around eleven, I again tried to pin down Allison Mather Hoyt, without success: she was at a client's, and there would remain for the rest of the working day. I also rang Martin's secretary to confirm the date for that evening. I spent half an hour following a whim in the firm's dead-file basement: I didn't stay longer; it was dank, damp and unpleasant; I could see why – as Kat had said – no one ever went down there. Then, reluctantly, I put my head down to complete the task I'd left over: reading the files on Westmoreland House.

It was less complicated than I had expected. A block of offices was in a condition so bad the tenants all had to relocate elsewhere for almost two years while remedial works were carried out. The landlord company's liability ran only from when it first had notice of the problem. There was a long period when notice could not be proved, until a link was disclosed between one of the directors and a previous owner of the block, who had certainly known about the defect. The argument was over the compensation for this period. Given the size of the block, the number of tenants affected, commercial rents and their temporary relocation costs, the difference ran the bill into real money.

What I also discerned from the file was that the barrister acting for the tenants was Russel Orbach, Queen's Counsel. Contrary to what is believed across the Atlantic Ocean, Queen's Counsel do not advise Her Majesty. The title reflects rather the majesty of their fees. A QC, or silk as they are called because of the special robes they wear in court, can command several thousand pounds for a single day's work: some of them can command that much for an hour's conference.

I'd known Russel since we were both young, progressive lawyers, undertaking work for the poor and seedy usually for no fee. He was one of the founding members of Disraeli Chambers, which was one of the groups of barristers, specializing in poverty, welfare and criminal defence work, established in the 1970s. His specialism was civil law: planning, housing, building, local government. He was very good at it indeed.

That was one reason why he was unpopular with his colleagues. Another was that he had refined arrogance to an art form: a martial art. Argumentative, four steps ahead of a discussion, also a Jew, and intolerant of the intellectually idle or deceitful. What he did best was make enemies. Eventually, his colleagues – whoops, sorry, comrades – summoned up sufficient courage to oust him from the group, at a meeting he was not invited to attend, on the basis of allegations he was not invited to answer. They handled themselves so badly, he successfully sued them for a substantial sum of money.

This is where he and I differed. I didn't mind that he would never forget or forgive their cruelty, or their cowardice. I would also like to be able to remember all those who have done me harm, but the list is too long. But I would have settled for the money and for the undoubted professional benefits that accrued – including his appointment as silk – after he left. Instead, years after the event, he still allowed his bitterness to eat him up, and his desire for revenge to dominate his life.

I knew, of course, that he no longer worked only – if at all – for the impoverished: but I had thought he had left landlord and tenant behind to concentrate on local government to the exclusion of all else. Given the number of tenants claiming at Westmoreland House, and the size of the damages, my first question was whether he would still be living in his compact, one-bedroom apartment in Highgate, or whether he'd invested some of the loot in something larger. I decided not to wait until the evening to find out, but rang him at work instead.

'Is Mr Orbach in chambers?'

'Who's calling him?'

'Mr Woolf. . .' I hesitated then, suspecting he might not otherwise take the call, added: 'From Mather's.'

There are few barristers – QCs or mere mortals – who will refuse a call from Mather's.

'Just a minute, sir,' the clerk sounded like he'd suddenly been doused in ego-massaging balm.

'Russel Orbach,' said a voice I was once sure I never wanted to hear again: 'Can I help you, Mr. . .er. . .?'

'Woolf. With two "oos", I added dryly.

Silence told me he'd got the point.

'What do you want, Dave?' He asked quietly: 'Why did you say you were calling from Mather's?'

'Would you have taken the call otherwise?'

'We'll never know now, will we?' He had recovered his composure: 'Well?'

'Yes, thanks, you?'

'That's not very original. What do you want, Dave?'

'I am working at Mather's, actually.'

'Not as a solicitor?' He was more outraged at the idea than Lewis had been. It isn't fair. Just because I think I'm a rotten lawyer doesn't entitle others to the same opinion.

I let the insult pass.

'I was wondering. . . I'd like to see you. Would you be willing to see me?'

'That would depend on why.'

'What would you say. . .if I invited you to dinner?'

Orbach lived alone. He sat in a chair overlooking his garden, at an angle from which no other properties were visible, a rare luxury in London. He slept, ate and listened to classical music: all on his own.

On his own, once a year, he went to Oslo, to stay with a family, and tour the Munch Museum where they changed the exhibits annually, with a woman old enough to be his mother, who indeed he called 'Mor', Norwegian for mother. I didn't know for sure that he had no friends, but that was the impression he gave and it's difficult to imagine whose choice of the relaxed evening might be to spend it with Russel, Josef Stalin excepted. This was the flimsy basis for my belief that I might be able to tempt him to meet me. I was taken aback when he replied:

'Where?'

'I don't know. I hadn't thought about it.'

'Frederick's. Camden Passage. Tomorrow night at eight o'clock. You book.' He hung up without waiting to see whether the time or place were convenient to me.

I asked Marion to make the booking and had just hung up on her when the door burst open and Randolph Mather presented himself, without appointment, warning or even a bouquet of flowers. He glowered:

'I want to talk to you, Woolf.'

I tilted my chair backwards. The hell with the job. This was personal.

'The thing is, Mather, I'm not sure I want to listen.'

'Now, look, Woolf. . .'

'I doubt that'd be much better than listening. You look. Kat was a friend of mine. She told me about you two. I didn't like it. I didn't like her going along with it, but I guess it wasn't really my business anyway. But that does not mean I have like you or tolerate you the same way. I read your divorce files, too.'

I watched his mouth fall open as he digested the import of the world 'too', wondering if it'd stop before it hit the floor: 'Oh, yeah, she'd read them. She told me. It doesn't do her any harm now for you to know that. But I decided I'd have a look for myself, to see what kind of scum you are.'

'You had no right.' He'd recovered his voice.

'Wrong. I had every right. I look at whatever I want. I look at whatever I think might give me an answer. Anytime you want to stop me, your firm can start looking for a lot of new business,' I spelled out the risk to their reputation.

Stupid he wasn't. He swallowed and nodded.

'Now we've got that out the way, whyn't you tell me what you came in here for?'

He nodded again, the bald-patch at the top of his forehead glistening in the strip-lighting:

'I know. . . I understand. . . I know. . .' Was he ever going to make up his mind? 'I know what Katrina must have told you. But. . .' He was changing his story about once a word. 'I didn't see her that night. Well, I did see her that night, but we weren't together. That's not quite what I mean.'

This guy was an allegedly articulate partner in one of the most reputable firms of lawyers in the country: there was hope for me yet. 'We were both here that night. Late, I mean. We. . . Well, we didn't ring down. I know we're all supposed to, but people don't always. If you're going to stay for just a few minutes after eight – well, I mean, most of us work late most nights of the week. You know the job. You were a lawyer too.'

I hate people using the past tense of my profession. It's my prerogative.

'I still am,' I reminded him dryly.

'Yes, yes, I'm sorry.' His attempt to ingratiate himself by treating us as members of the same club had backfired.

'You weren't going to stay for just a few minutes, were you?'

'No. It wasn't the first time. We went out for a drink about six, and came back just before eight. We had a couple of cases to talk about.'

'Which?'

'What?'

'Which cases?'

'Well, it was just one case actually.' He'd made love to her in the office. As he said, not for the first time. Under pressure, he admitted he got his kicks fucking her in Iron Ian's office, along the spacious sofa, across the king-bed-sized desk or sprawled out on the pure wool pile carpet.

He insisted there'd been nothing about it that was — he paused to look for the right word and descended pathetically on 'special' by way of euphemism for violent. Afterwards, they had separated while still in the building, both returning to their respective rooms, he to collect his things, she to catch up on some work. He hadn't seen her again. Ever.

He was a very worried man. Though all of them were civil lawyers, they watched enough television to appreciate there must have been an autopsy, and sperm would have been discovered. There was no doubt the police would want to know where it had come from. Well, whose. What wasn't clear was of what he was more frightened: the inference that might be drawn by the police, or that his father might find out.

I could have let him down gently. I could have told him the police already knew about him and Katrina. I could have told him that his father also knew. There was no need for his father to find out exactly where they had been accustomed to perpetrate their penetration. I could have reminded him she'd had her mouth blown

66

off, and the police were looking for a gangster, not a sex-slayer.

I thought for a while about all these things I could say to reassure him, then said:

'I can see why you're worried, Mather. I wish there was something I could say.'

During my silence, I think he began to appreciate some of the answers for himself. My reply told him one of two things. Either I was stupid, or I still wanted him to hurt. His eyes narrowed, his lips pursed just like Gauldie's, I recollected the meanness I had observed when I was first saw him. He had recollected it too.

'You think you're pretty clever, don't you, Woolf? You ought to be careful. My father isn't the be-all and end-all of influence.'

I studied his expression. He was already regretting what he'd said. I asked:

'Would that, by any chance, have something to do with other kinds of brothers?' Freemasons call themselves 'brother', like in a union.

'I don't know what you mean,' he threw his head back and rose and left the room in one, flowing movement. I watched him go, curious: What had he really wanted to tell me?

Martin shrugged, after I'd told him the tale: 'Who knows? Randolph moves in a mysterious manner.'

We were in the restaurant at Cannons, some hours later. I'd arrived late and found him pacing impatiently in the lobby. He had to sign me in, and pay for a visitor's card which I could use to enter the different facilities, like the pool, the sauna, the gymnasium itself or the bar. He steered me away from the stairs that would have taken me up to the women's changing room, and led me down to the men's.

I hate locker-rooms. All those male bodies, arses smaller and pricks bigger than mine, people walking nakedly, with assumed casualness, calling out to one another so fast and lah-di-dah I automatically scoured the floor for plum-stones. I picked a relatively discreet locker: Martin had his own regular spot.

Then he was standing in front of me, telling me to hurry up, in swimming trunks that revealed more than I had to conceal. There wasn't an ounce of fat on him. He rippled like in the movies. He shifted weight from one foot to another, a workout in its own right.

'I thought you could use the exercise,' he remarked: 'Swimming's good, but it wouldn't be enough. You ought to join, work out properly. And cut down on the alcohol.'

'I tried, but I never did get hooked on the good god body beautiful,' I admitted, somewhat unnecessarily: 'And I'm not likely to now.'

'Well,' he said cheerfully: 'If you don't now, there's not likely to be a lot of then in which to change your mind.'

'Thanks,' I muttered, clinging on to the bannister of the wet steps to the pool, terrified of slipping and making a fool of myself.

I paddled around the shallow end while he dived straight into the roped-off section for lap-swimmers. When he'd finished, he pointed to a separate hall:

'Jacuzzi?'

'Does it hurt?'

He shoved my shoulder lightly, and told me he'd catch up with me in the bar in forty-five minutes' time. I got the message: it would be exactly forty-five minutes. I spent ten in the jacuzzi, one in the sauna – how can people can do that to themselves? – three minutes in the shower, and half an hour getting a head start.

He arrived in company with a man with a nose so large, in America he'd have to register it as a lethal weapon.

'Dave, Tony,' he introduced us casually.

I rose to shake hands. Martin asked:

'What you would like to, drink, Tony?'

'I'll have a small whisky.'

'Dave?'

'Southern Comfort. No ice. No soda.'

I knew I liked the man. He read 'small' for his friend to mean 'large' for me. As we lawyers like to say all the time: *inclusio unius, exclusio alterius*. (I can't translate it because I don't speak Latin, but it means that if you qualify one thing, the qualification does not apply to another. What it really meant was: I got a larger drink.)

'I gather you work with Martin,' Tony said as we sipped our drinks.

'Sort of. What do you do?'

'Finance. A bit of this, a bit of that.'

'You have a mutual acquaintance,' Martin chipped in: 'Katrina Pankhurst. Tony is the former Mr Pankhurst, if you see what I mean.'

'Tony Galucci,' I muttered. It just hadn't occurred. 'Out of curiosity, Martin: do you ever do anything that isn't designed to shock?'

'Not if he can help it,' Galucci said gloomily: he hadn't found it funny either.

'I don't really want to talk about her,' he said, lifting himself out of his chair: 'I'm going to be late. I'm meeting Beat.' Unusual name, I thought: as in Beet Hoven?

'Squash tomorrow?' Martin asked.

'I'll ring you. Nice to meet you, Dave.'

I watched him leave until he stopped to chat with a couple of people still undressed for sport. He was an odd man; weaker that I would have expected Martin to be in partnership with, if Kat hadn't in effect forewarned me. Weaker, too, than I would have expected her to marry, without knowing she wanted a man she could run rings round. I asked:

'Who's Beat?'

'Beatrix Kelly, Beat for short. A splendid, and beautiful, accountant.'

I was shocked: I didn't know there were women accountants.

He went on:

'She runs Cross Course for us. You do know about Cross Course, don't you.' It wasn't a question. I nodded.

'Well, you see,' he leaned over towards me, speaking confidentially: 'Beat was Katrina's sister.'

'And Tony's not meeting her on business, is he?' Now I knew what Kat had been holding back. 'Tell me about Cross Course. What's it do? How'd's it work?'

'Like any other any similar enterprise. People bring us money. We turn it into more. It started as a sort of hobby; I went through a period when I thought I wouldn't want to stay in law. Tony brought in the contacts. That's what he's best at: meeting people. It's not big: just a handful of staff, and Beat. I don't have that much to do with it anymore; Tony and Beat run it between them and like a good capitalist, I sit back and draw my dividends.'

The club restaurant was the other side of the arches under the railway into which the gymnasium had been built. Martin ate fast, unhealthily so, faster even than me. It was a contradiction. He talked fast, too, with his mouth sometimes still full, before he swallowed whole chunks of steak each one of which would in my most desperate days have fed me for a week. He was amusing, talking about people I now knew at the office, dribbling bits of gossip, most of it irrelevant to my work but all of it thoroughly enjoyable.

'Do you know Russel Orbach?'

'The silk?'

'Yes.'

He shook his head, and neatly sprayed the apron of a passing waitress with red wine:

'I never met him. He's still a bit left-wing for our taste. Why do you ask?'

'I just thought you'd get along. He likes things which hurt people, too.

'Come on, Dave. Everyone loves gossip. It's half your living.'

'Right. So I can afford to be pious about it: I only deal in it 'cos I have to. What you'n'Orbach've got in common is, you don't bother to conceal how much you like it.'

'How do you know him? Ah, yes, I forgot: he was involved in that Disraeli Chambers' business.' He'd no more forgotten than had I.

'What would you say,' I asked hesitantly: 'If I told you it's been suggested to me that Andrew might be financially – uh – over-extended?'

He knew what I was suggesting:

'No way. I'm sure he and Marilyn don't confine themselves to their income, but there's no reason why they should. You've got to remember, when you're a profit-sharing partner in Mather's, your income can vary a hell of a lot in a year, and you don't know exactly how much you'll get till the end. So really people live against estimate, rather than actual income.'

'But you wouldn't think Andrew was actually in difficulty?'

'No. If you haven't already realized, my father doesn't approve of things like debt. If he found out, Andrew might as well change his name. But it still wouldn't convince him that Andrew could betray him.'

'What if I proved it to you?'

'The same. There's no chance. If he was a million pounds in debt.'

'Tell me about Randolph.'

He shrugged:

'Randy? What's to tell? He's aptly named. He's been through three wives: and through may just about be the operative word. They spoke not well of him when they left,' he added dryly.

'What or who's he up to now?' Katrina had not been the only string he played his bow on.

'Most of the female staff. He says baldness is a sign of virility, and he's trying to prove the point, I think. I'd feel sorry for him, if he wasn't enjoying himself quite so much.'

'And do they?'

'The staff? God knows. Who cares?'

It was difficult to discern how much was affectation, and how much he really meant.

'He wasn't that easy to follow, when we were young. He was clever at everything: school, sports, drama, art, music. Oxford. Mr Perfect. Mr "I'm in charge". That's what Randolph likes, you know: it doesn't matter what it is; if something's going on – and where Randy's concerned, something always is going on – he can't stand to be left out of it, and he has to be in charge of it. Andrew idolized him; he still does a bit. But he was much younger; it's different when you're nearly the same age. It's a general truth, isn't it? He joined the brotherhood young,' he added, assuming – correctly – I would know what he meant: freemasonry. 'By the time Randolph was at Oxford, I'd gone sour.'

'Which means?'

I had an idea, from my conversation with Kat, but I wanted to hear it from him.

He shrugged with false modesty:

'I had to leave school in a hurry. There was a fight. And some broken ribs. And a broken jaw, too, as a matter of fact.'

'Remind me not to invite you outside,' was all I said.

He laughed away his disappointment that I had not asked for the gory details:

'It's a thing of the past. I had a violent temper, and the skills to go with it. I still have the skills, but no longer the temper.'

'Great. So when you hit me, I'll know it was a perfectly controlled act?'

'When I hit you,' he said softly: 'You won't know anything. Not for a while, anyway.'

I shook my head disgustedly:

'You really do have a problem, Martin. You don't know who you are from one minute to another: macho bully, sophisticated seducer, skilful solicitor or maybe all three. You'll have to be suspect number one.'

'True, absolutely true.' He was not at all disconcerted: 'All you need is a motive.'

'Money? Family revenge? They're usually somewhere on the list.'

'I don't need the money, and revenge implies an extent of emotion that doesn't fit our family. We're a cold-blooded lot, like our father, I suppose. Do you know, my father has a half-brother, in America, who he hasn't spoken to for more than thirty years?'

Sometimes you want them to know how much you know, and sometimes you don't. I shook my head.

'They hated each other. My uncle had to emigrate, oh, about nineteen fifty. I'm not supposed to know anything about it, but he was something of a naughty boy and managed somehow to embroil my father in his affairs, professionally. Affairs I might add in which the police became involved. He fled the country and couldn't even come back for my grandfather's funeral. My father threatened to tell the police he was here if he did.' Lewis had been right.

'You obviously do know a bit about it.'

'A bit.' He didn't elaborate.

'Tell me more about Andrew,' I suggested instead.

'Andrew? Dear, sweet, precious, unimaginative, conservative young Andrew. Law at university, College of Law, Lodge member, straight to Mather's, lived at home until he got married.' He told me, as Katrina had done, about his apartment in town, the country house, the house-parties.

'D'you go?'

'A couple of times. It's fun. A lot of young women, a lot to drink, and otherwise. Maybe he's not so conservative in some respects now. The mind and much else boggles. Mind you, with Marilyn in charge it could hardly be otherwise. She was a deb and a model and she's still a gorgeous lady. I wouldn't mind,' he added, surprisingly crudely.

'Do you?'

'No. Somehow, I don't think father would approve. But the thought's crossed my mind, and I know for certain that it's crossed hers too.'

He was confident about his sexuality in a way I envied. I could see the attraction. He might have mastered his temper, but there remained a distinct energy that I imagined would be appealing to the sort of woman who wanted a man much more powerful than herself. Despite myself, I could see why Katrina had put up with him.

I waited to see whether he would volunteer information about Allison, and when he didn't I asked.

His brow furrowed as he looked for the right thing to say about his sister:

'I think she's probably the reason I could never settle down with anyone. I'm half in love with her. I mean, I would be if she wasn't my sister,' he corrected himself before I picked him up on a Freudian slip so classic I couldn't believe of him that it had been accidental: 'Kat came closest. Does that surprise you?'

He was fishing to see how much I knew about them.

'That's a trick question, Martin. You're trying to make "closest" sound like "close". It could mean anything; like, you went two nights with her, instead of just the one.'

'What are you? A solicitor, a private detective or a shrink?'

'There isn't that much difference. They're all people that people talk to. It's just that shrinks earn more.'

He smiled, but he'd lost interest in the conversation. He snapped his fingers at the manager for the check. I hate people who can snap their fingers: it's one of those macho things I can't do, like using fingers to whistle for a cab.

'Answer a question, Martin,' I asked while we waited: 'Has any of this got to do with freemasons? Your father and Gauldie are; Randolph and Andrew are. Are there others? Why aren't you?'

'That was several questions. I'm not because I think it's a load of rubbish. I don't like the way people become members: word of mouth, who knows who is a good chap. It's just not my style. Have you ever seen their regalia? As for your other questions: yes, there are several other freemasons in the firm. A lot of people joined – I suppose like Randolph and Andrew – because their parents were. Father was on the Board of General Purposes, that's the governing board. But Gauldie is much more powerful: he belongs to Royal Arch Freemasonry as well. That's supposed to be the spiritual side of it. It all brings in a great deal of work. As for your first question, no, I can't see what it's got to do with anything. I doubt someone's passing out secrets with Lodge Lists.'

'Why do you say you only suppose Randolph and Andrew joined because of your father?'

He hesitated for a long time before he answered. Then he smiled thinly:

'Let's say it attributes a degree of disinterestedness to Randolph that's somewhat out of character.'

'You really don't like him, do you?'

He hesitated again, then admitted disarmingly:

'No, I don't. So you should take everything I say with a pinch of salt. The truth is, I don't really understand Randolph: I never have. I don't understand what makes him tick.' Suddenly, sharply, a bit nervously, he laughed: 'That doesn't say much. I don't understand what makes me tick either.'

'Last question. Given the number of leaks on cases you've been involved with, how come you haven't tried to do something about it before? Why'd it take a killing to call me in – or someone?'

He frowned; thinking seriously – probably for the first time that evening – about his answer.

'I suppose, when something as serious as a possible leak happens, you think up a thousand other explanations, and put the idea out of your mind. D'you understand?'

I understood alright; it was how I'd spent half my life – avoiding reality. I said:

'And a killing can't be avoided quite so easily.'

The manager brought his bill, and he avoided a reply.

Unlike his oldest brother, Andrew gave me plenty of warning of his visit: he knocked at the door before he blew it open. 'You're spreading rumours I'm in debt,' he accused instead of introducing himself.

Kat's description of him as pretty was apt. I could also see why people prefixed him as 'young'. He was callow, pink-cheeked, a bright and beautiful blond, and as he stood in front of my desk, his mouth was turned up in a sneer that did his lips so proud if I swung both ways I'd want to lick it off.

I liked the way he'd leaped to the conclusion that what he'd heard was what I'd said: it was typical of a lawyer to ignore the possibility there might be another side of the account. As, however, he happened not to be wrong, I decided it would be unfruitful to point this out to him. I also lacked the incentive I enjoyed with Randolph to put the boot in. I said:

'It's a problem when you investigate in a closed environment. Everyone gets to hear every question you've asked, and starts reading a lot more into it than may be accurate.'

He wasn't very smart; he read my answer as a denial. I gestured to the uncomfortable upright and he sat down on it careful not to cut across the crease in his trousers.

'Coffee?' He nodded, and I buzzed Marion. I lit a cigarette before it arrived. He asked:

'Can I have one of those?'

He managed to get it alight with difficulty, laughing nervously:

'I don't usually smoke. Just occasionally.' I thought for a moment he was going to add I shouldn't tell daddy.

'Is it true, though?' I asked after Marion had been and gone.

'What?'

'That you're in debt?'

He flushed:

'Why have you been asking?'

I shrugged:

'Things I hear. Like, maybe, gambling?'

The colour drained from his face. I was sorry: he was much nicer to look at before.

'You don't like me, do you?' He said suddenly: 'You're trying to find something.'

I waited, without comment. It was news to me, but when people give me a headline, I like to hear the whole story.

'It's because of Katrina at the house, isn't it?'

I groaned inwardly: I'd asked her, and she denied it. Outwardly, I shrugged lightly as if it – whatever it was – didn't much matter to me.

'Look,' he said heatedly: 'I know things got out of hand. It was all a bit crazy. It wasn't my fault, honestly, you have to believe that. She didn't blame me. I talked to her about it, did she tell you that too?'

A lot of detection is like this. People think you already know something, so they tell you about it anyway. I

76

held up a hand: if she hadn't wanted me to know, I didn't want to listen to the details. She had said she had never been to his house. He'd said enough for me to get the general idea why it was something she wanted to forget.

'I asked you about money. Specifically, gambling.'

He shifted so awkwardly in the seat, I wanted to reach over and re-arrange his trousers. Maybe I should introduce Lewis to him, as a reward for getting it right about the absent Mather.

'I gamble a little. I can afford it,' he said without conviction.

'Andrew,' I said gently: 'I'll level with you.' Why should I be different? Everyone else was lying to me. 'I don't think it's got anything to do with Kat's killing. But you've got to understand, I'm under a duty to your father to find out what's going on in this firm, his firm. Money is a motive for leaking information. You understand me?'

He licked his lower lip:

'I'm not stupid. I understand. There's nothing I can tell you. Just, you're right, it's got nothing to do with Katrina's death. . . Or the leaks,' he added hastily.

I shrugged:

'Fine. There's something you don't want to tell me, so bad you don't mind your father finding out you've got a gambling debt bordering five figures,' I wanted him to be certain I really did know and wasn't just guessing: 'That's OK with me. You sure it's OK with you?'

He shut his eyes for a moment, as if I'd hit him. When he opened them again, he nodded slowly, like someone unsure what he wanted, but who didn't really have a choice. Which left me wondering: what or who could scare him more than his father?

Russel Orbach was waiting for me at Frederick's. There was one advantage to staying with Sandy; sometimes, she'd let me borrow her car. Tonight, I had to take the tube. I was, of course, late.

He was already at the table, and deep in conversation with a small, dapper Jew he introduced to me as the owner. It wasn't the sort of establishment I imagined belonging to a Jew: the table was in the lower room, glass-encased, with trees growing up the middle. The wine waiter wore a medallion and poured like he was on-stage at the opera. The waiters were the real M'sieurCoy they were only imitating at Cafe Pelican. The menu contained more sea-food than the Chief Rabbi had banned, and the special of the fortnight was tongue, which I also recalled from my distant past was the wrong side of *frum* (orthodox).

We made what passed with Orbach as small talk during starters. He asked:

'What sewers are you scouring at present, Dave?'

I asked: 'D'you see much of Lady Keenan?' The eye of the Disraeli Chambers' storm.

He asked:

'What are you doing at Mather's?'

I asked:

'Get much work from them, do you?'

Suddenly, without forewarning, he said:

'A woman was killed at Mather's. You're investigating. Why would they call in a private detective of their own? Whatever happened isn't the first thing they're worried about. There haven't been any earlier deaths, at least that I know about. They're worried about something else. What worries a solicitor? Leaks. You want to talk to me about Westmoreland House. You want to know how we found out about the connection.'

I couldn't help myself: I stared at him in frank admiration. I was supposed to be the detective. My duty of confidentiality to my client prevented me confirming this accurate assessment, so I merely said:

'Not bad,' which did as well as 'yes'.

The waiter brought our main course. It gave me a breather during which to think of what to ask next. I needn't have bothered. He was in complete control.

'What makes you think I'd know?'

'Because you like to know everything.'

He cut into his pork and shook his head with equal energy:

'Wrong. Sometimes, if you know where information

comes from, you can't use it, or you may owe a duty of disclosure to the court. So it may be positively necessary not to know.' I'd forgotten: he might not have minded seeing a few of his colleagues wacked off, but he was riddled with professional integrity. I'd spent the evening before with Martin Mather, though, which wasn't a bad way to warm up for a round with Russel Orbach: 'You're not saying you don't know.'

He smiled: Orbach enjoyed the game much more than the outcome.

His hair was darker than I remembered. And the beard which distinguished him from so many of his smooth-cheeked colleagues at the bar, where facial hair is frowned on. I asked about it.

'I had an operation, hiatus hernia. Do you know what that is?' I shook my head and he told me. It sounded appropriately vile. He went on: 'Anyway, as a side-effect, my hair started to grow darker. It was astonishing: I had dark roots and grey ends, as if I'd hitherto been dyeing my hair grey to look older. The consultant was delighted. He cut off some of it, so as to prove it hadn't been dyed.'

I hadn't noticed, but the owner was standing behind us, about to ask whether the meal was satisfactory. Instead, he laughed merrily:

'That old story,' he said.

Orbach explained:

'That's how we know each other. We share a consultant. The best in the business.'

I thought: it's a long way for a radical lawyer to travel. I meant him, not me: Frederick's; swopping medical stories with the owner and I didn't need to ask if it'd been on the National Health. He was inhabiting a different world than he used to, or than I was familiar with. But I dare say the Mathers would be totally at home here.

The owner sat down, invited by a movement of Orbach's left eye. I'm not sure what instinct made me ask, while he was still there:

'Are either of you a freemason?'

'Is,' Orbach corrected.

I scowled; Mather wasn't paying for Orbach to give me a lesson in grammar; no one was that rich.

The owner said:

'I used to be. Why?'

I shrugged and Orbach explained:

'My. . .uh. . .acquaintance is investigating a firm of solicitors with strong masonic links.'

'Oh, Mather's,' he said nonchalantly.

I was beginning to wonder why we bother to advertise ourselves as 'confidential'.

'What's Royal Arch freemasonry?' I asked.

I don't know if he would have told me or not, because at that precise moment the manager approached and whispered something in his ear which caused him to rise and apologize for leaving us. Unlike my question, it was probably something really important, like whether someone's beef was rare or not.

But Orbach answered:

'Freemasonry has two sides. There's the freemasonry everyone knows about, which is craft freemasonry and meets in Lodges, and there's Royal Arch freemasonry, which meets in Chapters. About one in three craft freemasons is Royal Arch. Craft freemasonry has a lot of ritual, but it's nothing compared to Royal Arch, some of which borders on the black magic.'

'I take it the answer is "yes", you are a freemason?' I confess I was surprised, though I'm not sure more that he'd join or that they'd have him. He reassured me:

'No, I'm not.'

'You know a lot about it,' I accused, before I remembered that I was talking to someone to whom an allegation of knowing something he wasn't supposed to – anything – was a compliment. He explained:

'One of the London Borough Councils – Hackney – conducted an inquiry into freemasonry. I did a job for them afterwards, and I had to read the report. Not because of freemasonry,' he added: 'I think the man who conducted the inquiry concluded that if there was organized freemasonry in the Council, it had to be a good thing, because nothing else was organized. So he spent most of his time writing about their management: that was what I was concerned with. But I read the stuff about freemasonry, too. It interested me, and I read some other books about it later.'

I tried to focus on what he was saying, but accidentally he'd managed to extract a splinter from the conversation with Katrina. She had said that Andrew Mather reminded her of one of the left-wing Council leaders. Russel talking about Hackney told me which: its leader was the chubby-cheeked would-be chilling challenge to Thatcherism she'd had in mind. Another unnatural coincidence?

'You still haven't told me about Westmoreland House,' I reminded him.

'No more I have. And you still haven't told me why you think I might be willing to help you – this pleasant occasion aside, which will hardly equal the bill you'd get if you approached me formally.'

I said:

'Well, Russel, I know how interested you are in truth and fairness and things like that.'

He grinned disarmingly.

'For auld acquaintance?' I tried again.

He shuddered: old acquaintances, in his framework of reference, usually meant old enemies.

'Katrina was a friend of mind,' I said suddenly, thinking honesty might be the best policy. Even if it wasn't accurately an answer to his question, it was both true and the sort of information that might well lead even a cynic like Orbach to help.

I should have known better. He laughed:

'I haven't yet paid everyone off for all my own friends who got hurt; why should I bother with yours?'

There was no alternative but to level with him:

'I figured, you still wouldn't be too keen on the whole history of Disraeli Chambers making headlines.' If in doubt, blackmail; everyone's got something to hide.

'That's better,' he said huskily: 'I just wanted to hear you say it. I don't like hypocrisy, Dave, you know how much I don't like hypocrisy.' His view of his erstwhile colleagues at Disraeli Chambers as hypocrites – not, it must be said, a view without firm foundation – had led him, in substance if not in any form susceptible to a criminal charge, to orchestrate the demise of some of their number.

I knew now why he was willing to meet with me. Disraeli Chambers had been his most painful experience: while he was a member; and, later, when he took his revenge. He still couldn't let go of the experience. I was a part of it. It was still the time or the event during which he had felt most alive. He used to live – I recollected – with a woman who was now a Member of Parliament, Margot McAllister. He told me once they had separated because he didn't want all the interference in his private life that went with a public profile. I wondered how she felt: to have to take second place to a wound in all probability he had inflicted on himself.

I knew why he was a skilful lawyer, though. The way other people found themselves talking to me about things they – erroneously – believed I already knew, I found myself talking to him. I told him about the leaks – not in any detail, but enough for him to feel gratified that his analysis of what I was doing at Mather's was correct. I told him about the firm's freemasonry connections, about which he already knew. I told him about Randolph's way of demonstrating desire, and about Andrew's apparent addiction to the gaming table.

He told me, which I already knew from the files, that neither Andrew nor Randolph had anything to do with Westmoreland House. He told me, as was from the files also quite obvious, that the leak had to have come from Mather's. In other words, he told me nothing new. Then I asked him:

'Everything I hear says Ian Mather ain't a man to take kindly to a gambling habit. And there's more to it than a gambling debt, I'd swear. So what I want to know is, who is Andrew more frightened of than his father, so much so that he won't give me enough explanation to stop me running to Ian with the story?'

'Jabulon,' he said.

'Jabu-who?' I asked.

'Jabulon,' Russel Orbach repeated like he was telling me the time of day.

'And who, when he's at home, is Jabulon?'

'You asked me – or would have done so if you knew anything about grammar: of whom is Andrew Mather more frightened than his father, and I am telling you – Jabulon.'

'Fine. That tells me a whole bunch. So who is this Jabulon guy?'

'Jabulon,' he explained: 'Is the god of Royal Arch freemasonry. . . Of course,' he added, as if it ought all along to have been obvious.

Chapter Five

'I'll wait in the car, shall I?'

I was hoping she'd agree. I don't like hospitals, hospices, homes or anything which suggests death, disease or decline.

I also had reason to expect to be told to stay in the car. A visit to meet one's ageing and unwell mother is an unconventional opening gambit between a man and a woman, whatever the basis of their encounter.

I was the man. The woman was Allison Mather Hoyt. For the last week, I had been trying to fix a time when we could meet. She was a busy lady, but finally, this very afternoon, she had said:

'I can see you this evening. I have to go to see my mother in the home.'

She said 'the home' as if I ought already to know about her mother's condition, which as a matter of fact I did.

'You can come with me, and we can talk afterwards. I'll buy you dinner. Alright?'

The words came out staccato: she was used to laying down the law, and to having her commands obeyed. I was tempted to tell her to piss off, but a number of things stopped me.

One was that it was becoming increasingly irritating that I hadn't yet managed to talk with her. Another was the nervous undertone I sensed beneath the assurance, which softened its blow to my pride. The third was: Allison Hoyt was – as Dowell had foreshadowed – a spectacularly gorgeous woman, and, surprising as this may sound, it is not often that a spectacularly gorgeous woman offers to buy me a meal.

We didn't talk much when we left High Holborn. She wove her sports Mercedes through the rush-hour traffic as if she was at Le Mans or maybe like Kojak after he reaches out to put the detachable siren on the lid of his car. The difference was: no one else was giving way. I spent most of the journey in a state of abject terror, tightening and re-tightening my seat belt, praying to a God I'd long since ceased to believe in. If the car-phone rang, I decided I'd jump out: it would have to be safer.

The home was in North London, Whetstone or Finchley – somewhere out beyond the realms of good taste, in the Prime Minister's very own constituency. But for the sign which announced it as a 'medical nursing home', it could have been just one more of the generous houses set back from the road which reminded me of the sort of property I'd been brought up in: wealthy suburbia, leafy, clean, two cars to a drive and a nanny for every other child.

'No. Come up with me.'

'But. . . I don't know your mother.'

She smiled grimly:

'She won't know you either.'

Her tone brooked no argument. I followed her in through the automatic, glass doors. As soon as we were inside the hallway, a glance to my right confirmed the Thatcher connection: a framed display of newspaper cuttings and correspondence recorded a visit the Prime Minister had paid to the home, a half dozen years before. My keen investigator's intelligence told me: this was a private home, not state-run.

Allison acted as if she owned the establishment. Maybe she did. Her mother's room was behind the first-floor nurses' station. I went in after her. The room was bright but boring: an iron-framed hospital bed sticking out from one wall, fitted utility wardrobe, plain painted wallpaper, there was a card-table in a corner on which had been set out portrait photographs of the family; by her bed, just a jug of water.

85

Her mother was white-haired and gaunt. Even covered by a sheet and blanket, she was evidently wasting away. She stared at the ceiling, and did not turn to greet her daughter, or move as Allison bent to kiss her taut forehead. Allison held a finger to her lips, to warn me not to speak. She pointed to a stool against the wall beside the window, opposite the foot of the bed. For herself, she selected a chair at the side of the bed.

We sat in a silence so loud I could hear my trepidation ticking over. Allison's mother was completely still; I could not see her breathe. Occasionally, she moved a muscle, or closed her eyes for a few moments. Once, she twitched, as if to throw off a fly I also could not see. After a while, Allison said:

'It's me.'

There was a long pause before her mother replied:

'It's no good. It's no good. What do you think?'

'I think it's no good, too.'

'You have to do it right.'

'There's no choice, mother,' Allison seemed to understand, even though I couldn't.

The hardest thing to take about her mother's nonsense was the physical strength and clarity of her speech. If she had spoken feebly, or perhaps with long pauses between individual words, it might have been less contradictory; it would have helped me keep in mind that she was past all recognizably rational life.

I watched Allison, rather than her mother. There was no mistake. She really was as good-looking as I'd thought. Tall, flaxen-haired, wide-mouthed, bright-eyed, dressed in a striped blouse and a light-grey suit — with high heels to match — that looked fit to burst in the right places, and disappeared temptingly in others.

Though calm, there were tears in her eyes. I thought of my mother, long dead, taken by cancer many years before, comparatively young: I had cried then, and now I couldn't remember crying for her since.

'You've got. . . The. . . Numbers. What do you think?'

'I don't know what you mean, mother.'

'Well, you ought to know. It's your job to know.'

'Tell me again.'

'It doesn't matter. Go now. It's no good.'

'I've just arrived. I want to sit here for a while. I've brought someone to see you. He's a friend of Daddy's. He's a friend of the boys.'

'Go away. You're stupid. You ought to know.'

The thing that struck me most was: she was astonishingly beautiful. Her facial features were so clear, distinct, as fine as ever I had seen or studied. I was in the presence of death, but a slow and painful death, borne with a dignity I doubted I could achieve in full possession of my faculties, let alone, as she was, in possession of next to none. I knew Allison's mother was only in her late sixties or early seventies. She looked the way I'd always imagined those in their eighties or nineties would look.

We didn't stay long. It seemed like just a few minutes, though afterwards, when I glanced at my watch, I realized we'd sat there for more than half an hour. Her mother had little recognition of who Allison was, and I wondered why she came here – as I'd heard, most nights of the week – to suffer the torment of fundamental alienation, an uncrossable abyss. But as she leaned over her mother to kiss her goodnight, her mother smiled and it was easy to imagine how this alone made the visit worthwhile.

Then, when she whispered to her mother:

'I love you,' her mother replied:

'Me too.'

I didn't wait for Allison. I bolted down the stairs two at a bound, and rushed out into the car-park, gasping for air, fighting back tears, leaning finally against the car, my head resting on my sleeve. It brought everything back: my sister's 'phone call – 'come now, not much longer'; the three of us in the hospital ward; after, they'd cried, and I, to my ever-lasting shame, had walked away, not to let go until I reached home and could weep and weep and weep in private until the sobs came out dry. It had been as if there was nothing left between myself and infinity.

I think my tears made Allison's superfluous. She

looked at me curiously, but didn't say anything while she unlocked the car, and slid behind the wheel, waiting for me to join her. I felt a fraud: I was supposed to be mister hard-boiled, and I'd just disclosed I was barely cooked.

We drove, as we'd started out from High Holborn, in silence, towards Highgate, where she lived. After I'd calmed down, I said, by way of explanation:

'My mother died.'

'Yes. I guessed. I'm sorry.'

'I'm sorry about yours, too. How long has it been?'

'A year like this, but two or three years in all. I keep thinking it can't be much longer. But her heart's as strong as an ox.'

'Is it always this bad?'

She laughed:

'Bad? That was good. She didn't hit me tonight. Sometimes, she's so violent they have to restrain her.'

'She. . . . I hope you don't mind me saying this: but she's incredibly beautiful.'

'Yes,' she sighed: 'She was always a beautiful woman, but never so beautiful as now. It's so damn, damn unfair. Sometimes, I just can't cope with how unfair it is.'

She drove no less adventurously than before, though there was now little traffic on the roads. When we stopped at lights, she said:

'The hardest thing is: she knows. I mean, she knows she's alive, She knows she's in a bad way, she knows it's all gone – her life until now – and all she wants is to die. When it started, after we put her in the home, when she was more lucid than now, she told me so, she begged me to make it happen, there were two months when she simply wouldn't eat. They put her on an intravenous drip – I didn't want them to, I wanted them to let her go. But by the time I won the argument, and they took the drip out, her mind had deteriorated further, and with it her will – her will to die. Now I think she blames me, because I haven't helped her die, because I can't do anything to release her from. . . It. . . This.'

We pulled up at the Highgate Village Wheelers fish

restaurant. Like magic, there was space outside, which she seemed to take for granted – a lady for whom magic happened all the time. She'd booked a table: they knew who she was, no one asked her name, the manager greeted her warmly. He led us to our table and asked whether we wanted a drink before our meal.

Allison shook her head:

'Wine with it.'

It was time for self-assertion:

'I'll have a large Southern Comfort. No ice. No soda.'

'I've heard you're a drinker,' she was polite enough to wait until the manager had departed to investigate my peculiar order before she made her comment.

'I've heard you ain't,' was my less than witty riposte.

'What else have you heard?'

'That you're an extremely hard-working solicitor, very clever, so clever that you might have made partner even if you weren't who you are. And I've heard it said there are people who've been with the firm long enough to remember you once smiled, though nobody's putting money on it.'

She had to fight not to lose the bet:

'I don't see a lot to smile about, do you?'

'Yes, sure. You're a lovely woman, you're rich, you drive a Mercedes, you're having dinner with me – hell, what've you got to complain about?'

The waiter hovered; we ordered fish; she ordered wine.

'Does it make you feel nervous. Mr Woolf? Being taken out by a woman, I mean?'

'Nope. It makes me nervous being called mister, though.'

'What do people call you normally? Hey, you?'

'On a good day. Waddayawant the rest of the time. Try Dave. I promise it won't bite.'

She examined me curiously, much as she had outside the nursing home.

'I've heard a lot about you, too, Dave.'

I waited. We were on my favourite subject. She made me beg.

'So, tell.'

'Let's see now. I've heard you were kicked out of your previous practice by your partner – Sandra Nicholl – because you were too stoned to know what time of day it was. I've heard you've been scratching a living as a private detective and but for the debacle at Disraeli Chambers would probably be waiting outside someone's home right now trying to serve them with a divorce summons.'

She paused to take stock, then continued:

'I've heard you're supposed to be some sort of left-winger, but can't decide which. I've heard you're now having a scene with your ex-partner, but can't resist hopping into bed with anything in skirts.'

I winced at that, but could guess the source: the late and momentarily less lamented Katrina Pankhurst. She continued blithely:

'I've heard Randolph was so pissed off about your appointment he actually came in on time, to try and talk my father out of it, and Andrew dared contradict Iron Ian for the first time since he stopped wetting his pants. Martin says he quite likes you and doesn't give a damn, but if the other two care that much about it and the money's right, he wouldn't mind handling a contract on your life.'

As she spoke and gathered pace, she finally gave way and grinned:

'It must be nice to be so popular, Dave.'

'I dunno. I never had occasion to find out,' I sighed: 'How come Martin'd take the contract? He need the money?'

'No. But he's awfully into that sort of butch pastime, haven't you noticed?'

'I gather he doesn't hang out in seedy, Earl's Court gay-bars. But that doesn't say much.'

'I feel closest to Martin, though that doesn't mean much. Andrew's the one who comes to talk to me most: cry on big sister's shoulder. But I don't see much of any of them – socially, I mean, we work together a lot. You've probably realized by now that feelings aren't high on the Mather family agenda. We don't talk much other than work. And I don't know if

Martin realizes he's the only one I actually care about. Did you know he goes to a gym three nights a week?'

'Yup. He thinks I ought to do the same,' I added wryly: 'Seems to think I ain't fit,' I patted the Sahara of my stomach.

She examined me critically:

'He may have a point.'

I shrugged:

'It's hard enough work just staying drunk, y'know?'

For only the second time, she smiled:

'Yes, I'm finding out.'

Contrary to what I'd said I'd heard, or perhaps for that reason alone, she'd drunk more of the first bottle of wine than me. Reading my thoughts, she signalled the waiter to bring us another.

We'd finished the main course, and I slouched back in my seat:

'Why've you been giving me the run-around at work?'

'Why not? I hadn't made up my mind what use you were to me.'

'Lady, you got balls. You're supposed to be use to me, not the other way around. Anyhow, how come you found out all that shit about me?'

She shrugged:

'Second nature. D'you ever think of this: I'm a Mather; I'm his child as much as they are; and Randolph's been married, and Andrew's still married, and I've been married, but I'm the only one who gets to change her name, and now nobody even knows I'm a Mather anymore. You know, the old Avis line: we try harder.'

'What happened to Hoyt?'

'He was a bastard. I still spend at least ten minutes every day wondering why I married him, and then the same again wondering how come so many of my friends married shits just like him. I figured finally: there's a lot of truth in Freud; we're all looking for our fathers; and our fathers were all shits. Maybe fatherhood is just a shitty idea: it's a pretty fundamentally oppressive relationship – parent and child, 'specially a father and his children, don't you think?'

91

She'd poured and drunk the first glass out of the new bottle as soon as it was set down on the table. I didn't mind being asked and taken out by a woman, but I minded one who could drink more than me. My bladder was full but I was scared that if I got up to empty it, I might miss the best part of the programme.

'I try not to think about it. I know I wouldn't want children. . .'

'Why not?'

'Hell, I don't know. They might grow up to be like me. That's a good enough reason, isn't it? You didn't have any children with Hoyt, did you?'

'No and for the same reason. They might've grown up to be like him. Or me. Ah, shit, I'm drunk, you know that don't you, Woolf? Is that what you're waiting for? To get me pissed so I'll spill all the family secrets – or the firm's – which is the same thing. Or are you trying to get me into bed?'

'You didn't tell me what happened to Hoyt,' I avoided her questions, mostly because I still didn't know which was true.

She sneered at my cowardice, and got up:

'Back in a minute', she slurred.

I'll tell you – in the interval – what I sometimes think is the true reason I can't settle down with Sandy. It's embarrassing, because it's so shallow. But. I love legs. I don't mean Sandy hasn't got good legs: she has excellent legs. But she's short, and they're short, and when I mean I love legs what I mean is I love long legs. Legs like Mather's secretary's legs. Legs like someone you're sitting opposite on the train and you start at the high heels and your eyes climb up her tights until they disappear and all you want to do is follow.

Legs like Allison Hoyt's, as I watched her weave her way across the restaurant, wishing I could go with. I was thinking about this so hard, I forgot to take the opportunity to go to the toilet myself.

The waiter hovered:

'Will you be requiring dessert, sir?'

I didn't require dessert, but I wanted dessert. On the other hand, I didn't know if Allison wanted dessert.

At this particular moment, I figured our relationship was decidedly rocky. Was it worth risking what might be left of it by making the wrong decision? I ordered profiteroles, for both of us.

'Give me a cigarette and I'll tell you what happened to Hoyt,' she said as she sat down again.

'I didn't know you smoked,' I pushed over to her the pack of Camels I'd left out on the table.

'I don't. Just once in a while,' she said, just like her kid brother.

'Tell me about Hoyt, then,' I said when she'd finally – and with difficulty – got the cigarette properly alight.

'He was a salaried solicitor at Mather's, and if we'd stayed together then he'd probably've become a partner. When things started to fall apart, my father saw him and told him it wouldn't make any difference in the firm. Then Randy saw him, and told him he might as well start looking for a job. Then Martin saw him, and suggested he make a will before it was too late. Then Andrew saw him, and offered to find the money for him to set up in practice somewhere else.'

'And he did which?'

'Well, the only real choices were trust my father, or trust Andrew. He trusted Andrew. So Andrew helped him just like he said he would. He found someone else looking for a partner and Hoyt went quiet as a mouse to his firm.'

'And?'

'And then they all set to work. Hoyt and his partner started the firm with a thirty thousand pound injection of capital, Hoyt's share of which was borrowed, and an overdraft limit of twenty thousand pounds. A year later, they needed an overdraft of fifty thousand. A year after that, they needed an overdraft of a hundred thousand. Every time they got a new client, they lost two others.'

She paused to savour the story, then continued:

'By the time it was over, Alex personally owed the bank a hundred and eighteen thousand. Then – and only then – did we start to discuss the divorce. He's working at the Law Society now, earning maybe sixteen-eighteen thousand, and living in a one-bedroom flat in would you believe it Finsbury Park.'

Her eyes shone, not with pleasure but excitement:

'We Mathers, we have our own special little way, y'know?'

'And what's your own special way mean for me, then?'

She took her time selecting a reply. I watched her swirl them round like a selection of the finest dresses on a rotating rack in a store.

The waiter gave her time to think. He delivered the profiteroles pompously, with a performance so riveting it wasn't until after he left that she asked:

'What are these for?'

'I ordered what I wanted. I'll have yours.'

If I'd been asked to guess beforehand what her answer was going to be to my question, it wouldn't've come out as it did:

'You wanna sleep with me, Woolf?'

This time, she left no room for me to avoid the proposition. I stuffed the last of my profiteroles into my mouth, and pulled her plate towards me.

I don't think my hesitation pleased her. She expected the same obedience in her personal life as professionally.

I chose my words exactly, with the sort of attention to caring detail that only committed self-interest could secure:

'Yes. And. No. I think you're extremely good-looking, very sexy, and physically there's not much more I'd rather do than go to bed and play with you. On the other hand, you're a pain in the arse, ruder than I am, and care even less how much damage you do to a person's feelings. For a relationship, I'd probably take the chance; for a screw, I'd rather jerk off.'

As I spoke, the blood drained out of her face, and the resemblance to her mother became more marked. There were no smiles left at the dinner table. She bit her lower lip, to stop herself showing hurt. Inside, I screamed out to apologize, touch her, comfort, explain

I'd had to say all that to get clear of the clutter and confusion by which our evening had been marred. Instead, I grit my teeth, rose, bowed mockingly, and said:

'I'm pig enough already not to hang out with other pigs. We might suit each other, but we don't need each other.'

I left, proud of my resolve, calculating that as and when Sandy and I got back together, I could turn it into something she'd be proud of me for, and regretting I hadn't had the time to finish my second dessert.

I was still waiting for a taxi when she came out. At first, she ignored me, and unlocked her car as if I was no more than a passing member of the dirty raincoat brigade. She couldn't carry it off, though, and instead of getting in behind the wheel, she turned and dangled the keys:

'I'm too drunk to drive. Will you take me home?'

I shook my head, not to say 'no', but meaning it wasn't a good enough apology.

'You're right, Woolf, you are a pig. I'm sorry I'm one too. Will you please take me home?'

She reached inside the car and inserted the key into the ignition. Then she walked around it as stilted and careful as a drunk, and settled herself into the passenger seat.

She lived in a characterless, but modern and probably expensive apartment development near enough she could have walked if she was really worried about her ability to drive. There were half a dozen low-rise blocks, surrounded by a low wall, flat-roofed, insipid red-bricked, aluminium windows, entry-phones, pallid plants, turfed plots, a handful of lock-up garages and signs which said 5 m.p.h. and which I ignored. I parked at the back, contradicting an instruction to 'Leave Garage Doors Clear.'

At first, she headed for a door, then she swung around and pointed up a grass bank:

'Go on, lead the way.'

I did as bid, though not without stumbling badly enough to stain the trousers of the new suit I'd bought in anticipation of Mather's money. She took off her heels before she clambered up after me.

'Where are we going?' I whispered.

It was an adventure. A trespass. Children exploring an abandoned house.

'This way.'

Beyond the apartments, in the middle of the gardens, was a fenced-off section. She held a finger to her lip, as she had done in her mother's room, but in entirely different vein. At the gate, she fiddled for the right key, unlocked it and held it open for me, before pushing it gently back behind us, reaching through the bars to close the padlock.

It was a swimming pool. She took me to the end furthest from the apartments, and sat down on the grass, pulling me down beside her.

'It didn't used to be fenced,' she said quietly: 'But a couple of years ago, some people went for a midnight dip – and a bit more. The older residents didn't like it, so they fenced it off a few days later.'

'Local kids?' I asked idly, wondering when and if she was going to let go of my hand.

She giggled:

'They thought.'

She stood up, still holding my hand so I had to do the same. She pulled me up and pressed herself against me snaking her free hand around the back of my neck until, all arguments aside, my lips met hers and we kissed open-mouthed and wet, like guzzling ice-cold water on a boiling hot day. She stepped back as suddenly as it had begun, letting go my hand, pushing my head away so she could see into my eyes, as puzzled and as curious and as wounded as if I had grabbed her.

Before I could protest my innocence, though, she had stripped off the jacket of her suit and let it fall on the ground. I was still wondering what her game was as she unbuttoned her blouse and peeled it off proudly revealing full breasts held up by a half-bra. Then the bra came off.

'Come on,' she hissed: 'You too.'

She didn't wait to see if I did as I was told, but lowered herself into the water, drawing in her breath sharply at the cold.

It brought back a memory, so old and in parts so revealing, that I'd conveniently managed not to think about it for several years.

In my early twenties, keen and unfulfilled, I'd met a woman in a Mayfair coffee bar and we'd talked and talked until the early hours of the morning. Gawky and unsure, I'd said to her as we left:

'Let's walk through the Park.'

There were no barriers to prevent access to Hyde Park; just a low fence a midget could've stepped over. We walked, occasionally hand in hand, down to the Serpentine Boating Lake. When we reached the hut from which boats were hired out I invited her:

'Let's go round,' thinking maybe I'd score a kiss or cop a feel.

As soon as we were standing on the wooden jetty she cried:

'Come on,' pulling her dress over her head and diving into the water before I realized my luck.

I followed. We swam out first towards one of the tiny islands, but were scared off by cackling geese. Instead, we swam to the middle of the lake where the rental boats were moored for the night. I climbed into one and it was her turn to follow me. Scared, I said to her – little realizing how commanding I must have sounded:

'Lie down,' so we shouldn't be seen.

She obeyed; I did the same; I slipped a hand under her head, to protect it from the hard and wet deck. After that, I couldn't have cared less any longer whether or not we were seen from the shore.

It is the postscript to this tale that embarrasses. A few weeks later, I was in the same coffee lounge, chatting to – or up – another woman. I can't remember the first one's name, but this second one was Lindsay. When we left at closing time, I said:

'Let's walk through the Park.'

With markedly less enthusiasm than I or my previous night-walking companion, she agreed. I wasn't worried. I knew the magic formula.

'Let's go round,' I said when we reached the boathouse.

This time, I had to take the lead:

'Come on in, it's fine,' I called from the water.

Hesitantly, Lindsay did so. I didn't bother with the island, but swam direct to the cluster of boats in the centre and, equally single-minded and determinedly, clambered in to one.

She swam around the boats, hung onto mine with one hand, but refused to climb in with me. Eventually, I gave up my desperate design and, frustrated, jumped out. The oarlock went straight into my armpit, so fast and so hard I hardly felt it. Clutching my arm to my side instinctively, the way a chicken without its head carries on twitching for several minutes more, I doggie-paddled single-pawed to the shore.

Back on the jetty, Lindsay helped me dress, and took me to St George's Hospital. I was dazed and still unsure just what had happened. They cleaned me up, and gave me a shot of Pentathol. My only recollection of the hospital is of the doctor saying:

'If it had gone an inch deeper, you would have lost the use of your arm for life. But that wouldn't have been long, because you would have bled to death by the time you got to shore.'

Lindsay walked me home – to the same rented, basement apartment I still occupy – and assisted me into bed, bringing me a hot milk drink to see me off to sleep. I have no memory of her leaving, only that as I lay there, still under the drug, and she sat at my side, I said:

'It's too late for you to go home. Why don't you stay the night?'

There were no boats in the swimming pool at Allison Hoyt's estate. No boats, but Allison floating, teasing, encouraging me to sink my overweight body into the uninviting cold, night water.

I shook my head:

'Uh-huh. You can catch a cold if you want, I've money to make in the next few days.'

Eventually, she realized I was not going to give in. Sulkily, she climbed out and slipped on her blouse and skirt without bothering to try and dry herself off. Without a word, she let us out of the enclosure and we slid back down the grass bank, landing close to where I'd left her car. We stood there for a moment, each hesitating for different reasons.

I didn't want to go inside. I knew what might happen, and how difficult it would be to put up any resistance. She was as appetizing stripped for service as the description in the menu. But it still felt wrong.

On the other hand, I'd hardly endeared myself to her so far and willing though I'd been to walk out when she gave me the excuse in the restaurant, she had apologized. If I now left her in this ambiguous position, I'd be the one at fault.

I can only guess at her reasons. Torn between persisting with the play she had initiated in Wheelers and pushed further at the poolside, or accepting – with whatever ill-grace she could muster – the apparent rejection. But after all, I'd only refused to join her in the water, so I wasn't that surprised when she tossed her head towards a back door into the block.

'Come on,' she hissed: 'I'm freezing.'

Her apartment was locked up like a New Yorker's, with three different bolts before we could get in. It was a surprisingly small flat: the entry lobby was the dining area off which led doors to the kitchen, the living-room and a short inner lobby which gave onto two further rooms and bathroom. She told me to go into the living-room and pour myself a drink:

'Me too. Brandy.'

There was no Southern Comfort. I had to make do with Drambuie. I could hear the shower running in the other half of the apartment. I wondered if she was waiting for me to bring her drink through: I'd already seen all she had to offer, but inside would be that much more intimate.

She didn't bother dressing. She curled up in her

bathrobe on the sofa. I was safely ensconced in a matching armchair. She was the first to break the long silence:

'You gay?' she slurred.

I grinned:

'Not that I'm aware of. It's like a man saying a woman who won't sleep with him is frigid, isn't it?'

She inclined her head graciously:

'Fair enough. But you were turned on downstairs,' when we'd kissed: 'Is it Sandy Nicholl? Or scared of AIDS?'

I lit a Camel:

'If the Big C don't get you, the Big A will.'

'We could use something,' she made her final offer. She – correctly – read my silence on Sandy to mean I'd brushed her first question aside as not worth answering.

'No. It's not that. I'm not really scared of AIDS' I laughed nervously: 'More like scared of you.'

She savoured this admission for a while:

'That's the damn problem. You all are. I'm surrounded by men who're afraid of me, sexually. It's sexist. Like, if I'm a successful lawyer, I can't possibly have enough left to be a successful woman too.'

'Maybe,' I shrugged: 'But you already told me what happened to the last guy that got involved with the boss' daughter.'

'You're not going to stay, are you.' It wasn't a question; more like an accusation.

I shook my head again:

'Nope. Sorry. You must know part of me wants to.' I was finding it increasingly difficult to hold hard to my resolve: 'I've got to go. I'll pick up a cab on the street. Really, I'm sorry. Maybe, some other time,' I tailed off lamely.

She followed me to the door, biting her lower lip, holding her bathrobe tightly together. At the door, she took my hand:

'We wouldn't have to do anything,' she seemed on the verge of tears: 'Can't you see? I'm lonely. I'm scared.'

It still felt too close to a command for comfort.

'I know. We all are,' I said as I opened the door.

Chapter Six

I was an inch out the door when she accused:

'Just like you walked out on Kat.'

I froze. I said, without turning:

'I didn't walk out. I wanted to stay. She made me leave.'

But I was not telling the whole truth and she had made her point so I pushed the door shut with me on the inside.

'You have to level with me. If I'm going to help, you have to tell me what you know. Do you understand?'

She bit her lower lip, and nodded. She crossed the room and put her arms right around me and hugged me and said:

'Later. Please.'

After all the come-ons and turn-downs of the evening, I was in no condition any longer to refuse. I let her lead me by the hand to the bedroom, where she turned down the cover of the bed and climbed in quickly, like a little girl waiting for daddy to kiss her goodnight.

At the time, it seemed like it went on for ever, far longer than I knew it or I could. When finally we had finished, we lay there, drenched in sweat, gasping for breath and holding on tight, relieved we hadn't drowned.

After a while, she let go and sat up beside me. I was drifting off to sleep. When I awoke, an hour or so later, I was alone. I could hear her taking another shower. She didn't return to bed. Instead, she made us each a cup of tea, and we sat in the living-room, she in her bathrobe, me with a towel wrapped around my waist, talking the way we should have spent the evening talking but I was glad we hadn't.

'Tell me who else knows.'

'Knows what?' She asked dully.

'Knows you leaked the report.'

'How did you know?'

'I figured it out. That's my job. There were precious few people who qualified for plumber of the year award. You were one. The money motive didn't hold: the plaintiffs were relatively poor people, represented by solicitors on legal aid who wouldn't ethically be able to pass on a bribe even if the parents collectively had the cash. The odds against finding one parent, with enough money for a bribe, prepared to shell out and share rather than make a private deal, are infinite.

'For a long time, I concentrated on the freemasons: they're supposed to be into sharing secrets, aren't they? But it wouldn't add up: you'd have to find two good freemasons – one either side – and that was hardly likely.

'Then there was the notion of some sort of grudge motive, but that had to mean whoever it was wanted to see Latimer walk out on Mather's which wouldn't tie up with who had the opportunity. None of you would want that: it's a lot of regular money on account to say good-bye to. Besides, I said to Kat, it's a classic case for a bleeding heart leak. Once I started thinking that way, it narrowed down the field: I'm not sure any of your brothers have got a heart, and John Gauldie's belongs to freemasonry alone. I was looking for a connection to a deformed child.'

I swallowed my tea: 'But it's all the same, isn't it? Deformed child needing constant care and attention. Mother beyond all reason in hospital. They're just different forms of disability, which make life hell both for those who suffer from it, and for those who have to look after them. . .'

'We had the money,' she interrupted: 'Most of those parents didn't. Imagine what it's been like for them. Especially the women, the ones who have to do the day-to-day caring.'

'I'm not criticizing you did it, Ali. I might've done it. But I need to know who knows.'

I'd already guessed the answer by the time she said, flatly:

'Only Katrina knew.'

'And that's why you're scared?'

She shrugged but didn't reply.

'What you haven't told me, why do you think there's a connection?'

'I don't know there is. But Katrina was scared. She told me she was; she told you so.'

'Now you tell me,' I insisted gently.

And so she did. She told me the bits and pieces she had picked up not merely over the last two or three years, but back in the family and the firm history. It was the account of a child, still trying to work out why grown-up life wasn't as much fun as she'd been brought up to expect.

She told me about her Uncle James, who she had never met and of whom her father would not speak. From her mother she drew a picture of a man who scorned the rules by which everyone else had to live, and who viewed his younger half-brother with a mixture of amused contempt and patronizing protection. A man who might one day turn up at dinner-time, uninvited, and remain for the evening, eating and drinking everything that was available, but that had been laid out for everyone else. On another, he would take them out to expensive restaurants, insisting that even the young child Randolph eat the very best.

She knew from her mother, too, that her father had mixed feelings about James. James was older. He had known a time when their own father was not so wealthy, when they had still been living in Glasgow, until after Ian's father's second marriage, to Ian's mother. When they moved south, Ian was still living at home, but James took off on his own, in and out of one venture after another.

Ian had served in the war, with distinction; James had secured a medical deferment on unknown grounds that were probably corrupt. Afterwards, when Ian and

103

John Gauldie set up the firm, James was their first, and for a while best, client: it was the time when the brothers saw the most of each other. They were very close, and Ian would not hear a word against James.

One day, Ian had come home, silent and brooding. Ali's mother had known beforehand that there were problems concerning James, but in those days, and given the sort of relationship she had with Ian, she had been told nothing about them. Shortly after, James disappeared and when Ali's mother brought up his name, she was told to forget him, to forget he had ever existed.

Naturally, to the children as they were born and grew up enough to acquire a scent of the story, it was exciting, rich terrain for the imagination: a spy, lost in foreign parts, imprisoned for service to his country or at the other extreme for crimes too unpleasant to mention. Randolph affected the superiority of the only one who 'knew' his uncle, but it was a pose: James had gone when Randolph was four or five years old.

'I've heard,' I offered: 'That he maybe wasn't honest.'

'I know.'

'How?'

'Martin. Martin went to the States when finally he qualified. It was his treat, his reward.' After the long route to qualification.

'How did they meet?'

'I don't know much. I know my father made him promise not to look for James, and I know Martin met him. He'd never tell me, except he insisted he hadn't broken his promise, so it must have been an accident or a coincidence.' She no more believed it than I was supposed to. 'He only said he's very rich and that he – Martin – realized it wasn't all honest. But he said James was beginning to put his money into legitimate activities.'

I pushed a little further:

'I've also heard. . . Perhaps, violent?'

She frowned:

'Where did you hear that? Martin's never. . .'

'No, not Martin. Someone else. Don't forget,' I said: 'I'm supposed to be a detective.'

'Was it Dowell?'

'Why'd'you ask that?'

'I don't know. I just get a feeling about him. Like he knows more than he lets on.' She was probing me.

My turn to shrug:

'Maybe. He's no fool. A long way from. D'you know he has a law degree?'

She shook her head, uninterested.

'He shouldn't be underestimated. I've made that mistake.' A mistake that saved my life. 'Anyway, what's to hide?'

She wasn't really listening. She was starting a whole new train of thought. She said:

'I don't trust John Gauldie.' She said, and stopped, needing a prompt.

'Why?'

'There's something devious about him. Sometimes I think he hates my father.'

'I thought freemasons are supposed to be about brotherly love?'

'Sometimes I think he's trying actively to undermine my father. Randolph looks up to him more than he looks up to father: he's influenced Randolph more than father has, and much more than father realizes. That makes it true of Andrew as well. My father is much, much the better lawyer, intellectually, but John has always conducted the greater share of the litigation. He's tactical: they admire that more than they admire father's type of law. But it goes beyond that: there's a loyalty to Gauldie that transcends even their loyalty to my father.'

'They've been partners for ever. Surely. . .'

'No, no, you're wrong.' When she shook her head to emphasize her point, she was even more beautiful. It was hard to continue the conversation instead of bringing her back to bed. 'Of course he never says anything. But I've seen the way he looks at my father sometimes. He's a thousand miles away and he's not listening but he's thinking and what he's thinking is how much he wants to be the senior partner, how he doesn't want to have to account for himself to anyone else, how he wants it to be his firm.'

'He must own a major slice?'

'Not that big. It was always my father's money, from his father – maybe from James, too. Probably not actual cash; probably just from his work. He brought all his 'business associates'. I've looked in some of those old files, right back to the fifties, and they're fascinating. Hundreds have a file note: referred by James Mather. If you include them, he was our biggest client before Latimer. But Gauldie handled almost all of them, while my father chased the better class of client, the old masonic families, the banks in the city, established companies.'

'How well do you know Latimer?'

'Not very. He's a remote figure. I've met him, of course; he's very charming. He got his start in this country, did you know that?' I nodded. It was all I did know about him. 'We did all his early work, and it just grew and grew. One of our solicitors went to work full-time for him.'

'A partner?'

'No. Initially, there were only four partners. One died young, and the other retired a couple of years ago. That's why Randolph's third in line – which is a big gap from John Gauldie.'

'What about Latimer?'

'John Gauldie's always handled his work, like he did my uncle's; well, for years now with Randolph. But if there's any issue – oh, I don't know, like over money, fees, the way a case has been conducted, a really major decision – Latimer won't talk to anyone except my father. That's who he really trusts, even though it's John who's done all the work. I think that's what John resents. He's nearly sixty, but so far as the firm's principal client is concerned, he might as well be Ian's articled clerk.' I knew the feeling.

'So why doesn't your father allow him a greater share, or a greater say?'

'He relies on people, but he doesn't really trust any-one, father, not anyone.'

'Not Martin?' I could understand him not trusting Randolph. But Martin was supposed to be the favour-ite.

'He's never approved of Martin's investment com-pany and even now Martin's not especially involved in it, he resents it.'

'What do you know about it?'

It kept cropping up, in the background and some-times in the main frame too. I'd sensed its relevance when Kat had talked to me; then Dowell had referred to it; and Martin had produced Tony Galucci like a heavy hint.

She smiled:

'Do you know the origin of the name?'

'No.'

'It's Katrina. It was a childhood nickname of Katrina's. The person who runs Cross Course – Beatrix Kelly – well, she's Katrina's sister.'

I said:

'I don't get the name.'

'I don't know how it started. Beat is Katrina's older sister and it was something silly she called Katrina when she was tiny but that stuck. Maybe because she was always cross or always chose the difficult path or some-thing like that. Originally, the company was Martin's, and it was called something else – I don't remember what. Beat had been in America, then she came back and went to work with Martin, which is how Martin met Katrina and how when she finished her finals she got offered articles with us.'

'Did Martin know Beat in America?'

'I don't think so.'

'And Galucci?'

'He was a business contact of Martin's, which is how Katrina met him.'

I shook my head:

'You people certainly believe blood's thicker than water.'

She didn't reply. Just stared at me as tears welled up

and began to flow down her cheeks. It wasn't, perhaps, the most tactful way of putting my point. I went over and sat beside her, putting my arm around her shoulder, stroking her hair.

'Ali,' I said gently, anticipating that the end of the conversation was approaching: 'Are you telling me all you know?'

'I don't know anymore; I don't know what's relevant.'

'What about Andrew. How much is he involved in everything?'

'Everything what?' She sniffed, pulling away. She got up and walked to the cabinet, from which she extracted the Drambuie bottle I'd damaged earlier. She held it up. I'd never refused before and could see no reason to start now.

Her question wasn't looking for an answer. She was saying I had no better idea what 'everything' was than she said she had.

I tried on her the same as on Martin:

'Maybe he's got money troubles.'

'Why? What makes you say that? What do you know?' She asked all in a bundle.

'I hear he gambles.'

She snorted:

'Tuppence halfpenny.'

'You sure?'

'Sure I'm sure. He likes the glamour – or she does; they like the late nights and the bright lights and the beautiful people with money to burn; but he's as Scot as the rest of us.'

Next morning, she dropped me off at home so I could change before I came into the office; neither of us wanted to be seen arriving together. My home was full of surprises: post that wasn't all bills, and a flashing answering machine. The machine hadn't seen so much activity since six debt collectors tried to contact me on the same day.

One of the calls was from Dowell: he'd be in to see me at Mather's at eleven. He sounded terse, less than friendly. The hour was odd: the pubs still wouldn't be open, even in the city. Another call was from Sandy, repeating that she wanted to talk with me: it was important. The letter that had attracted my attention as soon as I came through the door was addressed in a small, neat hand, in an embossed envelope. I extracted a single sheet, only a small part of which had been written on, in the same economical hand:

'The settlement allowed the landlords six months to find the money. We had to agree because they would otherwise have gone into liquidation; it wasn't certain we would get the money at all. They did pay, but a few weeks later someone bought the company – very cheaply, I hear. The question is: who? R.O.'

Signing himself with his initials was not an affectation: while an ordinary barrister signs his full name to a written opinion, a QC signs only initials.

I was not especially surprised to hear from him: I had not expected him to let it end with our dinner. Like Lewis, he had still to prove that he knew something others didn't know. I had a good idea what I would find out when I looked into who bought the landlord company: the same name that kept cropping up, Cross Course, was, I figured, bound to feature somewhere in the transaction. Later on, Dowell willing, I'd go down to Companies House and read me some records.

I made it into the office just in time for Dowell. I passed Allison on the stairs. Out of anyone else's hearing, she said:

'Are we going to meet tonight?'

'Sure, if you'd like to.'

'Maybe it would be a good idea for me to come to your place.'

'Why? It's really not very nice.'

'I just thought, well, I've got the car, and. . . You get a better idea about someone from where they live.'

I wasn't sure she'd like the ideas she'd get about me from my basement. But she had a point when she mentioned the car. I compromised:

'Whyn't we say you'll pick me up, and then we'll stay where seems best?' We agreed she'd come over after the nursing home, which meant around half past nine.

The brief exchange reminded me I had yet to return Sandy's call: I couldn't go on avoiding her forever. The trouble was, I still didn't know how I wanted a conversation to turn out; Ali wasn't making it easier to decide.

Marion buzzed me Dowell was on his way up: I asked for coffee for two. She said she'd already offered, but he had refused. She took it I still wanted mine. I told her she took it correct and I'd take it – and his – black. As I hung up, he came in. He had one of his men with him. I didn't know him: they all look alike to me.

"Morning, Tim,' I said, cheerful with cause: 'I gather you don't want any coffee. Sure?'

'Certain, thank you, sir,' he said more formal than since the first time we ever met. I hate it when people call me 'sir'; I know it can't be real respect, so it has to be sarcasm.

'This is Detective Constable Pratt. He'll be taking a note of our discussion.' He looked at me defiantly, daring me to make a joke about the officer's name. If my coffee had arrived to wake me up, I probably would have.

'The trouble is, Tim,' I said, incapable of calling him 'officer' or 'Inspector': 'There's only room for one extra chair.'

'So I see,' he said slowly and mournfully: 'Pratt will have to stand, then.'

I thought I saw a twinkle buried deep in one eye. He had seen the office at the same time I had; he knew as well as I did it couldn't take two spare chairs. He didn't mind Pratt having to stand. It made it a little easier for me to pretend to behave seriously.

'What can I do for you?'

'I was wondering if you have spent any time down in the basement, sir?'

I frowned: how did he know that?

I nodded.

'When?'

I told him.

'And how long were you there?'

110

'Maybe half an hour; maybe a bit more and then again maybe a bit less. Why?'

'If you'd just answer my questions, sir. Are you quite sure that you might not have been there for somewhat longer?'

'Sure I'm sure,' I'd picked up the expression from Ali.

'Did you smoke while you were down there?'

'There's a no smoking sign.'

'Yes, sir. And did you obey it, sir?' I winced: he was laying on the 'sirs' with a trowel.

'Of course I didn't bloody obey it, Tim. What's all this about?'

The no-smoking school is vicious, unfair and utterly sadistic. In the good old days, it was much more democratic: we all got a little bit ill every day, those of us who smoked only marginally more so than those who enjoyed, free of charge, the second-hand benefits. Now, there are no smoking signs every place you go. The effect on an inveterate smoker is inevitable: it is a constant reminder of an addiction which makes you want to light up another, long before you would otherwise have done so.

Dowell opened his briefcase and – at precisely the moment Marion Mortimore brought in my coffees – extracted a polythene evidence bag, containing a large number of half-smoked butts. He swung it distastefully across the desk at me and asked:

'You recognize the brand, I take it, sir.' Camels.

Marion put my coffees down, wrinkling her nose:

'Disgusting habit, I say.'

She removed my ashtray from the desk and waved it dramatically in front of my face before dumping the contents unceremoniously into the metal trash-can behind my seat, sending up a cloud of ash. I sighed; it was going to be one of those days. There was only one plausible reaction: I lit a Camel and blew smoke at them.

After she had left, Dowell asked:

'Do you think these might be yours sir?'

'You gotta be kidding. I can't afford to smoke that

many in a half hour. Nor can I afford to waste half
of them.'

He sighed:

'Very well, sir. That's all I have to ask you at the
moment.'

He turned to his assistant:

'That will be all, Pratt. Wait for me downstairs, will
you?'

'Right, guv.'

I pulled a face behind his back as he left:

'Do people really do that?'

'What?'

'Call you "guv"? Like on The Sweeney.' The Sweeney
= Sweeney Todd = Flying Squad; back in the seventies,
when the occasional British television production was
still worth watching.

'That one studied The Sweeney instead of going to
school. He's perfectly named,' he scowled.

'So what was all that about?'

'Just what it seemed. You're the only one here smokes
Camel. We found about ten, twelve butts. I had to estab-
lish if they were yours.'

'What if I'd said they were?'

'Then it wouldn't have suggested that someone hid
out down there for quite a long time, would it, arse-
hole?' I relaxed: we were back to normal. Whoever had
hit Kat had entered during the day, and waited in the
basement until the time had come to go upstairs. What
that led to was:

'How did he know no one ever went down there,
and how did he know she'd be here late?' The second
question was more interesting than the first, which was
a matter of general knowledge and general good taste.

'I'd say, yes, it's interesting.'

I muttered:

'Randolph.'

I'd already told Tim about Randolph's visit to see me
and the information he had wanted to seem reluctant
to disgorge.

'Seems that way.'

'What about day visitors? Are they all checked in?'

'Mostly, but not if they're just in and out: like messengers, for example.'

'So who got messengers that day?'

'It's not recorded. The doorman remembers a couple specifically, and he says there isn't a day when something or other doesn't arrive from one of Latimer's companies – often more than once. Usually, things are left off at reception, but sometimes something has to be signed for by a solicitor or a secretary. Then they'll send them up rather than ask whoever it is to come down. Time is money, remember?'

'Yes, thank God,' I was being paid for my time for a change.

'What's new, Dave?'

I leaned back in my chair, wondering what to tell him:

'You ever heard of James Mather?'

'Another legal luminary?'

'More like illegal. Would you be able to look back at files in the late forties and early fifties?'

'If it's worth my while. Why?' I outlined what I had learned. I also asked:

'What about enquiries in America?'

'They're not easy to pin down. Too many jurisdictions. You end up going from pillar to post. Local police, state police, immigration, customs, Organized Crime Task Force, Attorney-General's office, FBI, IRS, DEA, HAND.' I raised an eyebrow to query the last: I'd heard of all the others, even the Internal Revenue Service and the Drug Enforcement Administration.

He smiled wryly:

'HAND. Have A Nice Day. It's the one they always mention last. Just before they hang up.'

'Will you try?'

He shrugged:

'What do you want to know?'

'What he's up to, I suppose.'

'What are you saying?'

I shook my head:

'Nothing, really nothing. Just, well, if you know

113

there's a villain somewhere in the shrubbery, don't you like to have some idea what part he might be playing?' Another mixed metaphor to scatter with Kat's ashes.

'What else?'

'What time do gambling clubs open?'

'The Clairmount? Around the middle of the day. Why?'

'Again, I don't know. But would you have any serious objections if I paid a visit? I'm curious about this debt of Andrew's. He's hiding something; his sister says no way would he gamble that high.'

Again, he shrugged: why not? As he left, I thought it was all most suspicious: he was being too co-operative by half; it was entirely out of character to let me follow up my leads myself. He preferred to claim them for himself. I sighed: I had enough mysteries to worry about without that too; it would have to wait its turn.

I was just about to leave for Companies House when the outside line rang:

'Dave Woolf.'

'Sandra Nicholl,' she said dryly.

'Sandy. Hi. I was going to ring you. How'd'you know I was here?' The last sentence would have earned me a ten minute reprimand from Russel Orbach.

'A good guess. Once I realized you were working again, it wasn't that hard to work out what on.' I never said she was stupid.

'We ought to meet,' I said.

'What a good idea. I wish I'd thought of it.' Ouch.

She said:

'I'm ringing from the Law Society. What about lunch?' Double ouch. I couldn't lie my way out of it: my lies last in her presence like ice in a blast-furnace. We arranged to meet in the only place either of us could think of on the spot: the Freemason's Arms, where I'd met Katrina.

'I, uh, was figuring maybe you wouldn't want us to be seeing each other if I was working on it,' I said lamely, once we'd settled into a corner with our respective refreshments: white wine spritzer for her.

'And for the month before? Maybe you were waiting

for the case to begin?' Sandy has a tongue you could circumcise with.

'Fine, you wanna row,' I downed my drink: 'Let's have a row already.' I got up to fetch another. I can't fight with Sandy when I'm sober: it's an unequal contest; I'm not saying I win when I'm drunk, but at least it don't hurt so much.

She looked at me curiously when I returned, like she was trying to figure out what she'd ever seen in me. I wondered if she'd tell me. I reached out and took her hand:

'I do love you, you know.'

'Yes, I do know. It's not about that, is it? I'm getting too old for all of this, Dave; I don't want to spend my fortieth birthday wondering whose bed I'll be sleeping in, or sleeping in my own alone.' It was hard to think of her as beginning the approach to forty: she looked ten years younger.

'What do you want to do, Sandy?' I didn't want her to say it, but I could neither say what it was she wanted to hear nor else could I bring it to an end myself.

'I don't want to give you an ultimatum, Dave, but I can't keep on like this. If you can't – oh, shit, I don't know – I want to say "grow up" but it seems such a trite thing to say. Just that, though: grow up; we're both getting older; we've both got to start settling down or we'll wear ourselves out. Think about it, Dave, think about what I'm saying. And remember, if you don't want me, someone else just might, y'know.'

She jumped up, grabbed her handbag and left the table so fast I didn't have time to ask if she was going to the lavatory and coming back, or leaving altogether. After another quarter of an hour, I got the message, finished my third and somewhat belatedly followed her out of the pub, vaguely thinking – hoping? – she might still be in the street, waiting for me. It was lunch-time crowded: everyone else in the world was on the street, except Sandy.

I could no longer face the idea of reading fiches – microfilmed records. My alternative for the afternoon

115

appeared a lot more attractive. (I try to avoid the word alternative in case I misuse it. Years ago, I was at a meeting with Russel Orbach. Someone launched into a tirade in which she claimed there were only three alternatives. Russel brought her to a standstill by insisting emphatically that she was wrong. Once he had everyone's attention, waiting to see how he would flaw his opponent's argument, he said: 'There can only be two alternatives.' I'd looked it up when I got home and – as usual – he was right. Now you know why people love him.)

The Clairmount was a bright, white modern building not far from Knightsbridge, which also meant I was half-way home. The main door was open, but there was so little activity inside I wasn't sure the gaming rooms were. I was glad I was wearing my suit: the place was plush enough that even Ian Mather – if I could picture him with a gambler's green eye-shade drawn down on his forehead – would be comfortable. I told the man at Reception I'd like to see the boss.

'What would that be in connection with, sir?' Another smart-arse.

'It's private. Perhaps you could give him my card?'

He studied it disdainfully, but handed it nonetheless to a uniformed messenger and jerked his head towards a door. In a few minutes, the messenger returned and led me in.

'Mr Woolf?'

'Right. Dave. Mister makes me nervous.'

'Private detectives make me nervous,' he smiled disarmingly and gestured to a seat. He looked vaguely familiar, but I couldn't place him, and when I asked he denied that we'd ever met.

'Would you like something to drink?'

'Depends what's on offer.'

He waited. I asked. He didn't even raise an eyebrow. He took a bottle from the bar and poured me one, pouring his own from another bottle I couldn't see the label of.

'This is very civilized. People don't usually offer me a drink when they don't know what I want.'

He shrugged:

'Private detectives don't come to a club like this threatening trouble. I have – uh – too many good friends just outside the door, ready to come to my assistance.'

I held my hands up:

'I'm strictly non-violent. I'm sorry: I don't even know your name.'

'Michael Matheson. Mike. How can I help you?'

'I'm working for Mather's, the solicitors. I think you know one of them.'

He didn't say anything. Who owes gambling money is supposed to be as privileged as any information held by a lawyer: more so than much of that held by Mather's. Until someone welches on a debt: then the clubs like to go very public indeed.

'I think he owes you a lot of money: let's say eight to nine thousand pounds.'

'If you already think you know that, why are you asking me?'

'It's a funny thing, Mike, but a couple of the people who are closest to him insist there's no way he'd be that heavily into a gambling debt. How does it tally with your experience of him?'

'As you say, I know who he is. If he owed me that much money, he'd be good for it, wouldn't he?'

'What is that you're drinking? Cold tea?'

He chuckled:

'Apple juice. Do you want a refill?'

'Sure. D'you never drink?'

'I have one at about eight o'clock, and then a couple again between ten and midnight. That's the maximum on an ordinary, working day. It's a lot easier to pour myself something than to explain.'

'How long have you been in this racket?'

'A few years.'

'And you own the club?'

'My name's on the licence.' Another barrack-room witness.

'I don't know a lot about it. How'd's that work?'

'You have to declare any financial backers to the

Commission; they can refuse your licence, or revoke it, if they're considered undesirable.'

'And yours is the only name on the licence?'

'Correct. And as it's a matter of public record, no, I have no declared backers.'

'You must be a very successful man, Mike. It's a lot of club, a lot of expensive central London property, for a solo operator.' He didn't rise to being called a liar. I said: 'I got a friend owns a club, maybe you know him? Lewis.'

'I know him. He comes here once in a while. Why?'

'I dunno. I was thinking, maybe, you might like to give him a call, check me out, y'know?'

He tilted back his chair much as I like to do behind my desk, only he had lot more space. I saw his eyes dart downwards. He invited me:

'Come and have a look.'

The desk – from my side – was solid oak. From his, it was solid screen. There were twelve small screens, on which he could see, I presumed, every part of the club.

'Let's say for the sake of argument that I ring Lewis, and he says you are a good chap and I ought to help you. Is he going to give me some special reason? Like I'll get my kneecaps shot off if I don't, or you're the Commissioner's son and I'm in trouble come licence time?'

'I wish. No. But he'd probably say I was a friend of his and any help you could put my way would be something he'd view as a personal favour.'

He laughed out loud:

'You know Lewis. The godfather. He's a character: he gets away with it, too. You still haven't told me what you want to know. Or why.'

'Why's not so difficult: you've already been inter-viewed by the police about young Andrew's where-abouts.' Even I was doing it now: young Andrew.

'That's what you're investigating?'

'Right. For Ian Mather. So we can say I ain't investigating to get Andrew into trouble.'

'I've already talked with the police. He was here that

118

night. I'm quite certain of that: in fact, I could prove it to you.'

'How?'

He smiled.

'These,' he gestured below his desk: 'Are all on video. We video each evening's play, in full. Of course we only keep a selection.' He explained the circumstances when they might wish to keep a video: where there was contention over a game; where a large cheque had been paid and not yet cleared; on occasion, violence could break out, notwithstanding the genteel atmosphere he sought to maintain; and, of course, when the police came around to check an alibi.

'Alright. Show me.'

He hesitated for a moment, then nodded: he hadn't expected me to call the boast, but if he refused it'd look like he had something to hide. He crossed the room to a large, locked cupboard, where I could see several racks of videos, neatly labelled presumably with dates and by gaming room. He picked one out and slotted it into a video machine next to the cupboard, switching on a television set that was independent of the screens hidden in his desk. I remarked that the set-up as a whole must be costly:

'Tax deductible,' was all he said.

He had to play with the fast forward and reverse for a while before he found Andrew.

'Who's the woman? His wife?'

'Which one?'

I pointed to the one I'd meant, but as I did so glanced at the other, at the same table but not necessarily with them. She also looked familiar, though again I couldn't place her. Matheson confirmed my first choice as the former model, now Marilyn Mather. She and Andrew made the perfect pretty pair.

'And the other one?'

'Anabelle de Peyer,' he hopped from one foot to another, uncomfortable where I was leading him. Last picture of her I'd seen, she was wearing a lot less. As I turned away, I saw yet another familiar face: to my surprise, Anabelle de Peyer's companion of the moment was none other than her sometime assistant legal adversary, Christopher Wainwright. I remembered what Katrina had said: Martin only took the case on because Andrew and Randolph had claimed to be too close to it. I began to wonder just what that meant.

I think Matheson was hoping I'd got enough, because he started to say:

'If that's all. . .?'

I sat down again:

'I don't think Andrew ran up that debt. I'm thinking of telling Ian Mather about it. My guess is, he won't let Andrew pay and he'll put you to proof.' What I meant was: he wouldn't get paid without establishing exactly how the debt arose.

He understood. He tossed his options around like a salad. He could call my bluff, in case that's all it was, but he was likely to be out of his money for a while at best, and perhaps for as long as a law suit. He could ring Andrew, and find out just how much influence I really did wield, but that meant admitting how much he'd already told – or, rather, shown – me. He could consult with whoever really owned the club, which I didn't think meant talking to himself, but that wasn't what I was supposed to think. One way or another, I was trouble, and all I wanted to go away wasn't a lot more than he'd already given me.

'No source. Not even to Ian Mather. Right?' I nodded. My fingers weren't crossed, but my toes were. It never occurred to him I might want to tell the police. What everybody knows about private eyes comes from movies, t.v., or books, when we're always at war with the law.

'The debt was Wainwright's. Andrew guaranteed it. Not that night, but a few weeks ago. I had to call it in. I'm not going to tell you anything else. That's it.'

It was enough.

Chapter Seven

As we planned to eat near my house, we had parked on the Square where I live. Walking back from the restaurant, Ali wanted to stay, rather than drive us both up to Highgate. I could think of no good reason why not. Though still tired from the previous night, we had energy enough to practise doctor-and-nurse for an hour or two before, this time, she drifted off to sleep ahead of me.

I was still lying awake, enjoying the notion and occasional touch of the bright and beautiful brand new body beside me in my bed, when the good reason we shouldn't have stayed rang. It was nearly three o'clock in the morning. I grabbed the 'phone quick enough to stop it waking her. I greeted the caller with the warmth he or she deserved:

'What?'

'I think you'd better come in to Mather's, sunshine,' said the voice of the only policeman I've ever even been tempted to refer to as friend, and that while I was still suffering the post-operative effects of the removal from my shoulder of a bullet.

I repeated:

'What?' But I was already beginning to guess.

'More a question of who,' he said, his sarcasm designed to soften the news. I waited. He told me. I repeated in an altogether different tone:

'What?' And hung up. I thought: this is no fun any more; no fun at all.

I debated waking Ali, but she seemed so comfortable there was no point depriving her of a little while longer in innocent slumber. She had made me sleep on the side of the bed nearest the edge of the platform, in case she fell off: a new dimension to fear of flying. Carefully, I crawled around the bed and stepped cautiously and backwards down the stairs. The bed-platform, which I had built myself, was as solid as a rock: creak-free it was not.

I dressed, set the answering machine so that if the 'phone rang again it wouldn't disturb her, and scribbled a note, telling her I had to go out; if I didn't come back she should make herself coffee and simply slam the door behind her: I'd been robbed so many times there was nothing left to steal. I was about to tape it to the top of the bed-platform steps where she was bound to see it when I realized it was a bit curt. I added: 'love'. But I didn't sign my name nor even an initial, so it couldn't be used in evidence.

After I left the Clairmount, I'd had time to kill before she caught up with me, so I had decided to pay a visit on speculation to a house I was never otherwise going to be invited to. I was professionally pleased with my discovery, but personally uncomfortable: Andrew was the weakest of the brothers, the apple on the lowest branch, and Wainwright hardly counted at all. It was going to cause a lot of grief, to no obvious advance or achievement.

Martin's address proved to be a huge town-house in Maida Vale. As Kat had said, not so far from where she lived that he couldn't keep in condition while he ran around. From the solitary bell outside the front door, it was clear he occupied the whole house. I rang it long and hard, only a quarter-expecting him to be in, and so only a quarter-prepared with an opening line when he opened the door.

He scowled.

'That's a nice way to greet an old friend.'

'I took you to my gym, not my club. What do you want, Dave?'

'Not going to ask me in? Kat said you were choosy

about who you let in; not even her. What's the big mystery: you keep gerbils?'

I once knew a lady kept gerbils: in her bedroom. It was not a turn on.

He sighed:

'I suppose you'd better come in.'

I didn't say anything: for once, I'd run out of flip remarks.

It was a handsome house. I don't think I've ever thought a house was handsome before. It's a word I like to keep for when I look in the mirror extremely drunk. The hall was wide and though, like mine, it had no carpet, it wasn't because he couldn't afford one, but because the wooden slats were a prize feature, polished to a gleam, setting off a Persian rug the price of which would probably merit at least an honourable mention in despatches, and a couple of paintings that would not have looked out of place in the corridor at Mather's.

He led me into his study. It reminded me of somewhere else: Ian's office. There were a lot more wooden features, and paintings, but it was richly carpeted wall-to-wall, and the alcoves each side of the fireplace were lined with old-looking volumes, some of which he'd probably even read. He hesitated whether to sit behind his desk, or relax in front of the lit fire, in the winged, leather armchairs. To be helpful, I lowered myself into one of the armchairs without being asked.

'I suppose you want a drink, too,' he didn't wait for my answer either. He opened the bar of a redwood cabinet and reached inside almost without looking, to extract a fresh, friendly and familiar bottle.

'I thought you weren't expecting me?'

'I could say, I knew you'd be around at some point, but the truth is, I thought I'd see if I could find out what makes you tick. This seemed to be your major preoccupation, and therefore a good place to start. We haven't long, have we: you're meeting my sister shortly.'

'She told you?' I was surprised: I thought we were in agreement it wasn't something we wanted to advertise.

'It's hardly likely Sandra Nicholl rang to tell me.' That was another reason he reminded me of Orbach:

two out of every three remarks were calculated to wound. 'I told you I know everything that goes on.'

'Yeah. You never got around to telling me how you find out, though.'

'A man I once knew, who caught me by surprise, he said: "Never ask how someone found something out; it shows them you couldn't have done it; work out for yourself how it was done, and next time you'll be able to do it to them".' He settled down opposite me, true to his word trying out my sin for size.

'It's a nice line, but I don't know, Martin. I have a theory that people who claim to be able to find things out are really just very good at finding a use for everything they hear. Waddayathink?'

He chuckled:

'Very good. Can I use it?'

'Sure. I probably stole it from someone else anyhow.'

'You still haven't told me why you're here.'

'This is true. You still haven't told me why you don't like visitors.'

'I'm not sure the one equals the other.'

'Will you, though?'

'Tell you? Why? Why do you want to know? What part does it play in your investigation, Dave?'

'You know, just because I ask a question doesn't mean I know the answer. People got guilty consciences. They figure, a detective, he asks something, he already knows. So then they talk more than they need to. If I really did know, I'd've solved all my cases before I began. A lot of it's just, you know, poking around.'

'Great. I can tell my father he's paying you four hundred a day to poke around.' He paused, but couldn't resist: 'A lot of places.'

'That's vulgar of your own sister. I thought she was the reason no one else was good enough for you?'

'She's a grown up; she can do what she likes, with whom.'

'Yeah, I see. You've gone off her now she's slumming.'

'I really can't work out how much of your self-abasement is an act, and how much of it is an astute, accurate, objective self-assessment.'

'I have the same problem. Listen, I'll tell you. I only ever knew two ways to find a needle in a haystack. One way, you keep the pressure on until it pops out like pus from a pimple; the other way, you burn it down and rake over the ashes. Waddayathink?'

He grimaced:

'I think it's pretty disgusting either way. One way you get a face full of someone else's poison; the other way, you risk setting fire to the whole field. Aren't you worried about the damage you can do?'

'I didn't ask myself into thy father's house. That's another way of looking at it. It's a house of cards. Somewhere inside, the joker's been used, only the rules say you can't. Maybe the joker's the top card, you just lift it off and you ain't done too much harm; maybe it's only a little way down, and the harm's still repairable; maybe it's right in the bottom layer, and you've got to pull the whole house down. The point is: the rule got broken, and everything that's built on top of it deserves to come down with it.'

'Like the American legal adage: the fruits of the poisoned tree?'

'Yeah, I watch L.A. Law too.' If the starting-point of an investigation is unconstitutional, everything that results from it is inadmissible evidence. We're much more civilized and tolerant in England: the police perhaps get a rap across the knuckles, but it's up to the judge how much he lets the jury listen to, which is usually everything.

'It's an easy thing to say when it's not your own house.'

'Is that why you won't let anyone in here? In case they poison it?'

'Something like that,' he admitted. Suddenly, he seemed lonely. Why did a man like that live all alone? He was not bad looking, he was fit, he was wealthy, he had a beautiful house, he was witty. I had none of those things, and yet I now had Allison.

'Like I think I said, my upbringing wasn't a tale of mixed emotions – more like none at all. At least this

125

is mine, only mine. Now you tell me why you came here.'

I paused to think about it first. I had come as much to work things out for myself as to lay my news on him.

'It's your father's house of cards I'm dismantling. He's my client. I owe him a duty of care. If I find any of you had anything to do with Kat's death, I wouldn't hesitate to turn you over to the police, if I couldn't push you out of a high window first. But unless and until that's what I find, I've got to be careful, haven't I — not to do any of you more harm than you deserve. For your father's sake. Right?' He didn't say anything, so I repeated: 'Right? That's right, isn't it?'

He nodded slowly, and cautiously. As if he half-suspected what was coming. I expelled air, then held up my glass for another. He went to fetch the bottle: it'd be less distracting than repeatedly having to rise for a refill. He said:

'Only don't blame me if you're pissed by the time you meet Allison. Or is that why you've come here, to get pissed first?'

'I didn't think it was, but it's as good an excuse as any. Yes, I don't want to talk about work with her tonight.'

'You getting serious about her? Kind of quick, isn't it?'

'She's a special lady, like you said. Yes, I could get serious about Ali.'

'Then don't call her that to her face, or you'll be out on your ear.'

'God, not another one. Katrina. . .'

'I know.' Of course he knew: I'd almost managed to forget.

I studied the fire. I had only just appreciated it wasn't real. The flames were real, but the logs and coals weren't. When I was a kid, they had electric artificial fires that couldn't even fool me: bits of wire-mesh coloured charcoal, and a fan inside to give a light-bulb a mild, flickering effect. This was a century ahead. Now

I'd noticed, I could see the gas pipe leading into the fireplace.

Martin waited impatiently, refilling his own glass. I said:

'You like it, then? Is Wainwright a freemason?' He didn't quibble with my sudden change of direction, or answer about the Southern Comfort; I was finally and belatedly getting down to it.

'Wainwright? I believe so. Why?'

'Freemasons are supposed to help each other, aren't they? They call it "fellow-mason in distress" or something like that. It's part of their obligations.' The 'obligations' were what they called their membership oaths.

He laughed, and recited:

'"All these points I solemnly swear to observe, without evasion, equivocation, or mental reservation...under no less a penalty...than of being severed in two, my bowels burned to ashes, and...scattered over the face of the earth and wafted by the four cardinal-winds of heaven, that no trace or remembrance of so vile a wretch may longer be found among men..." That the sort of thing you mean?'

'I thought you weren't one.'

'I'm not. Shall I do another?' He went on without waiting: '"These several points I solemnly swear to observe...under no less a penalty, on the violation of any of them, than that of having my throat cut across, my tongue torn out by the root, and buried in the sand of the sea at low water mark, or a cable's length from the shore, where the tide regularly ebbs and flows twice in twenty-four hours, or the more effective punishment of being branded as a wilfully perjured individual, void of all moral worth, and totally unfit to be received into this worshipful Lodge..." One more?'

I nodded, fascinated.

'"All these points I solemnly swear to observe...under the no less penalty...than that of suffering loss of life by having my head struck off". When we were young, I used to sneak into my father's study and look at his books: it was most emphatically, strictly forbidden under threats just about as dire. So, naturally, I couldn't resist. But the others did. Maybe that's why I was never interested: you're not supposed to read all that rubbish until you're a long way in, by which time you've already swallowed so much of it, what does a bit more matter?'

'What have medieval weapons got to do with it?' I had just that day discovered a dead-end half corridor off which an alcove concealed a full suit of armour. I stopped to say hallo and introduce myself before I realized it wasn't going to answer back.

'Nothing so far as I'm aware. What made you think they did?'

'What you said, about Gauldie being the buff.'

He laughed:

'Gauldie's a buff about anything that looks good and makes money. He's profoundly acquisitive. He's the original poor boy made good good good. You should see his house. He didn't have money behind him,' like Ian: 'I think there's a sort of coincidental connection, an overlap perhaps: freemasonry and heraldry, insignia, coats of arms, symbols of authority, that sort of thing. English craft freemasonry started at the beginning of the eighteenth century, but the spiritual roots go back into the Bible: King Solomon's Temple. The real fanatics trace it step by step through the ages.'

He gave me another recital:

'"Father of All!

"In every age,

"In every clime adored

"By saint, by savage and by sage,

"Jehovah, Jove or Lord."

'I daresay Gauldie's interests overlap; that's all. The women in the firm tend to hate it, but no one else cares: if it makes Gauldie happy... It's worth a fortune, and it makes an impression on some clients: the old families, you know. Don't forget, though we're well-established now, we're a young firm, only postwar; between my father and John Gauldie, they used every trick in the book to grow so big so fast. You

128

haven't told me why you asked if Wainwright is a free-mason.'

'Would Andrew help him out, as a fellow-freemason, like to maybe eight, nine grand?'

'Your gambling debt?'

'Wainwright's gambling debt.'

'I see. No. Andrew has his good side, but that sort of generosity with money isn't it. The lady Marilyn likes the lolly too much.'

'In that case, I think perhaps Andrew's in a lot of trouble. Wainwright's blackmailing him. I don't know what for. Do you?'

His expression remained impassive. Instead of answering, he asked me:

'Why are you telling me about it?' Then he remembered to add: 'If it's true.'

'It's true. You just said it couldn't be friendship.'

'It's consistent with what I already told you: Andrew covers for him. He was originally Randolph's friend. Well his brother was. And I've never understood how Andrew got so close to him: they've nothing in common. So what you're saying fits.'

'You didn't tell me if you know what he was blackmailing him for.'

'No more I did,' he said softly.

'Tell me the truth, Martin. Do you know, or is this part of the "all-knowing, all-seeing" act?'

'I could say the same to you: do you know, or are you pretending to know in the hope I'll talk about it?'

I poured myself a fresh drink and glanced at my watch: we could sit sparring all evening and I doubted either one would come out much ahead. I said:

'No, I don't know. But I'll tell you what I think. Wainwright's been going with Anabelle de Peyer. Did you know that?'

'I heard.'

'He worked with you on the divorce case. I looked at the file. It was fun. You had p.i.s on her tail, and a very lovely tail it is too. Let's just suppose out loud that Wainwright got very turned on by her: hell, I did. Let's also suppose that after he's been to the lavatory and made love to a loo-roll, he decides he wants a taste of the real thing. OK so far?'

'It's plausible. You think he went to her offering information in exchange for a chance to get between her legs – and, as you'd say, very lovely legs they are too. Is that your theory? It hardly implicates Andrew.'

'No, it doesn't. That's why I don't think it's right. Wainwright's a conceited son of a bitch; I don't think he'd expect to have to pay for it.' I'd never spoken with Wainwright, but I'd seen him around the office, and I recollected Dowell's opening critique. Wainwright was another of these modern lawyers who look fit enough to give legal advice while running in the marathon. In my day, lawyering was a sedentary occupation, with occasional bursts of horizontal activity that were never enough to compensate for all the chain-smoking, continuous-drinking and waiting around to visit a client in the clink.

'Go on,' Martin prompted without contradicting me. I already knew he had no greater love for Wainwright. Then he interrupted: 'Wait. You're going to be late. Let's ring Allison and tell her you're here. Alright?'

'She'll already be on the way. Ah, right,' I had forgotten about the car-phone. Back in the days when I still owned a car, they didn't have mobile 'phones, or if they did, no one wanted me to find out about them. I'm a lousy driver at the best of times, and distracted by a call I doubt I'd've survived five minutes.

He punched about ten digits, like long distance. She must have answered on the first ring. He said:

'I think I've got your date here. Do you want to come and pick it up? It's going to be late otherwise.'

He chuckled, and disconnected.

'What's the joke?' I wasn't enjoying being tossed around between the Mathers, anymore than Kat had.

'She asked me to keep you sober enough to stay upright.' It wasn't quite the tender loving message I'd've liked him to have to relay. 'You've reached the point where Wainwright wants la de Peyer – an excusable impulse – and you don't think he'd expect to have to pay for it. You were going to try and relate this to my baby brother.' He did know. I was tempted to tell him to carry on the tale, but maybe I wanted to show off a little to my new girlfriend's big brother:

'I think he found something out about Andrew almost by accident, anyway by accident in his terms and blackmail came later, maybe once he realized he wasn't going to cut it at Mather's any other way. My guess is it was her idea. She probably let him have the first taste or two for free, to get him hooked – and I doubt that'd be difficult – and then she suggested he start to pay. Maybe she sung him a song about how she wanted the divorce over, she was only stringing it along because she didn't really believe her husband's declaration of assets: that's consistent with some of the previous correspondence. If she could only find out the truth for sure, the sooner she could be free for her new toy-boy. How'm I doing?'

'It's an interesting account. I wouldn't place it beyond the bounds of possibility.'

'So leaking was her idea. I imagine his first reaction would probably have been to refuse. Don't forget, he hadn't been that long qualified. It needs a sort of nasty, cynical confidence that only comes with experience; he'd still've been a learner, full of the high-sounding ideals they pump out at college. I think. . . I'll admit I'm guessing now: I think she had a way to persuade him that leaking wasn't that bad, that everyone did it some time or another, even. . .Andrew.'

I waited. He closed his eyes for what seemed like a long time, then started to speak, choosing his words carefully:

'Stonefrost and de Peyer were friends. Friends of Randolph, too.'

'Stonefrost was guilty, wasn't he? I mean, of what was written about him?'

'Yes. Beyond any shadow of a doubt. He'd been dealing to his society friends for many years. Everyone, even Randolph, did some of his dope, back when they were students or just out of college. Remember, this was the sixties or just after. No one thought it was a bad thing. It was admirable, appealingly piratical: we were stealing the world away from under our parents' noses. Most of us gave it up, gradually, and went on with our lives and our careers; I had less to do with it than others, because I didn't go to university, which was the hotbed.'

He took a sip of his drink, calculating his words carefully before continuing: 'But people like Stonefrost and de Peyer had nothing to go on to. They didn't have or want careers: they had family money, and expectations and all that was required of them in return was to marry and raise children – more sons – to inherit the family estates in due course. Boredom, greed, looking for excitement, hooked on sex, drink, drugs, travel, money. I should think in time they needed much more money than ever they were allowed by their parents. We've all known lots of types like that.'

'Speak for yourself. My druggies had plenty of things to escape from, not impatience to inherit.' He dismissed my objection with a wave:

'Really? That go for you, too? You were qualified, a partner in a practice – not a bad practice – what made you choose drugs, Dave?' I winced: I'd forgotten he had access to the firm's file on me. He went on: 'Randolph quit doing drugs early on, but not before our baby brother had been attracted to the glamour and the glitter: the night-clubs, coming-out balls, pictures in *The Tatler*, *Queen*, other magazines no one with a jot of intelligence would even open and that you only ever find in the waiting-rooms of Harley Street surgeons.' Me, I wouldn't know how to find Harley Street. 'Oh, yes, and then there were the gorgeous debutantes and models – like Anabelle, or Marilyn. It doesn't matter: it's a lot of stupidity, but no great sin.'

'Isn't it?'

'What do you mean?' He asked sharply.

'I asked Katrina if she'd ever been down to Andrew's house in the country. She said she hadn't. But Andrew told me she had. Andrew thought I had it in for him, because of that visit. Wonder what he meant, eh?'

He shook his head:

'I don't know. I never knew she'd been. With Randolph?'

'I don't know that. I wouldn't let Andrew tell me; if she didn't want me to know, then unless I have to, I don't want to hear. But I got the general picture: "things got out of hand", he said.'

He nodded unhappily, reading the same into it that I had.

'Andrew got into that scene, you're saying? He bought his drugs from Stonefrost, didn't he?'

'Yes.'

We were both lawyers; we both understood the implications. On the one hand, he was the perfect lawyer to represent the newspaper: he knew for sure that the libel suit should be lost. On the other, the implications of the action were serious – for him as well as for a lot of others. If Stonefrost lost, like Oscar Wilde, the police would have to investigate: who could say who might be caught up in it.

'Why did he take the case?'

'The News was bought out a few weeks before the action began. The new owners were old clients of my father. It was a big case, a lot of money; of course we took the case. Then Gauldie assigned it to Andrew. He tried to wriggle out of it – pressure of work and all that. But he wasn't under nearly as much pressure as others, and he could hardly tell Gauldie the real reason he didn't want to do it.'

'What happened?' I could guess, but I might as well have him tell me.

'Andrew tried to get it to settle. God, he was so unlucky: nine out of ten libel actions settle. But they were using some barrister who hadn't been in court for a while, a publicity junkie, who got all gung-ho about it. You know what the libel bar's like: they prefer to sit in chambers raking in their consultation fees and carving up the case with their opponent over a bottle of fine wine in El Vino's. He had the bad luck to get one who was looking for a scrap.'

'Is that the best you can say – unlucky? It stinks, and

133

you know it. If Andrew had an interest, he had no right acting.'

'Oh, grow up, Dave. We all make compromises with ethics every day of the week.'

'Some compromise: he leaked John equals Ron Fitzpatrick's record?'

'Yes.'

'How long have you known?'

'Known? Known for sure: about ten minutes. Suspected? Since the leak. But I'd never made the connection to the de Peyer case. There's something else you ought to know.'

He hesitated, but he'd started and there was no turning back.

'I don't think Andrew did it entirely out of fear for the personal consequences: after all, it might never have rebounded on him. It might: put Stonefrost on the spot, he was pretty much of a sneak, he may well have started trading names to the police. But it might never have happened. You got close to the rest of it earlier when you asked about freemasons in distress: Stonefrost and Andrew were in the same Lodge. I think Francis Stonefrost put a lot of pressure on him to find a way to help.'

'Ah.' It explained Andrew's fear of his father ever finding out. As well as whatever fury it unleashed over the breach of confidence, he would also be guilty of an abuse of freemasonry. I asked: 'And de Peyer?'

'I don't know that. But I wouldn't be surprised. We've acted for his family for a long time, and they certainly were. That's how father got their business, you see.'

'I thought people weren't supposed to join for reasons of self-advancement?'

'I don't think my father did. His father – my grandfather – was a prominent mason, master of his Lodge for many years, and a district grand master for a while. My father was a late child, my grandmother was my grandfather's second wife. I don't think they were very close; it was more a case of father wanting to emulate him.' Like Martin was emulating his father the way he'd set up the study where we sat.

He went on: 'But once you've joined, you're bound to get a lot of business out of it. People turn to their own; I've said that before, haven't I? If you actually believe all that crap, then you trust someone else who does. So, yes, he got the business of a number of old, masonic families, including the de Peyers. It was de Peyer who Stonefrost went out to stay with when he died.'

'I logged the location. It gives us game, set and match against Wainwright, doesn't it? And of course against Andrew.' I remembered something from our first evening together: 'You lied to me. You told me Andrew would never leak.'

'No. I didn't. I said he wouldn't leak if he was a million pounds in debt. He'd never leak for money, Dave, however much he likes the stuff. But he leaked out of some stupid, misguided sense of masonic loyalty, of fear for the implications, or both. And how far does any of it get you? It gives you two leaks, but there's two more to go, and what has any of it got to do with Katrina's death?' He didn't know I had now traced three, rather than two, leaks, and I wasn't about to tell him. Instead, I said:

'That's the connection I don't see, which is why I said I don't really want to use any of this, unless I'm sure it's necessary.'

'Does that mean you won't tell father?'

'I can't say that for sure. We've still got the problem of Wainwright. I can't just do nothing about him, can I?'

'Would you. . . Would you let me take care of it? It's really not your business, Dave; it's not what you're here to find out about. It's a family problem. I'll handle it.'

The doorbell rang before I got a chance to answer him, and Martin got up to answer it. Before he left the room, he turned and said:

'It's not necessary to tell Allison either, is it?'

'Necessary? No, I shouldn't think so. Why?'

He smiled winningly:

'She tries to sound a lot tougher than she is. She's fond of her baby brother. Please.'

It tied in with what she'd told me about Andrew crying on her shoulder, so I shrugged mine and gestured

135

for him to go let her in. I felt stale, and she'd be the welcome fresh air.

'Looking glum,' she said, leaning over to kiss me boldly, to show she wasn't inhibited by being in her brother's house: 'Maybe you'd rather I left the two of you to go on playing together?'

He hadn't followed her into the room, so I stood up, put my arms right around her and held her close, to feel the whole of her body next to mine and remember just how good it was.

Martin returned and coughed discreetly:

'Your drink, ma'am.'

He had made her a white wine spritzer: the same as Sandy drank. He had a couple of cubes of ice in one hand, which he dropped into his own glass before topping up his drink. I pulled a face:

'Do you have to?'

'Try not to cry. We can't all be big tough he-men who swallow it neat. Besides,' he sipped: 'Have you ever tried it? It's better. Go on,' he held out his glass. I shook my head:

'There's precious little to cling onto in this life. Leave me what I've got.' It was our last exchange on the subject that had occupied the evening until then.

We stayed only half an hour. Politely, Ali invited Martin to join us, and he dithered, drawing out his refusal while he watched how much I didn't want him to come with. Eventually, he declined:

'No, I've got things to do. Go on, children.'

That was how it felt. Let out to play. Away from all the adult, serious talk. We held hands as we walked to her car, and once inside, kissed again, hands finding other parts of each other to cling onto. She broke away:

'I'm hungry, and after all you've drunk, you need to eat. Come on.'

We dropped the car off outside my house, and walked down to the Fulham Road, where there are more restaurants than residents. You don't need to book, but you do need to be fast on your feet if you don't want to get hustled inside some real dumps. I had intended to take Ali to an American restaurant, but it had changed nations and now was Armenian. Only the sawdust on the floor looked the same. We ended up in a French pancake house, dutifully eating one savoury and one sweet pancake each, washed down with delicious, sparkling French cider, as unlike its English colleague as Perrier and seven-times re-used London tapwater.

'You were talking about Andrew, weren't you?' She said once we were settled.

'What makes you say that?' Either she had sixth sense, or she wasn't telling all she knew.

She shifted uncomfortably in her seat, but she still looked good enough to eat.

'I overheard the end of a conversation between Martin and Andrew the other day. It was more like a fight, and they don't often fight, those two. I was coming to see Andrew, and they stopped when I came in and Martin went off to the gym. Andrew wouldn't tell me what it was about and, well,' she laughed: 'It was only the day before yesterday, and I've been a bit preoccupied since.'

She reached out a hand to take mine: 'Happily so. I was going to try to talk to Martin about it today, but as soon as I went in to see him he wanted to know why I looked like the cat that'd had the cream. So I told him, I had.'

I shivered: I was getting horny listening to her; it felt unreal – like it was happening to someone else; I wanted it to be real.

'Tell me what you heard,' I said when we finally let go of each other before our pancakes froze.

'Martin said "it's got to stop" and Andrew said "it's not up to me". It might've been nothing: they could've been talking about a case.'

I frowned:

'You didn't think so, or you wouldn't be telling me about it.'

'So,' she pressed: 'Am I right? Was it what you were talking to Martin about.'

I gave her the only honest answer I could:

'I don't know. I thought I knew what I was talking to him about, but I'm not so sure now.'

Chapter Eight

The Lord, it is said, moves in a mysterious manner. (Martin said the same thing about Randolph.) All I say is, he or she isn't in Dowell's class. Throughout the case I had been disconcerted by his apparent anxiety to assist me in any direction I wanted to take; I knew it had to be a blind; nothing he ever does is that simple; if he was being helpful at one level, he was hindering me at another; he doesn't know any other way to operate.

By the time I arrived at Mather's, I had decided that, even if the case wasn't real fun anymore, I could still pretend. I reached this conclusion during a brief, but for the most part thankfully silent, cab-ride in to the city. I had no choice but to take a taxi: the London underground doesn't yet run all-night, though it's likely to do so as soon as the unions have been beaten into sufficient submission to make of it a profitable undertaking.

Because it was so late, and I had enjoyed no sleep at all, I wasn't quick enough as I climbed into the cab to close the window before the driver started to mouth off:

'Odd time to go into the city, isn't it? You one of these city-types like to get in ahead of everyone else? I had one in the back the other night, went into the office at four o'clock every morning, regular as clockwork. Only needed three hours sleep, he said. Know how he did it? I asked how he did it. He told me how he did it. I'll tell you how he did it. What he did. . .'

'Friend,' I leaned into the opening: 'I am going into

the city to look at a body. It's dead. It'll do without sleep forever.'

I slid the window shut before he could say another word. I could see his expression in the rear-view mirror. He was thinking. It was an effort. He was thinking: maybe I'm a doctor; maybe I'm a policeman; but maybe, just maybe, I'm the killer going back to make sure I really got the job done.

He still hadn't recovered either his composure or his conversation by the time he pulled up outside Mather's office, at the arse-end of one of a proliferation of police cars parked at excited angles. Two ambulancemen stood by their vehicle, smoking while waiting to collect the package. A lot of ambulancemen smoke. Why not? They're familiar with more effective means of population control.

The door was half-open but a uniformed bobby about half my age barred my way:

'Can I help you, sir?'

I shrugged:

'No, I don't think so.'

'Funny. Very funny. I can hardly keep from laughing. . .sir.' His face didn't change expression.

I sighed:

'That's what all the girls say. I'm from the cadaver collection corporation; I came for the corpse.'

'You sick shit,' said a familiar voice from within, pulling the door wide open: 'You've never actually seen one, have you? Come on; come in and lose your virginity.'

He was right: for all the deaths at Disraeli Chambers, I had not seen any of the bodies. The only one to have died in my presence had the courtesy to do so after I was shot and had passed out. Like everyone else, I've seen a million actors die, but only the occasional news-picture of a real person. On screen, the difference doesn't tell.

Unlike Katrina, he had not been shot. Whoever had killed him had twisted his head until it sat on his shoulders exactly the wrong way round. He was lying on his stomach on the floor, staring straight up at me.

'Take a good look, Dave; smell it.'

I wrinkled my nose, hoping he wouldn't notice I was also scrunching up my eyes. It smelled like a public toilet that hadn't been cleaned for a month.

'Lots of them let go at the last moment of a slow death. They lose all control. It all adds to the fun; you'll be able to make jokes about it tomorrow, I expect.'

I swivelled on my heel and headed for the real toilet. I thought I was going to throw up, but I didn't. I stood a long time over the basin, leaning my head against the cold mirror above. I was a little short of breath, but that was all. When I raised my head, I saw Dowell standing in the doorway, watching to see how I'd handle it.

'Let it go if you can. It helps.' He wasn't angry anymore.

I shook my head:

'I don't think I need to. What do you know?'

'Quite a lot, actually. He came in very late; around midnight. Signed in. Wasn't trying to avoid anyone. He looked happy the watchman said, like he'd had good news. He was dressed casually, not for the office, so he probably wasn't intending to stay 'till morning; it wasn't some kind of all-night work-jag. Anyway, that was hardly his style. He asked if anyone else was in and seemed a little surprised at first when told no, but then chuckled, like a private joke.'

'What about downstairs?' The dead-file basement. 'File' might have been superfluous.

'Nothing.'

'Earlier? Who was here?'

'Randolph. With a typist for a while.' He sneered: 'I suppose he was doing some dictating.'

His brother had said he was working his way through the female staff.

His man Pratt poked a head into the lavatory:

'Coffee, guv?'

'Yeah.'

'Me too,' I added; I would have waited forever if I'd waited to be asked.

Pratt glanced at guv who nodded wearily:

140

'Yes, yes, get him a coffee too. It might get a confession quicker than beating him up.'

'Guv?' Pratt was puzzled. I think he lived in a state of permanent puzzlement; Dowell was trying to drive him further into it and out of his life.

'Coffee. Two. Mr Woolf's room upstairs. Can you remember where that is?'

'Alright, guv, you know, alright,' he objected to the insult with all the articulation he could assemble.

As if we hadn't been interrupted, Tim continued:

'And Martin. Martin came in around ten. He and his brother were talking for a while. When the watchman went around, neither of them were here: he says. That's why he told Wainwright there was no one in. But.'

'But he didn't see them leave,' I finished off for him gloomily: I wouldn't mind if Randolph Mather had murdered Wainwright; I'd like to think of him having to spend the remaining years of his active life getting it where he'd hurt Katrina putting it. But I like Martin; enough that when I remembered his last words to me – that he'd handle the Wainwright problem – I knew I wasn't going to enjoy repeating them.

I stood at the window, staring out over unlit roofs, watching the moon awaiting the arrival of the soul of Christopher Wainwright, if he had one. I don't think I like death much, even when I don't like the dead person. It's a bit too final, too decisive, too unequivocal for my taste.

'Come and fetch me when they're done, OK?' he said when Pratt brought our coffees.

'Right, guv,' Pratt stopped sulking; he finally had a task that would stimulate and stretch him. He had to remember where to find Dowell for however long it took forensics to finish their work.

We sipped in silence. I saw what he meant: it was disgusting, far worse than a beating. Finally, he said:

'Waddayaknow, sunshine?'

Gloomily, I placed first one then another of my client's sons into the main-frame:

'He was blackmailing Andrew; I told Martin; Martin said he'd handle it.'

'Martin,' he mused: 'He's the one spends three nights a week in the gym, bit of a tough guy, right?'

'I heard.'

'And Martin was here this evening. Tidy, isn't it?'

'Look, Tim, you need a lot more than that. You said Wainwright didn't arrive until after midnight. Maybe Martin was shacked up with someone by then?' I was clutching at straws: no one had suggested Martin was currently seeing a woman, or for that matter a man; he lived alone, and that was how he liked it.

'Anyway, if the night-man didn't see them leave, he wasn't on the door all the time; which means either of them or someone else could have let someone in.' I reminded him: 'He's alibi'd for the night of Kat's death.'

'So? Different method, different motives.' At first, I thought he was simply playing with Martin; now, I began to think he was serious.

'What do you want him for? What about Randolph? Were any calls made out of here this evening?' Had someone rung Wainwright? Who?

'No and yes. Not through the switchboard, because though it's automatic, it lights up if a call goes out, and the watchman says not. But they've both got private lines.'

'I don't suppose,' I suggested without a lot of optimism: 'They're not on the test circuit, are they?'

He hooted derisively.

'They have places like Highgate on the test circuit 'cos they only make ten calls a day. Full of your lot,' he snarled unhappily. I winced: if he was resorting to racist cracks that low, he was really hurting over tonight's incident. I knew why: he always got angry when people dropped dead in the middle of a case; it offended his sense of professional pride; sometimes, it even interfered with his method. 'To put the City on circuit would cost next year's national debt. There's no way to tell if either of the private lines were used, by whom or to whom.'

'Watcha going to do?'

'Already done it. I've sent cars for them both.' I read 'both' as the older boys, not Andrew, whose potential involvement was unknown until I disclosed it.

'Great. You send one for Iron Ian?'

'Nah. I don't want him cluttering up the scene until forensics're finished. Besides, why shouldn't he get a few more hours' sleep? They say it's hard enough getting any sleep at all at his age.' It was unmentionably uncharacteristic for Dowell to show so much consideration. I decided not to mention it.

'What else do you know, Dave?'

I sighed: it was unfair; just because he had a badge, I had to go first.

'Remember the name Stonefrost?'

'Vaguely.' It was a lie. Tim Dowell either remembered things in excruciating, intimate detail, or not at all. The only thing he didn't remember was when it was his turn to buy a drink.

'Libel action. Drugs. Settled well for him, especially since he was bang-to-rights.' Guilty.

'Yes?' He stifled a yawn; I was boring him; he wasn't hearing anything he didn't already know.

'That was what Wainwright was blackmailing Andrew about. Andrew probably bought some dope from Stonefrost; also, they were members of the same Lodge; Andrew helped him win. Wainwright found out indirectly through a mutual friend, possibly another mason, called de Peyer. He was bonking Anabelle de Peyer.'

'Like you're bonking Allison Hoyt?'

'How'd'you know that?' I was genuinely shocked, wondering if he had a tail on me, or her.

'I didn't 'till now.' I'd fallen for the oldest trick in the book; the one I told Martin about; asking a question, banking on the accused giving you the answer.

'Pig. You want I should go on?' I sipped some more coffee: it didn't improve with cold.

'Go on. So far you've given me society, drugs and sex: does it get interesting?'

'Funny. She knew from her husband that Andrew Mather had done a no-no to help Maurice Francis,

Vice-count Stonefrost off the hook, so she persuaded Wainwright to do the same for her.'

'I seem to remember, when I studied law, there was something called "privileged information". Do they still have it?'

'We're living in different times than when you and I learned our law, friend. Today's lawyer is as involved in the market-place as his client. Privilege is just an extra edge he went a few more years to college to collect. You never heard of insider dealing? If you make money into the sole criterion of success, everything else takes second place: morality, ethics, honour, loyalty, even pure professionalism. Lawyers are no different from anyone else: just more so.' Tiredness was turning me philosophic.

'You're telling me what Wainwright's hold on Andrew was. Big deal. Blackmail is blackmail. They're all scum. If you're right, and Wainwright was blackmailing Andrew, I'm glad he's dead. I'll tell you something, son,' he could be philosophical too: 'We've all got things to hide. Our bad actions are as much a part of us as the good. When they get hold of what you want to keep a secret, they steal your soul. I hate them, every one of the bastards.'

'I don't get it, Tim. I'm giving you a lot of good material: motive, conspiracy, drugs, freemasons, you name it. You can get headlines for a month, your picture in the papers, your children can sell your autograph to their chums at school. How come you don't want to know?'

He looked glum:

'What've freemasons got to do with it?'

'Andrew is, Stonefrost was, Wainwright was, maybe de Peyer was: Jesus, man, it's staring you in the face. What is it about it?'

'It scares me,' he admitted, more easily than I would have expected: 'When you first asked me, I told you what I knew about them was enough to make me want to steer away from the subject. Unless you force me, I'm not going down that road.'

I snorted:

'And so the tax-payer gets value for money out of another of Britain's fearless finest? You're really that frightened of them?'

'If there's anything, any proof, I'll follow it as far as it goes, I will.' He sounded like he was trying to convince himself more than me: 'But I'm not stirring that pot of shit unless I'm certain I have to. Besides: how?'

'NG, Tim, no good. I've done some reading: since 1985, 1986, it's been their policy to co-operate with official enquiries. That used to mean just your lot, then there was that enquiry at Hackney which they co-operated with, and since then they've said they're willing to co-operate with other public authorities. You could find out if you wanted.'

'Yeah, and the minute after the minute I asked, someone at the Yard would know and want to know why. Like Woolard.'

I knew the case he meant. Woolard was a detective inspector investigating corruption in Islington. Freemasons were amongst his suspects, and some of them knew it. According to his own account, one day he received an unsolicited 'phone call from a man in the office of the Director of Public Prosecutions, enquiring how the case was going. It was unprecedented and totally out of order: in England, lawyers aren't involved in the police investigation, unlike America where the prosecutor is often briefed from the beginning.

Woolard accordingly went down, unforewarned and without the permission of his superiors, to DPP headquarters, and interviewed the official who had rung him. His belief was that there was a masonic connection: that a suspect had asked the man at the DPP's to help him find out, as a fellow-mason in distress, how close the police were getting. Within hours, Woolard was in trouble; within days, off the case; within weeks, off the squad and transferred – proverbially – to traffic control in Wembley, a part of London only marginally more relevant than Purley.

Woolard never gave up. He tried legal action,

press statements, television appearances, even a parliamentary petition. He became obsessed with it, and it finished his career. Dowell wasn't willing to follow the same route to loss of pension rights. Fear of freemasonry is insidious and effective: there has always been precious little hard evidence of actual corruption within it, or of abuse of membership. How can there be if no one is willing even to investigate?

In the same vein, I'd read in the library since the case started a book called *The Brotherhood*, an exposé of freemasonry. Its Prologue contained an account of how the book had been commissioned, and completed, before a change of ownership of the publishing company led to cancellation of the contract. The new owners were embarrassed, but open about their motives: their father was a freemason, and it would cause him concern if they published the book. He hadn't read it, or asked them not to; he didn't need to; they were prepared to side-step the issue rather than run the risk.

'What I told you about Stonefrost – that wasn't new, right?'

Dowell has a problem where I'm concerned. He likes me, so he doesn't like to deceive me. But he likes deception, in its own right, just as much. Instead of answering, he said:

'You asked about James Mather. Remember?'

'Gee, thanks for reminding me. I would've forgotten. What'd you find out?' I up-ended the rest of the coffee into the metal waste-paper basket behind my desk, in case I was tempted to try it again.

'The long-departed, much-travelled uncle,' he introduced: 'Is still wanted here, on a warrant thirty-five years old.' There is no Statute of Limitations in English criminal law.

'Apparently, he was in business with a fellow named. . .' He paused to refresh his memory: 'Kenneth Richardson.'

'Sort of business?'

'Import/export. The years after the war contained rich pickings for those who weren't too concerned about the rules.'

'I remember.' Believe it or not, I did: I remember rationing; some things didn't cease to be rationed until the early fifties. At least, that's what my parents said. Now I thought about it, probably for the first time in twenty years, it may just have been a ploy to keep our sticky little fingers out of the cookie jar for a while longer than the law rendered absolutely necessary.

'Anyway, things went a bit badly wrong, their vessel was impounded and the partnership was dissolved without the usual formalities; Richardson was found in little pieces in the back of a lorry. It seems, James Mather wasn't available to assist the police in their enquiries,' he used the traditional euphemism for being questioned under suspicion.

At the point where they actually go so far as to admit that someone is a suspect, they have to give him a caution, let him see a solicitor, and engage in other kinds of unhelpful, enquiry-obstructing exercises like producing the accused before a magistrate. So they have this preliminary stage. It's extremely British. The same evasion goes on all over the world, but in this country it is institutionalized to an extent that has its own formal standing.

'The odd thing was,' he continued: 'It was very hard indeed to get in and out of the country in those days. You couldn't just hop a 'plane to the States. And don't forget their ship had been snatched. The files just come to a dead end, like someone ordered it shoved in a drawer. We didn't even try to find out how he got away.'

'Has he surfaced since?'

'Not here. But he's well-known across the ocean. There's an open RICO file on him.'

'Rico?'

'It stands for racketeer-influenced corrupt organizations. It's a law they've got that allows them to indict the people behind the people behind the people, if you see what I mean.'

'Mafia-type thing?'

'Yes, though I think that must be the most abused word in American law-enforcement. I've heard it used for Colombians, Cubans, Costa Ricans, Canadians, even Polish. Did you hear the one about the Polish mafia?'

I waited. He sighed:

'I can't be bothered. It's extremely complicated and I don't understand it either. Something to do with having a contract notarized. But he's not considered active now, more like retired and protecting his investments. Lives in Miami. Not Miami Beach. They're different activities. Everything's a city over there: two men and a dog's a city; McDonald's and a petrol station's a city. Pardon me, gas station.'

'You're sure about not active now?'

'Listen, it's not easy getting information. Over there, they only give it out in trade. Hands across the ocean, special relationship, don't count for nothing. You have to half-hint the Queen's personally at risk before they give you anything. Anyway, it seems this guy has been into everything: drugs, yes, prostitution, yes, gambling, yes, pornography, yes, numbers. . .You know what numbers is?'

'Nope.'

'Me neither, but they always say it. At one time, this guy was the only non-Italian operating out of New York. It seems like,' he dropped his voice like Marlon Brando as Don Corleone: 'People showed him a lot of respect.'

'And all this you managed to get since today. . .yesterday? I would've thought it took you that long to find the files?'

He looked at me doe-eyed and sad:

'No, Dave, I didn't say I got it today, or yesterday.'

I had to extract one answer from another. Nothing I was telling him was news. He'd known about James Mather, and he'd known about Stonefrost. I played back my conversation on the first of these topics, and realized he had just fallen short of lying to me.

Pratt came back in, looking pleased with himself, like he'd finally found us after a long time looking:

'We've got one, guv.'

'Yes, Pratt, I daresay you have. Which one?'

'What? Oh, Martin Mather, guv.'

'Any trouble?'

'Nah; like a lamb, they said.' It was quite a long sentence for Pratt, and certainly more graphic than I'd come to expect.

'What about the other?'

Pratt shrugged: it wasn't an attractive sight.

'I dunno, guv. He's not there, is he.' His sole saving grace was that he did not add, though it would have suited: 'know what I mean?'

I looked at my watch: it was nearly six o'clock in the morning. Ali was still asleep in my bed, and I wished I was beside her. Dowell asked me:

'You want to say hallo?'

'Are your forensic people finished yet?'

'They should be. Why?'

'I was wondering about a wee trip to Hampstead,' where Ian Mather lived: 'Someone's got to break the glad tidings to him. Another assistant solicitor terminated without prejudice, who happened to be blackmailing one of his sons for leaking privileged information, with a background in drugs. Another son in the clutches of the constabulary. Maybe another on the lam. I should think it's the sort of thing he'd rather not read about in the papers.' I decided to try it out for size: 'Know what I mean?'

He grimaced: he didn't like it either.

'Next thing, you'll want a police car to take you up there.'

'Well, uh, it would help, at this time of the morning, y'know.'

I followed Dowell down after pausing to check an address in my files.

Martin was sequestered in his own office. That way he wasn't quite so legally in custody. But a uniformed officer was standing inside the door, not outside. He looked up, surprised to see me:

'I'm not sure my sister will appreciate your sense of priorities, Woolf.' For a slice of *sang froid*, it wasn't bad.

Dowell was conferring with the arresting officers – pardon me, officers who had invited Martin to assist in their enquiries. They left, I took it to go fetch Andrew. Dowell joined us before I could reply to Martin's quip. He cleared his throat, then said:

'Sir, I understand you were here earlier this evening. From ten o'clock. Is that correct?'

Martin said nothing, nor even acknowledged the question. He might be only a civil lawyer without experience of criminal law, but he knew enough form to stay *schtum*.

'Are you willing to inform me of what time you left here, sir?'

'About,' I corrected: 'Inform about.'

'Thank you, sir,' Dowell said to me, looking both grave and murderous: 'I think you understood my question, Mr Mather.'

Martin smiled pleasantly:

'Am I under arrest? This is fun: I've never been arrested before.'

'It's not a joking matter, sir.' On balance, I'm fairly sure Martin had managed to get under Dowell's skin.

'Yes it is, officer, if you've done nothing at all that merits the attention of the law. Do you propose to tell me what's going on, or do you not?'

'You are of course acquainted with one Christopher Wainwright, sir,' Dowell spoke slowly. Both the uniformed bobby and the uninformed Pratt were writing down every word of the exchange. I wondered if they'd included my intervention, and how a judge would feel about it.

'Did you see him this evening, sir? After you returned here at ten o'clock?'

Martin had gone pale, but did not reply.

'Will you tell me what time you left here, sir? Can you produce someone to confirm where you were between midnight and when my officers arrived at your house, sir?'

Martin bit his lower lip; for a moment, I thought he was going to say something, but he suppressed the impulse. Dowell shrugged: if that was how Martin wanted to play it, he could play too.

'I am informing you, sir, that Mr Wainwright was

murdered, on these premises, at some time after midnight, and that I am arresting you on suspicion of complicity in that offence. I have to tell you that you are not obliged to say anything, but that anything you do say will be taken down and may be used in evidence against you. I also have to inform you of your right to consult a lawyer and to have him present during questioning, so long as I do not consider that this will interfere with my investigation.'

'Her,' Martin said: 'Have her present. I want my sister. She's my lawyer. Will you tell her that, Dave?'

I nodded once. They led him away. Only after he had gone did I realize I couldn't telephone Ali: she was at my home, and the answering machine was switched on.

House didn't quite fit what Ian Mather lived in. Palace overdoes it. Mansion is closest. He lived on Redington Road, in Hampstead, where the midget properties start at a million. He owned a three storey, double-winged building which when I looked down the sides dipped sharply enough to tell me there was a fourth storey in the back. I could just about see the end of the garden, past the swimming pool, where the tennis court was. I didn't blame Andrew: if I'd had the choice, it was where I would have lived through college.

I rang at the bell and, eventually, a middle aged Latin woman, probably Italian, came to the door, opening it on the chain. Her eyes widened at the sight of the police car in the drive. I decided to keep it simple, and let her believe it belonged to me, or I to it:

'I'm sorry. I have to see Mr Mather. Would you wake him, please.

Like most citizens, she believed that a request from the police superseded orders from the Holy Ghost. She shut the door to unhook the chain, and as she re-opened it to let me in, I saw her finish crossing herself. After a minor hesitation, because the social rule book doesn't spell out where to dump a policeman who comes calling at six thirty in the morning, she showed me into the dining room and left me there while she went to wake the master.

A quarter of an hour later, she brought in a tray of tea and toast. I didn't wait to be invited, but helped myself. French pancakes are filling but, like Chinese food, don't last. Ten minutes later, as dapper as ever, the man himself joined me. I admired that he had taken the trouble to dress properly, and to shave, before descending. He apologized for keeping me waiting, acting for all the world as if it was the most normal way to start the day.

'I'm sorry to have to wake you,' I swallowed a 'sir'. I was beginning to like the guy, and to be seduced by his manners.

'I rise at seven in any event, Mr Woolf.'

'Shall I pour?' It would be my second cup.

'That would be most kind. Thank you.'

I could see where Martin got the *sang froid* from. He wasn't going to ask until I was ready to tell him. I said:

'I'm sorry to have to tell you this, Mr Mather. The police rang me.' I decided against explaining in whose company I had been at the time: it was another life. 'There's been another death. Another murder.'

'Yes.' He took his cup in both hands and fumbled to raise it to his lips. He had worked that much out for himself.

'Christopher Wainwright,' I put him out of his misery.

His hands were shaking so bad, tea was spilling everywhere except into his mouth. Gently, I took the cup away from him and replaced it on the saucer. He said:

'I see. It's a great shock.' Then, in a moment of uncommon honesty, he said: 'A great relief.' He'd expected me to announce the death of one of his children.

I let him sip tea for a while before I told him he wasn't that far off:

'I'm sorry. I also have to tell you, Martin's been arrested.'

'For. . .?'

'Yes.'

'It's ridiculous. Ridiculous. You must see that? You see that, don't you? Tell me you believe that,' his voice raised: 'Tell me,' he demanded.

'I believe it, Mr Mather.' I don't know whether I would have said it anyway, but as it was true, it seemed churlish to withhold his reassurance.

'Yes, yes, of course you do.' I wasn't sure he was going to survive my visit. It was worrying. I'd never killed one of my own clients. I'd once given a landlord a heart attack under cross-examination, but he survived and we lost the case. If Ian died, would any of the others be willing to keep on paying?

'We must get him a lawyer, a criminal lawyer, at once. Let's see, there's. . .'

'He asked for Allison,' I nearly said Ali: 'He was most emphatic he wanted her. You see,' I paused before plunging on: 'Wainwright came in expecting to see someone. That suggests someone sent for him. Both he and Randolph were at the office late. I don't think Martin had anything to do with it, Mr Mather, but I wouldn't swear he had no relevant information.'

'What are you saying, Mr Woolf? Are you suggesting that. . . Randolph?' His eyes bulged unhealthily, but he didn't go into the same song-and-dance routine about his older boy. I figured the wily old goat had a better idea about his children's quirks than I would have anticipated.

'I'm not suggesting anything beyond what I said. I think Martin wants Ali. . . Allison. . . because he wants to keep things in the family for the moment. I think he should be allowed to follow his own wishes for the time being.'

'He's not your son, Mr Woolf.'

It wasn't my house of cards, either.

'Yeah. OK But things aren't always what they seem. There's something suspicious about the speed with which Dowell latched onto Martin. You have to understand, Dowell doesn't really deal in anything simple, not even simple murder.' His Adam's apple bobbed: I don't think he had hitherto appreciated that

153

murders could be classified as simple. 'And anything he does, you have to work out what he's really doing.'

'What do you think he is really doing in this case, Mr Woolf?' He wanted to believe me.

'How much do you know about Cross Course, Mr Mather?'

'Martin's investment company? Why? What has that got to do with it?'

'I don't know that it does. But what I'm thinking is, what Dowell wanted wasn't Martin, but a warrant on Martin's premises: home and offices. He gets them automatically now. He didn't want Martin; he wanted grounds for suspicion.' Of course, he could always have broken in, like he had to my home and, once, to Sandy's office; but Dowell could tell the difference between us and a Mather.

He muttered:

'I never liked it. I never approved. I always said it would get him into trouble. People should do what they are good at, and stick at it. Have you ever noticed, Mr Woolf, how all the lawyers who get into serious trouble – sometimes, even criminal – are those who have been involved in other enterprises?' I didn't like to point out that this was tautologous: as a licence to practice law doesn't include a licence to commit crime, it follows that a lawyer involved in the latter has of definition stepped outside his job description.

Otherwise, though, I knew what he meant and agreed. They see their clients coming in, with all their problems, and they begin to think they can handle things better, without all the problems; they get cocky; they confuse knowing law, and being legal.

'Where is Randolph? And Andrew? Has anyone telephoned Allison to go and see Martin?' He wanted his sons around him.

'Uh, there's no answer from Allison's home number. Perhaps she's taken a sleeping pill.' Not bad on the spur of the moment.

'Randolph wasn't at home. And, er, I believe that Inspector Dowell has made arrangements for Andrew to be informed.' I paused to congratulate myself on my delicacy.

He wasn't fooled:

'Is he under suspicion, too?'

I took a deep breath, then said:

'I'm sorry, I'm very sorry. Wainwright was black-mailing Andrew. I knew. I had to tell Dowell. I hope you understand. . .'

He brushed my apology aside:

'Yes, yes. You have to do your duty. Why wasn't I told about Wainwright? What. . .?' He stopped suddenly and shuddered. He didn't want to know.

'I only learned last night.' I waited. He waited. Then he nodded for me to go on. 'I think it's possible. . . It's likely. . . I think Andrew leaked the information that made the News have to settle the Stonefrost litigation. Wainwright, er, found out about it.'

His shoulders were shaking. I wondered about calling for medical help. His hands were over his face. I said:

'Mr Mather? Mr Mather? Are you alright, sir?'

He wouldn't remove his hands. There was a strangled, gasping sound from within. It took me a long time to realize: the old man was crying. I got up and walked to the window, looked out at the police car still waiting to take us back into the City. The driver looked at me hopefully. I shrugged: not yet. When I turned around, Mather had brought himself under control. We neither of us made any reference to it. He said:

'Do you have more to tell me? I don't want you to conceal anything from me, Mr Woolf. Do you understand me?' But his tone was conciliatory; I think he heard me call him 'sir'; it could be the slip of my tongue that kept me on the case.

'Wainwright was, er, having an affair with the de Peyer woman. Wainwright told her about her husband's property. I suspect she told him about Andrew helping Stonefrost, to persuade him to help her.'

He was shaking his head from side to side, slowly, in disbelief:

'They are lawyers, Mr Woolf, lawyers. I brought up my sons to be lawyers; this is my firm. And... And people have breached privilege for their own, private ends. I cannot... I do not understand how it could happen, Mr Woolf. Do you?'

I poured out the last of the tea, equally: we each got half a cup. He gestured towards a bell on the wall and I got up and pressed it. The woman came at once with a fresh pot, without needing to be told. He waved away her offer to pour, and himself topped up our cups. Before she left, remembering he was a host, he asked me if I wanted more toast. I hated to say it, but:

'I've been up all night. Yes, please.'

'I asked you a question, Mr Woolf. It was not rhetorical.'

'What do I know, Mr Mather? I'm just a private eye scratching around for information. It's not my job to put it together.'

He snorted:

'Yes, I sensed your modesty as soon as I met you.' He was capable of sarcasm, too. 'Tell me something else, then, Mr Woolf. Do you know how the other leaks happened?'

'I've got a lead on one of them,' which reminded me I still hadn't been down to Companies House in accordance with Orbach's oblique instruction.

'And the other?' He wasn't going to eat evasion for an answer.

'I, er, yes, I have an idea. I'd say it was what we call a "bleeding heart leak", a sympathizer, someone who didn't like the idea of the parents remaining uncompensated.'

He met my gaze deliberately:

'And you are not planning to tell me who that was, are you?'

I'll leave the question-mark at the end of the sentence, though I'm not sure to this day whether it was a question, or an injunction. I said:

'No, I'm not. If you'll take it on trust, it won't happen

again, and there is no reason to pursue it. It has nothing to do with anything else.'

He licked his dry lips, though whether with relief at the position I had so willingly taken, or because it was totally out of character to take anything on trust, I similarly don't know.

'Mr Mather, there's something else I want to ask you. Was Wainwright a freemason?'

'Yes.' He didn't shilly-shally about confidentiality: the question of a man's membership is his own; he is, contrary to popular belief, entitled to disclose it, in appropriate circumstances and provided it is not for the purpose of self-advancement; once a man is dead, the knowledge may be made public by another.

'The way I remember it, it never used to be a big deal who was and who wasn't. I seem to recall when I was a kid, they used to list people attending Lodge-nights in the local paper.'

'Yes. That's correct. After the war, we became – I'm not really sure why – somewhat introspective, even secretive. It has done the craft enormous harm; it has generated suspicion without cause or purpose.' He filled in a gap: 'Andrew introduced him. I was opposed to it. I did not think he was the sort of chap we wanted. I thought he was joining for unworthy motives. I did not believe he would achieve the standing of a man in good repute. It seems, I was right.'

'But Andrew insisted? Could he do that – over your objection?'

'Freemasonry is Lodge-based, Mr Woolf. I belong to four Lodges, myself, and Andrew is also a member of two of those. But he was a member of a third, and it was into that Lodge that he introduced Wainwright. Now, at least, I understand why.'

'Would you be able... Would you know, or could you find out for me, about Lodge memberships: different people, who is or was in whose Lodge?'

'Why?' He snapped: 'What are you suggesting now, Mr Woolf?'

'Not a lot. I'm not suggesting a masonic conspiracy. But I think a few people have been a bit too connected to each other. I need to understand who and how much.'

He waited for me to elaborate. I didn't. He said, swallowing the discipline of a lifetime:

'I would need good reason.'

'Alright. I'll talk to you about it again. What about Chapters?'

He froze:

'That is an entirely different issue, Mr Woolf. I am not a companion of the Royal Arch.'

'But the Grand Secretary of Grand Lodge is also Grand Scribe Ezra in Grand Chapter, right?' I tried to keep a straight face as I gave the silly old scribbler his titles: 'And all the obligations, they say "Murder, treason, felony and all other offences of the realm being at all times most especially excepted".'

He was impressed:

'You've done your homework, Mr Woolf.'

'It's your time, Mr Mather.' Time and money.

'I, uh, I will have to think very carefully about this, Mr Woolf; I shall have to take advice.' I guessed who from: the ghoulish Gauldie.

It was time to go. I asked to use a 'phone, and tried my own number, just in case Ali picked it up. If she did, she wasn't admitting it, because I asked if she was there and nothing happened. When I got home, I'd get a recording of my own voice saying 'Allison, Allison, are you there? Pick the receiver up' over and over. I took a ride from the police car into town, but as we approached Oxford Street I asked to be let out. I reminded Mather I hadn't yet spoken to Allison, and he promised to contact her to go to Holborn police station where Martin was being held. I had another Mather to go meet first.

Chapter Nine

I'd taken down the address before I left the office. She lived in Mayfair, a block of flats in South Audley Street where only Arabs could now afford to rent or buy, but that had probably been in some part or another of her family for years of rent-controlled privilege. Though costly, it was run-down: impoverished gentility. There was no porter and I made my way up to her fourth floor apartment unhindered. I rang and rang at the bell; it was loud enough to wake the dead, and my thoughts were beginning to drift in that direction when she opened the door on the chain, enough to show herself enticingly alive.

'I'm sorry to disturb you, Mrs de Peyer,' I started the way I meant to carry on, by lying. 'I work for Mather's, and I need to have a word with you.'

'Do you have some identification?' Her voice was gravelly, from sleep and cigarettes, not sexily so.

I produced the bland and uninformative introduction letter I'd had Marion Mortimore type up for me when I began, and taken down for Ian Mather to sign. It was a shame he wasn't around at the time, but most solicitors' letters are in any event signed not with a real person's name, but that of the firm. One hand-written flourish – mine – looks much like another.

She let me in. She wore only a light dressing-gown and no evidence of anything beneath. I could still remember what beneath looked like. She led me into the kitchen and put on a coffee percolator with one hand, while she lit up with another. One of my hypocrisies is that while I smoke like a chimney, I ain't that keen on women who do. (My most profound residual sexism is: I can't stand women smoking cigars. It'd be like French-kissing my father.)

'What's all this about, then?' She asked boredly.

'Christopher Wainwright's been killed,' I said dead-pan and determined to dent the don't-give-a-damn tone.

Her teeth clenched, but that was it. Her hands didn't tremble as she poured coffee – for both of us. Her voice was level as she asked if I wanted milk and sugar.

'You don't seem very shocked.'

She shrugged, bringing half a breast into view for just long enough to make me want it to come out altogether.

'He's a casual friend. That's all. I'm very sorry. You said "killed"? What happened?'

'You knew about the other death at Mather's?'

'I can read.' She absorbed my answer: 'Do the police have any idea yet?'

'How would I know?'

'Because that's your job. I know who you are, Mr Woolf. I've been told about you.'

'No, not yet. I daresay they'll be round to see you.'

'When did it happen? Do you think they'll want to check on my alibi?'

'I should think so. It happened late last night. After midnight, anyway. Do you have an alibi?'

She laughed prettily:

'Sure. It's still asleep inside. Shall I fetch it?'

There was a smug twinkle in her eye: she wanted me to see who it was. I would have liked to have refused, on perverse principle, but I didn't professionally have that option. He was who I had come to see. I needed the visible proof that he was as greedy, as insatiable, as unconcerned for anyone else – ultimately, as out of control by any recognizable criteria – as I had suspected, and as almost everyone had, in one way or another, hinted.

As he entered, I picked up my coffee cup in a 'cheers' gesture:

'Breakfast with members of your family seems to be the order of the day.'

Randolph raised half an eyebrow while he poured

his own coffee and then, unexpectedly, refilled mine. I returned the hospitality:

'I just left your father. He's gone in to the office. I should think he'd like you to come in. I know the police would.'

'Yes,' was all he said.

For all the aplomb, I'd shaken his cool, though it was yet unclear whether with news of Wainwright's rapid removal from the rolls or my discovery of him *in flagrante* with Anabelle de Peyer. I wanted to know what he had that could attract so many women, some of them extremely delightful. Maybe there was something to masonic mystique after all; being had in a hood might be fun.

'Did Wainwright know about you two?'

'I've known Anabelle for many years.' That much coincided with what Katrina had said: he and Andrew had both claimed to be too close to handle the divorce for her ex-.

'What you're saying is, this isn't exactly the first time?'

'Correct. I would have to say, I don't think Christopher knew we still occasionally slept together. It, er, it is not what you would call a serious relationship, and of course neither of us is currently married.' He was saying he couldn't be a suspect either on the grounds of jealousy or to keep the affair secret.

'You were at the office late last night. With a secretary?'

If I'd thought it might annoy Anabelle, I was wrong; she chuckled throatily and amused.

'Working, you know,' he waved a hand airily: 'That sort of thing.' We weren't supposed to believe him; if anything, he was admitting my accusation, bragging about his capacity.

'When did you arrange this – well – arrangement?'

They exchanged a glance so fast I almost didn't catch it. He said:

'You still haven't told me where Christopher was killed.'

'At the office. He came in around midnight, expecting to meet someone, looking cheerful. My guess is, you rang him, and told him to meet you there; Mrs de Peyer said she was tired – not to come back. Is that about right?' It was a similar trick Katrina said Martin had once played on Tony Galucci; I began to wonder exactly what Ian Mather had taught them when he gave them each his version of the birds and the bees.

'That's what you say. Why would Mrs de Peyer need an excuse to tell him to leave?'

'I don't know,' I watched her while I answered him: 'But maybe he wasn't that easy to get rid of. You know? After all, she had what she wanted out of him a long time ago: since the divorce settlement; but she was still seeing him.'

They both understood what I was implying. She paled, but didn't let me draw her into it.

'I think you had better leave now, Woolf. I'm sure this is most distressing for Mrs de Peyer.'

'Yeah, sure, she looks distressed.' I was curious about something: 'Tell me, though. If you two have been such good buddies – bosom buddies, you might say – how come you didn't let her know about hubby's land in the Bahamas?'

He couldn't resist:

'That would be a breach of privilege, Woolf. It would be unthinkable.'

I met his mocking gaze:

'Yeah, right. Why didn't I think of that?' I waited a second: 'So you did know about it, then?'

I'd flushed out an answer; he flushed right back at me. He mumbled:

'I didn't, as it happens,' knowing how non-credible it now sounded. He tried to bolster his answer: 'That's the sort of thing I might have found out, that led me not to conduct the case. Conflict of interest. There's no evidence to support what you're hinting about Christopher either. You're guessing.'

He was fumbling.

'Whyn't we ask Anabelle?' I turned to look at her; she was better to look at than Randolph.

'I said, you'd better leave, Woolf. I meant it.'

I was too tired to fight. I got up to go. Something

else puzzled me, but I wouldn't get an answer this time around, even by default: if he wanted me to know he was with Katrina shortly before she was killed, albeit apparently reluctantly, why not admit he'd called Wainwright in? There is absolutely no better defence than an innocent explanation of the truth. Unless the difference was: he hadn't expected her to be murdered.

By the time I arrived at the office, Ali had been and gone, to Holborn police station where they were holding Martin. By the time I arrived at Holborn, she had gone with the police to Cross Course, to witness the search. I asked whether I could see Martin; they called Dowell at Cross Course and – still suspiciously helpful – he agreed. We were allowed to talk alone in a bleak, barred interview room.

He didn't look so chipper. No longer the swinge-breech. He needed to shave; his eyes were blood-shot, his shirt wrinkled, he wasn't wearing a tie. I said:

'D'they take it away from you?'

He held up a foot. He was wearing loafers:

'I think they were disappointed there were no shoe-laces to remove.'

'How's it going? They feed you?'

'Now I know why they're called pigs; the swill they eat.'

'You going to court?'

He shook his head:

'Tomorrow. You took your time getting Allison here,' he complained.

'Problem. She was at my house; answering machine. Sorry: I had to go see your father.'

'How is he?' He asked anxiously.

'He's a tough old buzzard.'

'How much did you tell him?'

'All I know, more or less.'

'What was the less?'

I shrugged:

'No reason to tell you either.'

163

'I thought you trusted me, when you came to see me last night?'

'I did. Until you lied to me.'

'How did I lie to you?'

'Well, I can't recall exactly if you lied. Same way you said Andrew wouldn't've leaked. What's the expression that guy used: "economical with the truth", is that it?'

He smiled thinly:

'If it's good enough for the government, it's good enough for me.' The man who had brought the expression back into contemporary usage was the former British Cabinet secretary, who happened to be giving evidence in a court at the time: this is what is meant by the integrity of the civil service; they don't deny being a bunch of lying shits.

'Andrew's more deeply in trouble than you said. Right?'

He didn't answer.

'You were too easy, Martin. You rolled over on his leak like you were doing me a big favour. But a squirt who knew Andrew'd leaked a bit of information on a case wasn't worth eight or nine grand, was he? Especially not to Andrew, with his affection for Mr Green,' a Hill Street coinage. 'While I was waiting for your father to come down this morning, I tried to work out what he needed to live like he does. I've got a fair idea of all your earnings: it isn't nearly as much as I expected. You've all had to pay your way into the partnership, by deduction from profits.'

It was the usual way to buy in to a practice. If Ian hadn't also been so tight, I would've been more surprised he'd made his children pay their way in. 'Anyhow, it didn't leave a lot of change to host weekend parties and buy a lot of drugs to keep the guests happy and high. You – I know where your extra loot comes from. And Randolph ain't spending money getting his kicks – quite literally – so I don't know what he's worth. But where'd's Andrew's come from, Martin?'

He still didn't answer, so I told him:

'He was more involved with Stonefrost than you allowed. That's why he had to stop it getting to trial, not 'cos he might've been implicated as an occasional user, but as a dealer. I think Wainwright found out about it somehow: I don't know how, yet, but I will.'

'I don't know what you're talking about,' he said flatly.

'Never drink coca-cola?' I asked.

He looked at me like I was crazy; maybe he ought to call a guard before I flipped completely. I ignored the expression on his face:

'Did you know: ever since they changed the formula for coca-cola, there's been a shortage of cocaine? They produced a lot of it – a hell of a lot of it – before, and it was processed and sold to the medical industry. It was of course perfectly legitimate, indeed a helpful by-product. Don't forget, cocaine became known to the developed world as a medicine: it was nearly Freud's first major breakthrough, for use as an eye anaesthetic, though someone else got it just before. Then he discovered its other qualities: he used to put his whole family on it, when they got depressed. I guess he didn't have the time to spare to analyse them out of it.'

'What has it got to do with the price of eggs?'

'A lot of that legal coke got ripped off. Along the way, or at end destinations. It wasn't in itself one of the major sources, because most of them are sewn up, but it was a side-line source. It used to get into this country via Haiti, until they deposed the Duvaliers. Since then, the Bahamas is a favourite route. People coming in from the Bahamas are like diplomatic bags, they don't hardly get looked at. My guess is, de Peyer's Bahamian property was bought with drugs money: that's why it was never declared anywhere. It shouldn't even have been on file at Mather's. It's why it couldn't come out in a court case.'

I waited to see if I had yet scored a reaction. In a way, I had. He leaned across the table, picked up my pack of Camels and extracted one for himself. I asked:

'How come none of you smoke openly? You're the third one to bum a fag off me that way.'

'Father didn't approve. His father died of cancer.' The funeral his uncle couldn't come back for.

We sat in silence for a time, while he savoured the cigarette. Prompted by the reference to his grandfather, I said:

'Tell me about James Mather.'

'What's to tell?'

'Why is Dowell interested in Cross Course?'

'You tell me.'

'My thinking is, maybe it's a laundry for your uncle's dirty money?'

He laughed out loud:

'You're crazy, you know that, Dave?'

'So tell me,' I persisted.

'Why not? It's something to talk about while we wait.'

When he'd finished his long period of articles, he had inveigled his father into funding a summer sabbatical in the States. The only condition had been that he not look for his uncle. Martin said:

'I didn't have to. He was waiting for me when I came off the 'plane.'

'How? How did he know you were coming?'

'I asked him just that. He's the one gave me that line about not asking how someone found something out but working it out for yourself.'

'And did you? Work it out, I mean?'

He shook his head:

'No, I was just a kid, really.' America's fate is to be excused as a youthful folly. 'It was all so exciting, I was tired at the time, it never seemed important to know. Someone told him, but I don't know who. I suppose, it wasn't that big a secret; it could've been coincidence. Maybe it's what you said: it wasn't because he was good at finding things out, just that he found a way to use it.'

'Go on about James.'

'Well, as I said, it was exciting. I was what – twenty-two, twenty-three? I'd stayed up the night before, then my first really long 'plane flight. I spent it chatting up a girl in the seat next to me; I didn't have enough experience to realize how common that is when you're travelling, how you can get to feel really close to someone that quickly, because, after all, you're going to go your separate ways as soon as you arrive. So I was very turned on when I arrived, and as I came through customs I was suddenly being hustled towards this old guy – and I knew immediately who he was, the resemblance is marked – and a limousine.'

He stopped for a moment, perhaps reluctant to share a story he had savoured in secret for such a long time. 'We drove into town. He had an apartment in the Dakota – the place where Lennon lived; oh, not then, of course. But it was his New York home. And he took me up and there was, you know, well a girl there, he said was looking after the apartment for him. And he told me to get some food, have a shower, get some sleep if I could – he'd come by for me the next day. That was what she was for: to help me sleep. It was unbelievable, it was like out of a movie. She was young, she looked like a college girl, not a hooker; but she was good, God was she good. Everything before, well, I wasn't a virgin – none of us were in those days – but it was like I'd been chewing someone else's stale gum.'

He paused to enjoy the memory, his face alight:

'It was the best time of my life, ever. He wanted me to stay with him: I don't mean in New York; he wanted to travel around with me. We compromised, and I agreed to spend about half the time with him – I was there for four months, but in the end I did spend most of it with him. It was just so easy: everywhere we went was first class; he had friends everywhere – you also know he isn't exactly a conventional businessmen, but his friends were all sorts. Once, we went to a party on the Cape, I met this guy everyone thought was going to be the next President: me, I was standing talking to him.'

His face shone still with the thrill:

'He had a family: a common law wife and a daughter, they lived in New Hampshire, and either she deliberately didn't know what he did for a living or they really didn't: the wife, I mean, the girl was still in her teens; she certainly didn't know. He didn't spend a lot of time with them. No one else was supposed to know about them: just me; I was his nephew; I was also family. And we went out to the West Coast: you know, we'd arrive, he'd make a 'phone call, there were people coming through the door before he hung up; tables at the best restaurants, the best seats at the ring, anything. And girls: for him, for me – they'd just appear. We went to New Orleans. You ever been to New Orleans, Dave? It's fantastic, maybe the most fantastic city of all: it's like all the best of Europe, condensed, but with all the historical hang-ups discarded. You cannot, you simply cannot have any idea at all what it was like.'

'It sounds like a dream?'

'A fantasy, more like.'

'How did it end? How was it left?'

He shrugged indifferently:

'It ended. He drove me, himself; usually when we drove he had a chauffeur, only I think the sort of machines he was best equipped to handle had triggers, not wheels. So he drove me down to Kennedy, from New Hampshire. And on the way, he made this big, long speech – sort of in bits, but I remember it as if it was one speech. About how the world was divided into three types of people. The bossed, the bosses and the bosses' bosses. He said no matter how high up you go, and how far back, when you come to someone who seems to be in charge, there's always one more behind.'

People behind the people behind the people.

'I think he was telling me, well, I know he was saying that's what he was: one more behind someone else. He was telling me to make my choices. I could live my father's way, according to a tight set of rules and with a narrow set of expectations, or I could live his: the hell with the rules, the whole world and nothing less was what I could expect.'

'And?'

He stopped to look for the right way to tell me. He went in at an angle:

'You read much, Dave?'

'Comics?'

'Do you know John O'Hara?'

'Maybe. Why?'

'I read this article about him. About how fed up he

was because he'd never won the Nobel prize for literature.' I sympathized: I'd never won it neither. Know what I mean? 'Anyhow, the article was by this journalist who'd gone to O'Hara's home one night, uninvited. It was some kind of anniversary, or his birthday or something. And he looked in the window of this big, country house, and what he saw was a ballroom orchestra, and there were no guests, just O'Hara and his wife, dancing alone.'

I shook my head to clear it: I hadn't slept; I was tired; that was probably why I couldn't see the connection.

'The way O'Hara was, that's the way I used to see my parents. All alone in the Hampstead mansion. It's been more acute since mother went into the hospital. What I'm trying to say, look at my choices. I could be like my father; big, rigid man, a freemason but no real friends; just rules, bloody rules. You don't want to know what it was like being brought up by him. Did you ever think what a coincidence it is we've all become lawyers? We were never given a choice, Dave.'

'You found James attractive?'

'Absolutely. Randolph was already well-set in his way: also a mason, heavily so, into the Royal Arch crap too, and. . .' But he didn't finish the sentence. Instead, he said: 'Following Gauldie: now there was another role model for me. Gauldie loves, in the following order: himself, money, power; himself, money, freemasonry. Randolph's admired him all his life. He loves hierarchy, authority over others, the ritual, the mystery.'

He quoted: '"We three do meet and agree. . .in love and unity. . .the sacred word to keep. . .and never to divulge the same. . .unless when three. . .such as we. . .do meet and agree. . .agree. . .agree. . .agree."' That's a bit of Royal Arch, but I don't know much, because Ian isn't.' Maybe Shakespeare was though.

'So you went the way of James?'

He shook his head:

'No. That's the point I'm trying to make. I didn't want to be like James either. There's something weird about the Mathers, Dave, it gets to us all. Something to do with my grandfather, I think. Trying to live up to him, experience what he experienced. He had it tough when he was a boy; he was the ultimate self-made man. He was hard. Insecure, I suppose, but they didn't use terms like that in those days. And Andrew... He was also Andrew,' he explained: 'And Andrew begat James and Ian and James begat Randolph and Martin and Andrew...'

'Ali? She appeared under a bushel, maybe?'

'I'm sorry, Dave. I'm not being very helpful. I'm just trying to explain. I did not take up James on his offer. Though, for a while I thought I might: it was probably part of why I set up Cross Course.'

'Why'd he make the offer?'

'At the time, I believed it was affection: he had his wife and daughter in New Hampshire; but he didn't live with them, and no son. I thought he wanted a relationship with me, for its own sake, you know?'

'But that isn't what you think now?'

'No, nor for a long time. I think he wanted a relationship with me not for its own sake, but in order to get back at Ian. He wanted to hurt Ian, by bringing me into his way of life and out of Ian's. Revenge. And, you know, I was tempted, I could so easily have done it. But that's what it would have done: hurt Ian, more than I could stand.'

'Revenge for what?'

'That's something you'll have to ask Ian.'

'Why'd you go to the office last night?' I shot at him.

'I rang Randolph at home; he wasn't there. I rang his private line; he answered. I wanted to talk to him, about Wainwright, about what you told me.'

'What'd he say?'

He didn't answer.

'He already knew, didn't he?'

He still wouldn't tell me.

'How'd I do otherwise?' I meant my earlier analysis of Andrew's activities.

'Ah,' he said sadly: 'I won't lie to you anymore, Dave. It's gone a bit too far for that. But... Well... There may be no love lost, but they're family. All I'll say is, you weren't wrong, but you weren't that right either.'

'For God's sake,' I snapped disgustedly: 'People are dying, Martin. It isn't like sneaking on a school-fellow.' Maybe it was though: to care about life and death, you gotta care about people; the thing about the English upper classes is – they don't care, period; sneaking on a school-chum betrays the code, which is far more serious than whatever might happen to the fellow himself.

I didn't get any answer because that was when Dowell returned. He wanted the key to Martin's house: that was where they were going next. Martin gave it him without argument. It was easier than having the door repaired. I told him:

'I'll talk to Allison. I'll see you later.'

Tim said:

'She's meeting us at the house. I don't want you there, Dave.'

'I've got other things to do.'

They didn't have an underground station marked Beat Kelly, so I got off at Bank instead. No one had been lying when they told me it was only a small set-up. There was a reception counter within the main, outer office, and from the number of desks and computer terminals, I figured most of the staff worked in one, open-plan environment. They were busily sorting out files into drawers: replacing them after Dowell's descent. There were only two doors off. One was ajar, and I could see it was a conference room. The other was shut. That was where Beat Kelly would work.

'Could I see her?'

'Do you have an appointment? She's been very busy this morning.'

'Yes, I know about that. And, no, I don't have an appointment. Tell her it's Dave Woolf. I think she'll know the name, but if not you can say I was a friend of her sister.'

I was shown in with a minimum of ceremony. Martin had said she was beautiful. He hadn't lied about that either. For a moment, I could hardly believe she was Katrina's sister. Her hair was much lighter, almost blonde. She was about two inches taller, and several inches smaller around the waist and chest. If her skirt had been a millimetre shorter, I could tell how the thighs compared.

'Yes, I've heard about you. From Katrina. And from Martin.' I sat down without waiting to be asked. She looked confused: 'The police took a lot of papers. Can they do that?'

'I don't know. Allison Hoyt was here with them, wasn't she?'

'Yes. But, well, she didn't seem to know either. We made them list everything. Is that what you came about?'

'It just seemed like time to talk.'

'Would you like some coffee? Or a drink?' She glanced at her watch; I didn't bother glancing at mine but said yes to the second. She didn't ask what I drank, but poured it out for me, and the same for herself.

'The first thing I remember Kat ever telling me about you was how much Southern Comfort you could put away.' There was the slightest accent in her voice. Notwithstanding the Irish name, I knew she wasn't, anymore than Kat had been Italian. She confirmed: 'I was married to an American called Michael Kelly. We're divorced now, well, isn't everyone?'

'I was never married,' I answered. I remembered: Allison said she had lived in the States.

'That's not smart. Marriage is the quickest way to someone else's bank balance.' She grinned and when she grinned she looked like her sister's twin. I felt a warm glow of belated recognition. Kat wasn't dead after all; just reincarnated with a lot less weight to carry about.

'Do you miss her?'

'I'm supposed to be the one asking the questions. But, yes, I do miss her, which is stupid because I hadn't seen her for a long time until just before she died.' I found myself telling Beat about the last evening together, and admitting out loud, as I hadn't admitted to anyone, why I felt guilty: 'I didn't have to go. I could've just stayed on 'till she was finished talking. It wasn't like I had a job to get up to in the morning. I could've slept on the couch.

172

But I wasn't comfortable about some of the things she'd told me.' I didn't elaborate.

She was only barely listening to my expiation. She said:

'I can hear her. "Play bodies" was one of her expressions. You can't live for other people. We've all got the right to make our own mistakes.'

'What are yours?'

She got up and poured us both another drink. When she returned, she took a pack of cigarettes from the bag hanging on the back of her chair, and offered me one. I was about to refuse when I realized they were Camels. I thought about asking how she'd like to get her hands on my bank balance.

'Michael, I suppose. No, that's not true. We had a time, for a while.'

'Why were you over there?'

'I went to work there.' She was surprised I didn't know. People think their mutual friends and acquaintances talk about them more than usually proves to be the case.

She explained: she was – as I knew – Kat's older sister; she was also bright, and ahead of her years; she had qualified as an accountant early, and decided to take a couple of years in America rather than go straight into practice here. She wasn't qualified to practise as an accountant in the States, so she worked in business.

'What kind of business?' She shrugged:

'Things a bit like this. Kat never said?'

'No.' Kat had been holding back; I thought because of Beat's connection to Galucci.

'Did she know what you did?'

'I got around a lot. I was in Colorado, I met Michael. I couldn't believe an Irishman in Colorado, but there were plenty. We went down to Nevada together, got married in a hurry, I was just a kid, I didn't know what I was doing: that's why, you know, I don't really like to go back over it all.' Another one to write America off as an adolescent indiscretion.

'What happened with Kelly?'

'Nothing. After a while, nothing happened; that was the main reason for getting divorced, so I came back here.'

'How long were you there?'

'Three, four years. It seemed like longer.'

'And then?'

'Then I met Martin, and Tony, and I liked their ideas and the way they were beginning – just beginning, then – to approach money and the market: don't forget, we're talking years before Big Bang.' De-regulation of the stock market.

She warmed to her theme: 'We've been so totally conservative about money in this country, that's why the early Americans to make money here could made so much so easily. Martin and Tony, they saw the way things were going, how much mileage could be made out of diversification, how much money could be made out of an enterprise that didn't give a damn about tomorrow, just wanted in and out. It's all like that now, but in those days it felt – oh, I don't know – I mean, being an accountant isn't exactly an adventure, and it had been exciting working in America so I was looking for something like this. The idea of conventional practice was anathema.'

'You said "early Americans": like Latimer?'

'Sure. But he wasn't the only one. Though, I guess, he made his start here, while others came over already successful in the States.'

'Some did it the other way around,' I probed cautiously.

'What do you mean?'

'I was thinking of Martin's uncle, James Mather. What do you know about him?'

'Martin's talked about him.'

'How did Kat feel about you and Tony?' I shifted gear suddenly enough to catch her with her guard down. (I think that one goes on the funeral pyre with the other mixed metaphors.)

She shrugged:

'It was no harder for her to cope with than Tony having to cope with Martin and her.' But she hadn't told me about it, and in the context of that conversation it was a distinct, not a casual or accidental, omission:

'Did you and Martin ever, er. . .?'

'No. And to save you asking, I'd rather die than do it with Randolph Mather.'

'But you knew about his, er. . .?' Talking to her sister made me coy about the details.

She blushed, bringing back more colour than she'd lost a couple of questions ago:

'Yes, she told me.'

I couldn't find it in me to ask her, as I'd asked Martin: what had she done about it? I wanted to think that it wasn't an entire irrelevance. I tried to construct a theory that linked his behaviour to her death: she was telling people; people minded; they were going to get him for it; he got in there first. It didn't make a straight line.

'Another question?' She nodded permission. 'Who do you think killed her, Beat?'

She shuddered:

'I haven't the first idea. I've thought about it; of course I've thought about it. If I thought I could pin it on Randolph, I'd kill him myself. I heard: you feel the same way. But he's alibi'd, and he's not concealing he was with her just beforehand. She never harmed anyone, Kat: she was bright, and chirpy, and I loved her more than anyone else.' There were tears in her eyes so maybe she was telling the truth; at least, she wanted me to believe she was.

I waited for them to subside, then I asked:

'Obviously, you know about Wainwright?'

'What about him?' The temperature dropped to somewhere below freezing. This time, I got up to pour the drinks. She grasped her glass with both hands, the way Ian Mather had been holding his tea when I gave him the news. She was younger; she made it all the way to her mouth without spilling a drop.

'Any thoughts?'

She shook her head:

'I didn't know him.'

I took a wild shot; they're my best. When I stop to think, I invariably get it wrong.

'What if I told you it was the same person that killed Katrina?'

If I'd had a camera in my hand, I could have convicted her; I didn't have a camera, and she was beyond confession. She slumped back in her chair, stared at me for a full minute, then hissed:

'Get out of here, Woolf; get out of here.'

I didn't move. Her eyes were bulging. I was an inch away from all the answers. She knew who had killed Wainwright, and now she believed she knew who had killed her sister. I waited for her to calm down. I waited for her to tell me.

'I can't,' she whispered: 'I don't know, I don't know. It was just a shock. It brought it all back, you see it brought it all back. That's all; that's it. I loved Katrina, Dave, I did, I really did. I wouldn't hurt her for all the world.' She made about as much sense as a masonic ritual.

'Beat, you have to tell me what you know. She was your sister, for Christ's sake. You owe it her.'

She shook her head violently:

'It won't bring her back, will it? I didn't know, I'm telling you, I didn't know anything about it.'

'I know, I believe that. But you do know now. What about the police? They're going to be round again. You might as well tell me.'

Time was operating against me. Every exchange allowed her to recover herself.

'There's nothing to tell. I'm sorry. I'm sorry,' she repeated dully: 'You have to leave now. I insist.'

I shrugged:

'I'll go, now, but it isn't that easy, you know. It – whatever it is you know, whoever it is you're scared of – it isn't going to go away like walking out the door.'

'I know,' she said dully: 'Don't think I don't know that much.'

I got up to go. I sighed:

'No, I'm sure you know that much, I'm sure you know more. You're cut from the same cloth Kat was, Beat. I want to help you, if I can, if you'll let me. People are getting killed for what they know, Beat; I wouldn't like you to be one of them.' I like to end on a subtle note.

She looked like I was discussing the arrangements for her funeral. Shaking, as I left the room, she was already reaching for the telephone, probably to call Tony. Or, a travel agent.

Chapter Ten

I had been lying to Beat Kelly from start to end: I did not know that the person who killed Wainwright had also killed Kat. The evidence pointed in the opposite direction.

'Person' wasn't really what I meant.

This is close to what I mean:

'The Juwes are

'The Men That

'will not

'be blamed

'for nothing'.

'Juwes' is not a misprint for Jews. 'Jubela, Jubelo and Jubelum – known collectively as the *Juwes*. In masonic lore, the Juwes are hunted down and executed "by the breast being torn open and the heart and vitals taken out and thrown over the left shoulder",' according to the author of *The Brotherhood*, the book that had almost not seen the light of day thanks to unfortunate fatherhood.

The subject was Jack the Ripper, who murdered a handful of prostitutes in London's East End in 1888: there's every kind of theory who done it, including the then Prince of Wales, but no one was ever caught or convicted of the killings. One theory is that freemasons were responsible. The relationship to freemasonry is evidenced by the eradication of the above nursery rhyme from a wall near one of the murders, by no less a personage than the Commissioner of Metropolitan Police of the time, a prominent freemason and a member of the Royal Arch.

In 1981, a scandal broke in Italy, America and all points between. It was known as P2. Not to overstate the position, a gaggle of Italian freemasons had put themselves in virtual control of the nation. (This doesn't mean as much as in a normal country: they change governments in Italy somewhat more often than underwear. But it's still something.) The implications rippled through the western world: they had three cabinet members, a few former prime ministers, several football teams of members of parliament, half the command of the armed forces, the judiciary, the police and the media, and a number of bankers.

The names have gone down in history: Gelli, Sindona, and Calvi, the man who liked to hang about Blackfriars Bridge. But the details have quickly been obscured. This isn't a history book so I'm not going to spell out the whole story, but these people were running the whole country, and everything that the wealth of a nation could buy. Ian Mather had scorned my conspiracy theory at its inception; but at the end of P2, the Americans decided not to act to replace all its involved officials, because of the effect it would have had on NATO (them what keeps you and me safe in our beds at night). That's how big it'd grown.

I made two more stops before I went back to the office. The first was to Companies House where I learned I was wrong about Westmoreland House: Cross Course played no traceable part in it. The second was to Hackney Town Hall. I'd tried to find the report about freemasonry at the council that Orbach had mentioned, but it wasn't in any library or bookshop so, undaunted, I decided to go to the source.

It was about five o'clock when I arrived. No one stopped me at the door, but there weren't many people around. English local government doesn't like to work late; it's not a rule, just a convention. I wandered down long, bland corridors, poking my head into unlocked rooms. If there was anything to steal, I could have stole it blind.

I was just emerging – fortuituously empty-handed

179

– from a room marked 'Chief Executive's Secretary' when a woman came out of the next door office.

'Can I help you?' she asked politely.

I was surprised. She was smart, attractive, in her mid-forties, and spoke with an accent more polished than I would have expected of a secretary in what is variously referred to as the People's Republic of Hackney, 'Ackney, and the Lodestar of the Lunatic Left. I don't normally go for older women, but she could prove the exception.

'Uh, yeah. You had an inquiry here, a while ago, about freemasonry. D'you know anything about it?'

'I seem to remember something of the kind,' she said dryly: 'What about it? It was a long time ago, and not very significant.'

'I was wondering – how does someone go about getting a copy of its report? I understand it was made public, is that right?'

'Yes. But why would "someone" want a copy? It's very lengthy, and extremely tedious.'

'I'm, er, interested in the subject.' I felt like I was being hauled up to explain myself to the headmistress.

'Do you live in Hackney, Mr uh. . .?'

'Woolf, Dave Woolf. No, I don't.' I swallowed a 'Thank God'. No one wants to live in Hackney. The worst thing is the road-planning. Most people born there are still trying to find the way out.

'Does that matter?'

'Hackney residents are entitled to a copy free of charge. Others have to pay.'

'You've still got a copy, then?'

'Good lord, yes. Hardly anyone was interested in it. By the end, I don't even think the author was. There were hundreds of copies printed, and most of them are now used to prevent subsidence in the basement.'

'Listen, I've been looking for somewhere I can get one. Can you help me?'

'The Council's Secretariat receives requests for copies. But I'm afraid there'll be no one there at this time. You'll have to write to them.'

'Aw, shucks,' I batted my eyelids: 'I still have trouble making the loops on all those letters.'

She was not impressed. I tried again:

'Listen, I'm a solicitor. It's really important to something I'm working on, not against Hackney,' I hastened to add. 'Is there any way I could get a copy now?'

She sighed:

'I suppose I ought to seize the opportunity to reduce the stocks; it probably won't come again. I still have half a dozen in my room. You'll have to pay, though.'

Oh, yeah, I got it: everyone's on the take. Reluctantly, I pulled out my wallet. She shook her head:

'A cheque please. Payable to the London Borough of Hackney. I shall give you a receipt.'

That was when she led me into her room. Not, as I expected, the room marked 'Secretary', but the one next door, without a marking. She walked behind a huge desk and familiarly opened a drawer, from which she extracted a key, which she used to open a cupboard. She pulled out a massive, yellow-bound volume and offered it to me. She must've been stronger than me, because I could only just carry it. She sat behind the desk while I wrote my cheque, and scribbled a receipt on a sheet of headed notepaper. Curiosity got the better of me:

'You're not the Chief Executive's secretary, are you?'

'The word "secretary" is redundant.'

'I suppose it happens all the time? Sorry.'

'Oh, no, Mr Woolf: it never happens. I do not allow it to happen.'

I left the room backwards, bowing courtly: ma'am, your 'umble servant.

When I got back to Mather's, Allison still hadn't returned from Martin's house: there was a message to ring her there, or go over, she'd wait for me. Dowell must have left if I would now be welcome. I wanted to see Ian Mather first, but he was in conference with Andrew. I was glad not to have to be present. Marion brought me two mugs of coffee, as she had done ever since that was what I asked for the day Dowell came to see me.

I was having difficulty thinking straight. That had been the morning after I'd first slept with Ali. It felt like a month ago, but it was only the day before and I hadn't slept since.

The atmosphere in the office was thick enough to cut with a medieval sword. Randolph, apparently, had been questioned by Pratt, and released: he had an alibi that Pratt would much prefer to spend several hours interviewing. I knew it would stand up. I sent Marion out for a fresh cream donut before I starved to death.

While I waited for Ian to finish with Andrew, I leafed through the report. As Orbach had accurately summarized, most of it reflected its author's concern with the want of organization within the authority, rather than his commission to discern how much of it was rotten with freemasons. I am no more interested in local government than in any other kind of organization that tries to tell me what to do. For this reason, I flipped quickly through to the part of the report that concerned the ancient ('antient') order of freemasons. I paused at a few passages.

One of them described the initiation ceremony in terms by now familiar. There was also an explanation of Jabulon. He was said not only to be a secret God, but secret even to most of the membership. The name was apparently a composite of Jehovah (the angry God of my youth), Baal and Osiris, the Egyptian God of the dead. I don't know who Baal was: maybe he dealt dope.

My eye was caught by a heading 'Donkey Whipping. It is not generally believed, however, that there is any basis in the rumour that Freemasons whip donkeys, give poisoned sweets to schoolchildren, or drink boiled nail-clippings.' I wasn't amused: I was still eating.

Freemasons claimed to be 'men concerned with moral and spiritual values, who accordingly can be regarded as having taken it upon themselves to cultivate their own moral improvement. . . The notion of "good citizens" recurred. . . They. . .invite men who they considered to be "of good reputation"...to join.' I was out.

The contradictions were reflected in a passage which referred to John Poulson, who represents corruption in English local government about the same way Mayor Richard Daley does in America, subject to the minor difference that Poulson got caught and the major difference that a lot more money was up for grabs in Chicago. 'Commentators will commonly remark upon the membership of Freemasonry of Mr Poulson; yet one of the principal judges who condemned and sentenced him for his activities was himself also a Freemason, and prominently so...'

Relevantly, the report recorded: 'It is hard to resist an impression of Freemasonry as constituted of generals and their foot-soldiers...' This was the description Orbach had lifted: it did my heart good to realize that even he could sometimes stoop to plagiarism.

The analogy fitted with the conclusions I was beginning to form for myself. The way I saw it, the real danger was not the institution itself, but what men made of it. People with an attitude to life that relished ridiculous robes, raunchy ritual and obscene obligations, nonetheless enjoyed access to alleged secret powers and esoteric mysteries. Boys will be boys; it was a recipe for abuse and corruption, and ultimately and inevitably for evil.

Marion buzzed me to say that Ian was free. I wandered down the stairs. Andrew was just coming up, ashen-faced. Our eyes met; his were bloodshot; he had been crying. For a moment, I thought he was going to strike out. He raised a hand then, suddenly, thrust it towards me. Nervously, I took it. He said:

'I have to take a year off. Then he'll decide if I can come back,' he laughed uneasily: 'If I was anyone else, I'd be out on my ear.' As Kat said, even Ian could not resist spoiling him.

'No hard feelings, then, Andrew?'

'No,' he shook his head: 'To tell you the truth, it feels like a great weight has been lifted off me. I've been here since I left college; I know I've let him down; it's been a strain. I don't know how Marilyn will take it, but for myself, I'm just relieved the deception is over.'

'Is it?'

'What do you mean?'

'Your father's suspended you for leaking, right?'

'Yes?'

'I just hope he doesn't have to suffer anymore unpleasant surprises, Andrew.'

He stared at me, trying to work out how much I knew. He said:

'I don't think. . . I won't treat you like an idiot, Woolf: you've proved you're not, whatever we thought of you when you arrived. Obviously, there are things yet to come out: I didn't kill Wainwright, and you still haven't solved Katrina's death. But whatever else there is I think I've seen the worst of what I will have to take the blame for.' He was only following orders.

'I don't suppose you'd care to enlighten me? Tell me what other surprises there might be?'

He went white as a sheet:

'I would, Dave. I would. But. . . I can't betray. . . Oh, hell. No, that's all, no.'

'The brotherhood? Is that what you were going to say?'

He shook his head, his lips pursed:

'I wasn't going to say anything. Just, well, as you said, no hard feelings.'

We shook hands again – normal, not masonic – and I proceeded to the old man's office. Old was right: he'd aged twenty years in the short time I'd known him. I wasn't sure I hadn't too. He gestured me to a seat. He said:

'Would you like a drink, Mr Woolf?'

It was uncharacteristically generous; I hoped he wouldn't deduct it from my bill:

'Sure.'

'What would you like?'

'I, er, drink Southern Comfort. No ice. No soda.'

He looked puzzled:

'I don't believe... Uh... I don't think I've ever heard... That is to say, I don't suppose we...'

'Sure you do. Marion Mortimore's been keeping stocks since I arrived.'

'I'll try.' While we waited, I told him about Southern Comfort, the peach-based American liquor that made it out from the mountain stills. We both needed a few moments away from the trauma.

His secretary brought in our drinks. He was drinking scotch, of course. Her legs hadn't improved in the intervening decades, but then again, they were no worse than I remembered. I sighed. He said:

'I understood, uh, that you were presently seeing, uh, someone.'

I studied him carefully to try and discern how he felt about it: was it a warning, or a blessing? He smiled wanly:

'Mr Woolf, if one of my children is a little bit happier since you arrived, I am not going to object. After all...' He tailed off: the rest weren't. 'The first day you came to see me, I said some things of which I am not particularly proud. I hope you will accept my apology.'

'Why?'

He looked surprised. It wasn't the answer he expected. I explained:

'I don't mean why should I accept it: thank you. I meant, why are you apologizing?'

'At the time, I said there was no one left for me to trust. So I had to trust you. I'm not pleased by everything that has happened. How could I be? Another young person is dead. But sometimes it is necessary to cause pain, in order to cut out the cancer.' Given how he felt about his father's death, I was taken aback by the metaphor, but at least it wasn't mixed.

I pressed my luck:

'Earlier, you said if I gave you some names, you'd find out about their masonic connections.'

'I said I would think about it. I said I would take advice about it.'

'And?'

185

'I was advised that it would be inappropriate, Mr Woolf.'

'Without even hearing my reasons?'

'That was what I was advised.' I saw the twinkle in his eye: 'I didn't say it was what I would do.'

'If I told you. . .' He'd suffered a lot for one day, and the next piece of news wasn't going to act like a balm: 'The final leak was Westmoreland House.'

He nodded for me to go on.

'Because they had to settle, the landlords were way out of their depth. They were next to bankruptcy. . .'

'Liquidation,' he corrected. People go bankrupt; companies go into liquidation.

'Yeah, great. The point is, suddenly, they were available – and were bought up – at a snip.'

'I see.' He picked up his drink and sipped it before gesturing for me to go on.

'The company who bought it, they're a Latimer enterprise. Topcent. Heard of them?'

'No,' he was genuinely surprised.

'Well, it's a property holding company, and one of the few that doesn't carry his name. But there is no doubt at all he owns it.'

'I see,' he repeated, absorbing the information. This time, he didn't ask me to carry out any analysis: he could manage on his own. The point Martin had made in his defence was the point I was now making: the leaks we knew about were no more than the tip of the iceberg.

'Who do you want to know about, Mr Woolf?'

I passed him the list. Most of the names would by now come as no surprise: his oldest and youngest sons, for example – I wanted full lists of their Lodges, and Chapters; Stonefrost, de Peyer, the Wainwright brothers; John a.k.a. Ron Fitzpatrick; Gauldie; Latimer. I included Galucci, too. There was one name guaranteed to cause something more than a mild frisson: James Mather.

'What has my brother got to do with this, Mr Woolf? He left this country almost forty years ago. I have had no contact with him since.'

'Except when he wanted to come back for your father's funeral; I gather you were the reason he couldn't.'

He picked up his drink again, but put it back down without touching a drop. I watched admiringly: it was something else I've never been able to do. He waited for me to go on.

'I don't know... There's a lot I still don't know... But you and your brother fell out pretty badly, didn't you?'

'Yes,' he was having difficulty breathing.

'Would you care to tell me why?'

'It's not necessary.'

'I think it is, Mr Mather.'

'It's painful...for me to talk about.' I waited. He sighed. I wasn't going to let it go.

Most of what he told me I already knew. He had looked up to James, since they were children; it had never occurred to him that his brother was in any way dishonest, not even his exemption from military service during the war.

James' youth had passed at a time when their father, though not poor, was still a long way off rich. James had made it for himself, independently, and Ian admired that. When he established the practice, James made sure they got the early work that made the difference. Ian was glad to get it; proud to be trusted by his successful older brother.

Most of the work generated by James was handled by Gauldie; some of it by Ian; some of it by assistant solicitors – that which was of no real significance. Ian himself never had a clue that there might be anything amiss with his brother's business. Then, for Ian out of the blue, a ship was seized, and Richardson – James' partner – disappeared. James alleged that the ship had been seized for minor infractions of the regulations. That wasn't what the police intimated.

'James came to see me. He was trying to make everything sound like a misunderstanding, or that it was Richardson's fault, he'd been duped by his partner. But it didn't add up, and I kept finding flaws in his case. It was my job, Mr Woolf, he was coming to me as a lawyer, not as his brother. He, well, he didn't take it well: perhaps he didn't like the idea that I could find fault with his. . . Reasoning overstates the case. . . He took another tack.'

I didn't like to tell him he had created a nautical pun, splendid in the circumstances:

'He admitted there was a lot he had never told me about his business, and he, well, he wouldn't deny he was implicated in Richardson's death. I wasn't a criminal lawyer, Mr Woolf, and this was not a criminal practice. I told him we would not act for him. It was, perhaps, wrong of me, but I had begun to build up a clientele who would not wish their solicitor to be seen acting in a case involving smuggling and murder and much more, especially not when the accused was the solicitor's brother. Soon afterwards, James disappeared abroad. That's all.'

'You always call him your "brother". He was your half-brother, though?'

'Yes, but we were like brothers, we were very close. That was why. . . He was upset when I wouldn't accept his account, and angry when I wouldn't act for him; he felt betrayed. I think. . . I know. . . He talked to our father, but he adopted the same attitude as I, as James – anyone who knew him – should have expected.'

'James was a freemason, wasn't he?'

'Yes,' he whispered: 'He introduced me into my first Lodge.'

'The police investigation, at the time, it came to a sudden end; they made no real attempt to track him down – or even to find out who helped him get away. Did you use any influence?'

'Certainly not, Mr Woolf; that is not my understanding of what the craft is about.'

'But he wanted you to, didn't he?'

He sighed heavily:

'Yes. By time time, I had the connections, amongst my clients. . .'

'You've always been craft masonry, but he was Royal Arch as well, wasn't he?'

'What are you saying, Mr Woolf?'

'It's possible. . . Someone else. . .'

He knew who I meant. He didn't deny the possibility. The full implications were only just beginning to dawn on him. Though his brother's activities had come as a shock to Ian, they could surely not have constituted news to the man who regularly conducted his affairs: John Gauldie. But all Ian said was:

'How could it have anything to do with, uh, recent events, Mr Woolf?'

'Someone told me, well, he was quoting your brother,' I saw no reason to tell him who; one more shock for the day might finish him off. 'There's always people behind people behind people. D'you understand what I mean?'

'I don't understand what you're saying.'

'Everything that's been happening, it's connected, it has to be. It would beggar imagination to believe it was coincidence. Things don't happen in threes as the saying goes,' I suppressed the temptation to wise-crack 'except Royal Arch ceremonies'. 'We're talking about a lot of things that have been happening here; drugs are involved – Stonefrost,' I added quickly, since he still did not know of Andrew's added involvement: 'Cross Course – the police are definitely suspicious, and so am I. Now Latimer behind Westmoreland House. Two deaths, sir.' It didn't hurt so much the second time I said the magic word. 'Your brother, well, let's just say he's been as crooked over there as he was here.'

He nodded once, to say he knew: I didn't doubt he'd kept a distant eye.

'James swore he'd get back at me. I never believed. . . I always thought. . . Just bluster. . . I always thought. . . We were so very close once,' he repeated. The fullness of his brother's revenge, and the extent to which he had himself been played for a patsy, had finally sunk in.

'You shouldn't leap to any conclusions, Mr Mather,' I tried half-heartedly to reassure him: 'I may yet be wrong. You've got to understand, I can't work it out without asking the questions.'

His voice was clear, though his skin looked like the clerks could use it if they ran out of parchment:

'Leave me now Mr Woolf. Leave me alone to think.'

I didn't want to; I wasn't sure that he didn't mean 'Leave me alone to die', and if I'd been him, I might have been feeling the same way: I was telling him he'd been betrayed by his two oldest connections – Gauldie and James. He waved me out without allowing any more argument. But he kept the list that would allow me to make my case.

I wasn't tired any longer. Beyond tiredness. High. Spaced. At an entirely different level. I spent a couple more hours at the office, sorting my thoughts, and then went over to Martin's house where I found Ali. She had been waiting for me, sitting in front of the phoney fire, nursing what I didn't think was her first gin and tonic, and that's where she went back to after she let me in.

'Pretty neat, huh?' I pointed to the fire.

'It all is,' Ali slurred, meaning the house.

'Mind if I look around?' It was no more than idle curiosity, to understand Martin better.

'Why not? Everyone else has.'

'D'they take anything?'

'Documents. Just documents. I made them list them out, one at a time, sheet by sheet. Your friend wasn't amused. He gave the job to one of his officers. He seemed to have some difficulty knowing how to write.'

'But I bet he gives great cosh.'

'Huh?'

'Never mind. You going to show me round?'

'Sure.'

She took me on the grand tour. It was a big house for a single person. Two upper floors each with its own bathroom, and between them three bedrooms. The attic access cover had not been replaced, which gave me an excuse to clamber up the steps and poke my head inside. It was completely empty: not even the old cartons, bits of broken furniture or empty cases that most houses would have. A man without waste.

On the ground floor, in addition to his study there

were a large knocked-through living room that also served as a dining-room, a cloakroom and an open-plan kitchen, utility and breakfast area that made me think that maybe it wouldn't be all bad to have money and a real place to live. Steps led down to the boiler in the basement.

I had not expected to see or find anything; after all, Dowell had spent half the day searching. I asked Ali:

'D'you ever stay here?'

'Once. For a short time during the breakup.'

Married people do that. It's not 'my' breakup, but 'the' breakup; the big moment, the big one they presume everyone they ever talk to knows about and understands. It's sad. Life stopped, and had to start again. It spells out the whole story of how stupid it is to get that tied to someone else.

We were in the kitchen. She opened the refrigerator to get more ice for her glass. I said:

'Don't you think you've had enough?'

Her eyes flashed, and for a moment I thought she was going to start yelling at me not to tell her what to do. Then they glazed over. She placed her glass in the sink, and came and put her arms around me, right around mine, the way she had that first night.

She leaned against my chest, and nibbled at the buttons of my shirt, sticking her tongue inside to lick my chest. She removed one hand from around my body, and placed it between us, gripping me to tell me she knew how I was responding. I had a flash of Randolph and Katrina, fucking in his father's office. This seemed equally inappropriate, and for that reason equally exciting. I whispered:

'Do you want to go upstairs?'

She shook her head, moving backwards into the breakfast area, pulling me with her, until she was standing right up against the solid-oak table. As we kissed, she put her hands behind her, to lift herself up so she was sitting on the table edge. Her skirt was no more than an inch below her waist. I slid my thumbs inside the band of her tights and panties, and lowered them, following them to the floor until, kneeling between her legs, I could slip off her shoes and remove her underthings altogether.

She put a hand on the back of my head but I didn't need any encouragement. She was wet and warm and welcoming. With one hand, I undid my own trousers and when I stood up I went straight into her hard, fast and furious. She fell back onto the table, flinging her arms out to grasp its edges while I tore at her buttons and roughly pushed her bra up over her breasts.

From the moment I entered her, it was a fight against time, we were both on the verge. It went on like forever, until neither of us could stand it any more and we came together, gasping and screaming and – dare I think it – full of love.

I stood there feeling eminently foolish. My pants were around my shoes. I was sticky and sweaty. I could see oozing out of her the evidence of our intensity. Usually, I hated to see it. I'm not into the natural, animal aspects of sex: I like the high, the tension, and the release, but you can keep what comes after. Yet now what I felt like doing was collapsing to my knees and burying my head in her again until I had licked her clean and we could start all over.

Instead, she pulled her knees up to her chest, and rolled free of me, trotting straight to the cloakroom before I could catch hold and tell her what I was thinking. Her one glance into my eyes told me she knew, maybe she liked it, but she didn't want to hear. With a fixed, foolish, wry expression on my face I stood in front of the kitchen sink to wash, and used sheets of kitchen-towel to dry myself before I pulled my clothes back up. I had to watch out: what I was beginning to feel about Allison Mather Hoyt didn't fit into any chapter of the teach-yourself tough-guy manual.

I heard the toilet flush, and then she emerged, smiling, from the cloakroom:

'Your turn.'

When I came out, the kettle was boiling.

'Tea?'

'Sure. Why not?' It was true. I didn't need a drink. I didn't even want a drink.

'What d'you want to do?' I meant, for the rest of the evening.

'Come home with me. I'll make us some supper. You're tired, you need to sleep, have a bath, we can go past your place first to collect some clothes, I'll look after you.'

She meant she didn't want to be alone. I didn't blame her. One of her brothers had been flung unceremoniously out of the firm; another was languishing in jail. It wasn't what was normally meant by a hard day at the office.

Chapter Eleven

At Mather's, whenever someone spoke about Latimer
the man, as distinct from Latimer as shorthand for one
or all of his enterprises, they always said, 'himself –
pause – himself' in awe, like they couldn't believe he
really existed.

I didn't get in to work the next day until after midday.
Ali went in earlier; she had more to steal, so she left me
a spare set of keys big and heavy enough to gratify a
prison warden.

The atmosphere in the office was alive with tension,
gossip and intrigue. If you wanted to know what people
were thinking, the two places to bug were the women's
and men's lavatories.

It was not surprising. Everyone now knew that
Andrew Mather had 'withdrawn' in disgrace; they
also knew that Martin was under arrest, and what
for. There were journalists and photographers camped
outside the door though, unflatteringly, none of them
asked me for an interview nor took my photograph.
Martin had already been arraigned, and returned to
police custody while further enquiries were made,
rather than sent to Brixton on remand. Whatever the
outcome, he personally and the firm as a whole would
suffer irreversible damage.

As if this wasn't enough, Ian Mather had disappeared. He had gone from the office the night
before to the nursing home, where he had spent
a private hour with his wife. It made me appreciate that Ali had skipped her visit, waiting for
me at Martin's house instead: would her mother

even know? Did she know Ian had been to see her?

Afterwards, it seemed he had driven home, asked for a suitcase to be packed, made some 'phone calls and departed in a taxi without leaving any forwarding address or contact number. Enquiries of the other Mather offices achieved nothing more than to spread insecurity and concern.

I had a number of options how to proceed, but I didn't yet trust my judgement, I was still tired, and shell-shocked. Instead, I asked for and was provided with a typewriter, and I put my head down to the tedious task of writing up everything I knew to date. Before I took my next step, I wanted there to be a record.

Late afternoon, Marion Mortimore told me I had a visitor. He wouldn't give a name but she insisted he was harmless. Reluctantly, I agreed to see him; I wasn't wearing my bullet-proof vest.

'Mr Woolf?'

'Yes. You are?'

He took a card from his pocket and handed it to me. He was from the United Grand Lodge of England and had a title something like Grand Dragon or Grand Vizier; I only knew it wasn't the Grand Secretary a.k.a. Grand Scribe Ezra.

I was disappointed: he didn't look evil. He looked more like a salesman, or a clerk. If he had come to put the frighteners on me, they'd have to send someone my own height.

'Last night, Mr Woolf, I received a telephone call from Mr Ian Mather.'

'Where from? What time?'

'I don't know where he was telephoning from. It was about nine o'clock. He telephoned me at home.' It didn't need all my skills as an interrogator to draw the details out of him. 'He gave me a list of names, and some instructions. I should say, he asked me to speak with the Grand Secretary before I complied with them, and I have of course done so. The Grand Secretary was unavailable last night.' Probably wearing an apron while washing up the ritual tools of the craft.

He continued: 'The Grand Secretary has confirmed Mr Mather's instructions, and I am accordingly authorized to give you the information which I believe you need. I do so, Mr Woolf, on the strict terms, which Mr Mather assured me, that you will only use this information so far as it proves necessary for your enquiry, and will reveal it to no one, other than Mr Mather, or the police should criminal charges ensue. The Grand Secretary personally asked me to confirm this.'

'Yes,' it wasn't the time to be funny: 'Why, though? Why are you going to tell me?'

'I am going to tell you because I have been instructed to do so,' he avoided blandly. He was not, however, a mere Grand Messenger, so he couldn't help asserting himself. 'Mr Mather told me that you are investigating most serious matters, possibly criminal. It is our policy to co-operate with the police and public bodies in such enquiries. In the circumstances, and as it is Mr Mather for whom you are working, it seemed appropriate to extend that co-operation to you, on the terms as I have relayed them.'

'Put another way round, if I'm right and there's a masonic link, you're going to carry the can anyway; you might as well seek the credit for co-operation in completing the case. Right?'

'That is a cynical view; the craft does not encourage cynicism. I have the list of all the names you asked about, and of the members of their Lodges. They are complete lists, Mr Woolf: the names of many people with nothing to do with your enquiries are included.' I got the feeling he wasn't too keen on this extension of co-operation.

'And Chapters?'

He licked his lips nervously, then his head tweaked as he agreed he had brought me Chapter connections too. I held out my hand. Reluctantly, he extracted from his jacket pocket an envelope which he passed over the desk to me. I grabbed it before he could change his mind. I hardly noticed him go.

Before I left for the day, I took a call from Dowell.

He refused to meet me for a drink, so I knew he was serious when he asked me:

'Do you know where either Beatrix Kelly or Tony Galucci are?'

'Nope. Why?'

'They seem to have, let's say, taken offence at my visit to their office yesterday. I wanted to ask them some questions. They are "unavailable".'

'They don't seem relevant to what Martin's been charged with,' I observed.

'Really? Surprise me.'

'Ian Mather's done a bunk, too. You think he's run away with Beat? Or Tony?'

'I thought they would have gone off together.'

'Where did you learn that? During the course of your enquiries? You're not supposed to ask him anything about what he's already charged with.'

'Says who? His sister was here, I can ask what I like.'

'Not for a date, you can't. Was it?' To do with what he was charged with.

'I used to think you were just an idiot, Dave; now I think you may be an *idiot savant*.' Once in a while he liked to flex his education; in his job, the opportunities did not come often. I wanted time to think over what he was saying, so I let him explain. 'An idiot has an I.Q. of 25 or a mental age of two; an *idiot savant* is the same, but he's got one or two exceptional additional skills. Like mental arithmetic.'

I need a calculator to add up change from a pound.

I decided he might not thank me if I told him maybe someone – and maybe that someone was me – had put a scare into them that would send Superman into an otherwise unplanned orbit around and around and around the world. Instead, I said:

'You know you got the wrong Mather, don't you, Tim. Either one of them could have let someone in.' I'd said the same thing before, but maybe he hadn't heard me.

'Golly gosh, I wish I'd thought of that.'

'You will, Oscar, you will. So why're you holding him?'

'There's two things I could say. I could say: if I've got the wrong Mather, which one do you think I ought to have? Or: it depends on what I want him for. Then again, maybe I could say both. 'Night sweetheart, sweet dreams.' He put the 'phone down suddenly, either to taunt me, or because someone else had come into the room.

Sometimes, I get a lucky break. As I was leaving, I saw himself himself in the hallway, talking urgently with Gauldie and Randolph. It was too good an opportunity to pass up. I approached; Randolph rapidly left.

My first impression was wildly inappropriate. He brought to my mind a humourless Russian revolutionary bureaucrat: steel-rimmed glasses, closely shaved, cropped greying hair, thin and small. He was about twenty years older than me, approaching sixty.

'Mr Latimer, I'm Dave Woolf.'

'Yes?' He didn't look at me, but at Gauldie for explanation.

Gauldie muttered something unbrotherly beneath his breath, and then said:

'The matter of Miss Pankhurst.'

'Mrs,' I corrected in spite of myself: 'That and related incidents. I was wondering if I could talk to you,' I hurried on, before Gauldie could deny me thrice: 'I think it's quite important for me to do so.'

Latimer cleared his throat to give himself himself time for reflection. He looked again at Gauldie for guidance, but, remembering what Ali had told me about the real repository of Latimer's confidence, I quickly contributed:

'I work for Ian Mather, Mr Latimer. Last time I heard, I still had his full confidence.'

He nodded almost imperceptibly, and said:

'Tomorrow morning, my office, seven o'clock.'

I swallowed, gulped and was building up the courage to explain that I couldn't stand up straight at that time of the morning, let alone think or talk, as he left.

'What do you want to trouble Mr Latimer for?' Gauldie snarled.

'That's my business, isn't it? I report to Ian Mather, not you,' I retorted. As you have gathered, I like and respect Gauldie an immeasurable amount: immeasurably small.

He looked down at me, nostrils flaring, eyes glaring, like he wished for nothing so much as to put me on an altar for a ritual sacrifice.

'What is your game, Gauldie?' I asked, as innocently as if I was offering him a drink: 'There's something going on with you, and I wish the hell I knew what it was.' I didn't want him yet to appreciate just how much I'd already managed to put together.

'You're ridiculous, pathetic,' he snapped, turning on his heels and returning to his office where, I assumed, Randolph was waiting for him.

It was a good thing I was seeing Ali again that evening, not only because she could fill me in on the line of questioning which had been followed during the day, but also because I had forgotten to find out where Latimer's office was.

I knew Central Towers well, from the outside. I remembered when the concrete and glass monolith had been built, and then when it was left empty for years as it anticipated and patiently awaited the boom in commercial property values. At one time, it had been occupied by protesters drawing attention to insufficient and inadequate housing. On another occasion, anti-nuke activists let down banners, and floated ten thousand balloons, from the roof.

I suppose I was vaguely aware that it had been brought over the years into commercial occupation, though in ignorance of by whom, and overwhelmed by indifference. I had not known that almost half of it was occupied by Latimer International and its related companies. I had not known, therefore, that the top floor was given over entirely to Sterling Latimer personally, as both office and living space for his visits to the United Kingdom.

For once, I wasn't late. At least, when I arrived at the

main entrance to Central Towers, I wasn't. It took me five minutes to get permission to use the elevator, ten – including a frisk – in the top-floor security lobby, another ten minutes in the outer office and quarter of an hour in Latimer's own waiting-room, while he finished his previous appointment. At what would have been seven in the morning, I was not the first.

No one apologized for the delay. He operated like the legal system, where more work is listed before a judge than he can handle, to make sure that if a case falls short, not a moment of judicial time is wasted, even if it means wasting everyone else's.

I'd been brought two cups of coffee to keep me occupied. By the time I was shown in to Latimer's office, I badly needed a leak.

I'd never seen an office so big, not even Ian's. We were in a corner of the building, and two walls were solid glass. Crossing the room was more exercise that I'd taken all year.

Latimer was seated behind a desk – entirely bare of papers – so big I couldn't even stretch across it to shake hands. He didn't look as if he wanted to mingle fingers anyway. There was something fastidious about him; his hands were finely-structured, his skin was sallow and his movements as considered as his words.

'Sit down, Mr Woolf, and tell me how I can help you.' He was being what Americans call 'old world courteous'.

'D'you mind if I ask you a personal question?'

'I'm listening.'

'How much are you worth? You see, I never met anyone as rich before, and I'd like to be able to tell my grandchildren that I once met someone like you.'

'Are you married, Mr Woolf?'

I shook my head.

'Well, then, you're unlikely to have grandchildren,' he declined to answer my question. 'Now I'll ask you a personal question. How much are you worth?'

'You want to tell your grandchildren you once met someone that poor?'

He chuckled pleasantly:

'*Touché*. Tell me why you don't want to make more money, Mr Woolf. Your income in the past year has been less than the staff on this top floor alone earn in a week. It has been considerably less than I earn in a day. Yet I'm told you are very good at your job.'

'Who said that?' I protested. I'd sue for slander.

He waved a hand airily:

'Never ask how someone knows something, Mr Woolf; it shows you couldn't do it; work out for yourself how they could have found it out, and next time you'll be able to do it to them. You still haven't answered my question.'

'I guess, well, I'm sort of choosy about the work I do. And a lot of the time, my clients don't have much money. Anyhow, what's it to you?'

'I like to know the people I deal with.'

'Apparently,' I was thinking of the access he had obtained to my accounts.

'Now tell me what you really want?'

'Sure. It's just one question, really. I want you to tell me who told you it was Katrina Pankhurst who leaked the LCP report.'

He stared back at me evenly and calm:

'What makes you think anyone told me that? What makes you think she did?'

'She didn't. I asked who told you she had. What makes you think someone told you she had is she's dead.'

He absorbed my ass-backward answer:

'I understand she was a friend of yours?'

'Yes. A close friend. As a matter of fact, a some-time lover and I wouldn't have minded resuming the relationship. She was a fine woman, Mr Latimer. Not perhaps the most beautiful, and probably not the most brilliant. But she was the sort of soul who makes living almost bearable. Did you ever meet her?'

'Once or twice in conferences, I think. And I agree with your description: not that beautiful, not that brilliant, but a good person.'

I expelled air: he was responsive.

'You just said, she didn't leak my report. Are you sure of that?' His eyes narrowed.

'Yes, one hundred per cent.'

'Will you tell me who?'

I shook my head:

'It's someone I like.'

'Mr Woolf, if you did not have the confidence of Ian Mather, I wonder if you realize just how dangerously you would be behaving?'

'Sure. I'm saying you're responsible for Kat's death. That's what you're referring to, right?'

He frowned and nodded. I added:

'I didn't say you had it done, did I?'

It was his turn audibly to exhale.

'A lot of people would say you're not making a lot of sense, Mr Woolf.'

'You don't, though.'

'I might. It depends what you think.'

'I think. . . Let's see: I'd like to continue putting things obliquely, it's more fun, isn't it?'

He struggled to suppress a smile, and failed:

'I can see why Ian relies on you, Mr Woolf.'

I raised my eyebrows:

'I can't. Nevermind. I think I've worked some things out, and I think they make such a pretty fit with Kat's death that I can't resist the connection. It starts years ago, doesn't it? When you first came to this country, as a front-man for James Mather. It took me a long time to get there, and more than time – I had to do quite a lot of reading. Suddenly, there's this young Yank, without a penny to his name, and he's doing business with too many people who used to do business with James Mather. How'm I doing?' I shot at him, suddenly beginning to lose confidence in my own theory as I rehearsed it aloud for its very first performance.

'Go on, it's fascinating,' he said; 'perhaps my publishing house could give you an advance. . .' For fiction.

'You've got his name, money from America, names of people to talk to here, and above all, probably his one true commandment, you're to use Mather's as your lawyers. Right? He says: don't trust anyone else; and when push comes to shove, if there's a real issue you need real advice on, don't settle for anyone less than my brother. Right? He also says: my brother's straight, straight as a die; but you'll get plenty extra help from Gauldie. He's greedy; don't be put off by the formal front; he'll bend the rules. Especially for a "brother". After all, he used his contacts to get me out of the country. Right?'

That was three rights, so I paused for confirmation. I settled for absence of denial and continued:

'My guess is – and I admit I am guessing now – you were far more successful than either James or you ever dreamed. You were ahead of your times in your attitudes and approach. You arrived maybe twenty years before other American businessmen and corporations; they really started to eat up England after the International Monetary Fund had to bail out the Labour government in the mid-seventies and made external investment a condition.

'Anyway, your style took off like a freaked-out firework. You went public, probably because Ian Mather advised you to so strongly you couldn't resist without creating suspicion; you bought in Europe, you even made contacts behind the Iron Curtain. You had some wonderful breaks from Gauldie, too: for a slice of the action, he could be disgustingly indiscreet about his other clients, and things he picked up on the masonic vine.

'All the time, there's James Mather lurking in the shadows. I'd say, he's probably become an embarrassment to you. You certainly don't need him now, and haven't for maybe ten to fifteen years. When the companies went public, there was an additional problem. It's quite one thing to use a private corporation like a private bank, but next to impossible when it's subject to the sort of scrutiny Latimer International and its offshoots have to suffer in the name of stock market flotation.

'That's where something like Cross Course could be useful, only it wasn't called Cross Course then. Beat Kelly was pushed in the right direction ...' I held up a hand: 'She didn't tell me anything. I don't want to read she's also been giving blow-jobs to bullets.'

He said softly, speaking for the first time since I began to lay my jigsaw pieces down on his desk:

'I thought you said you accepted I did not have Katrina Pankhurst killed?'

'I do. It's not you I think had it done. I don't actually think you knew what was going to happen to her, or even guessed, though whether a jury'd feel the same is a different question. But it definitely wouldn't be true now, if anything happened to the sister, would it?'

He curled his upper lip inside his lower teeth and scratched nervously:

'Go on. You understand, I am not admitting to anything you say.' He didn't deny knowing Beat; but he didn't seem to know she had beaten it.

'Sure. The way I see it, Mr Latimer, you probably haven't broken any laws in this country that I give a damn about. I don't know about your past, or care beyond curiosity. If you got a start with dirty money, I couldn't care less. I'm not even sure money comes dirty and clean.

'I think Gauldie made a mockery of professional privilege in your interests, but that's a matter for my client and I don't suppose he'll want to broadcast it. I'm curious, though: how much of it had to do with freemasonry?'

'Both the Mather boys were freemasons, and I joined too when I arrived, on James' advice. It was an easy and quick way not only to meet people, but also to create a conservative impression.'

'How involved was James?'

Latimer laughed:

'James Mather is involved in everything and nothing. He's a rogue, a complete, charming rogue. I should say: a dangerous rogue, but I think you've worked that out for yourself. He belonged to freemasonry for the same reasons he told me to join: front, image, contacts. In those days – don't forget, we're talking about the forties and fifties – it was a very respectable organization, everyone in the City and commerce, too, belonged.'

'You're being very candid about it,' I lied: 'Don't you get excommunicated or something if you tell an outsider?'

'You have to be a mass murderer to be expelled, Mr Woolf, and that's only if at least half your victims are fellow freemasons. I haven't been to a Lodge meeting for more than a decade. I would describe myself as having left the freemasons, because I've long ago stopped needing them, but rather like the Catholic Church, once a freemason always a freemason. They don't let you leave.'

'You've been talking about craft freemasonry, right? You said: you haven't been to a Lodge meeting for years.'

He met my gaze from a new dimension. My next question remained as yet unspoken, but the conversation was being carried on notwithstanding. He dared me to ask it. He was right: since I'd read the material brought me by the official masons, I'd been shitting myself. One of the names by which the freemasons refer to God is 'Great Architect' (of the Universe): he was currently working up a design for my tomb.

I cleared my throat:

'Ammi Ruhamah.'

When he didn't answer, I said:

'Didn't I pronounce it right?'

The new, and noticeably less accommodating Latimer said:

'Why do you think it won't be the last thing you ever pronounce, Mr Woolf?'

'Aw, shucks, you were supposed to answer "Jabulon".' When he didn't smile, I thought it opportune to mention: 'There's nothing we're talking about that isn't already written down, and copies where even you don't own. And they are all signed, and marked by me, as written in contemplation of death.' As I was talking my own ritual language, I explained: 'Statements made in contemplation of death are admissible in an English court of law, Mr Latimer.'

'Go on, Mr Woolf, go on with what you say you've got written down.'

'The Prolistic Chapter of Improvement is one of the oldest Chapters in Royal Arch. You were exalted – that's the phrase, isn't it? – a member in. . .' I consulted my notes: '1967. Gauldie was a member; so was James Mather. Later, both Randolph and Andrew Mather were introduced to it; so also Maurice Francis, Viscount Stonefrost, and two others who I'm concerned with – Robin de Peyer and Stephen Wainwright. . .'

'Wainwright?' He asked before he could help himself.

'Stephen, not Christopher. He was, is, was Christopher's older brother. That's how Christopher knew a lot more that he ought. There are a lot of other members – only, they're called Companions I think. I was barking up the wrong tree: I thought at first it was all to do with Lodges, but it's Chapters that matter. What is it about the Chapter that leads it into conspiracy?' Warren, the Commissioner of Police who'd covered up for Brother Jack, was a companion of the Chapter, and therefore maybe Jack too; Prolistic was reputed to have enjoyed closer contacts with P2 than any other English masons.

To my considerable surprise, he answered me:

'It's the belief that the only real power is secret power. You put your finger on it a while ago, by accident: you said that once Latimer was a public corporation, it couldn't channel Mather's money. Public power, public money – they're the same thing, of course – is publicly accountable: people can see how you use it. But the power, the money, that people don't know you have. . .' He didn't need to finish the sentence. 'Ian, on the other hand, is committed to freemasonry as a moral influence. That class of freemason positively craves the respectability that open wealth brings.'

'How much did – does – James Mather really believe in it?'

'I don't really know, Mr Woolf. He might; he might not. It depends on whether he found it useful. James never needed an excuse to chase money or power, or anything like freemasonry to encourage him.'

'And you?'

He struggled:

'What do you mean by "believe"? Some people use the word to refer to a religion, some to a system of government or economics, some to refer to whatever they hold most dear. I joined first craft masonry, then Royal Arch, because that was the way ahead for me. It was expected of me.'

'How much has it got to do with your business now?'

'Nothing that matters.'

'That's what I figured. How come you never broke free of it, or of Mather?'

A shadow passed over his face like a cloud:

'You think you know who had Katrina Pankhurst killed, don't you, Mr Woolf?'

'You're frightened of him, right?'

'You don't cross James Mather, not so that he'd know. I'm a very rich man. I could afford to hire bodyguards for twenty-four hours a day. He could still reach me.'

'The police? You must have enough on him?'

'Presuming the police are to be trusted, which would be a foolish presumption, I still doubt it. He's not what you would call candid about his activities. But weigh it up. All I have had to do for the last ten or more years – and you were extremely accurate about that – is to continue to treat him as a friend. And why not? Where would I have been without him? I was running a small time nowhere business when we met. Look at me now. I made my devil's pact, Mr Woolf; you've read Faust.'

Faust? Batfaust? Superfaust? Faust Street Blues? L.A. Faust?

'How come he knew about the leak? How come you gave him a name?'

'I think it was pride, mainly. He knew about the leak because he likes to stay in touch. It's always been part of my job to keep him in touch with his family.' Hence, Martin's good old welcome to the good old U.S. of A. 'He's a very old man, now, Mr Woolf. He doesn't have much to do but his mind is still as active as ever.

'He lives in Florida, in an apartment at the top of a block he owns, part of which contains a hotel he owns, in which there is a bank he's not supposed to own but does, with shops, lawyers, accountants, a sauna and massage parlour he also owns. He has the bodyguards, not me. He has to have his apartment and 'phone lines swept for bugs every couple of days, not me. He sleeps a lot; he isn't allowed to drink much anymore; he can't eat anything but totally bland food; I don't suppose he can still have sex.

'So he calls me often, to stay in touch, to talk, to feel part of it all. And I tell him things, things that are harmless but sound important. And I told him there'd been a leak; he had to know something was happening, even Latimer International dropped a couple of points when the size of the settlement was announced. And he asked where the leak had come from, and when I said Mather's, he demanded to know more, who.'

He lowered his head:

'I had no idea he would take it the way he did. I had no idea until I read about the Pankhurst woman's death. It ought to have been just business. He took it personally. Mather's is still his main point of connection. He has no family over there.'

'I thought he had a wife and a daughter?'

'He had a wife and a child – I don't know a daughter. They lived somewhere in New England. They were kept very separate. I never met them. The way I heard, they never knew what he did. After the wife died, he wanted to bring the child into his life, but as soon as he – she – realized what her father really did, she cut him off totally. Much like Ian.'

I shook my head slowly, in awe:

'You're making me feel sorry for the guy. Jesus, we're talking about a killer. A gangster. Someone who has just had a friend of mine murdered. And I'm sitting here, feeling sorry for him.'

He smiled:

'I've described him well, then. He has that quality. He's very hard to hate until he turns on you, and then it's probably too late for you to do anything about it. It's all over.'

I shuddered:

'I think I'll be happier leaving him out of my life. How do you feel about Ian?'

His lips twitched, as he thought about the answer:

'Sorry for him, really. He is a moral man, the sort of moral man he thinks everyone ought to be and if everyone could follow craft masonry they would be. I feel sorry to have participated in a degree of deception on him. For all of these years, he's been helping his brother without knowing it, and against his declared wish to have nothing more to do with him, and I have been one of the two main agents of that.'

'Two? Right, Gauldie.'

'Correct. Mr Gauldie. Since I like Ian, and admire him, I naturally regret that. But that's been business, too. To do as much as people like James Mather have done, and people like myself – though I hasten to add that my style is very different in the respects that concern you – we cut personal corners to suit commercial ends.'

'I'm not sure I completely understand Gauldie.'

'I'm not sure anyone does. You can't go through life, Mr Woolf, treating people as if they can all be reduced to a set of rational rules or a logical progression. People do one thing, and that's where they start the next step from. Gauldie went along with some sharp deals in James Mather's early days, and when he came to whatever was the next choice, it wasn't such a big step more. Isn't that what we all do? Did you plan to quit law when you snorted your first gramme of cocaine?'

He was re-asserting himself by displaying the extent of his knowledge about me. I sensed the interview was drawing to a close. There were a few more answers I needed. I said:

'Let's talk about Beat Kelly, and Tony Galucci. I've been very slow about it. The way I see it, I think the way you're telling it: James ain't a man to take no for an answer?' He nodded, curious to see how far I could take it on my own. 'Once he failed to seduce

209

Martin to his way of thinking, to make his deal like he made with you – Faust, was that the guy? – he still wanted Martin's. . . What? Soul? Integrity? Name? Whatever it was that would give him his revenge over Ian. He could've broken Ian, by influencing business away from him, but that wouldn't have been nearly as good.

'So he directed Beat at him. Maybe he thought Martin would fall into bed with her. I would, given half the chance. I don't know how much Beat knew: maybe it was casual to begin with; I've got this nephew, don't mention my name – there's a family estrangement. But take a look at what he's into, he and his partner Galucci, it's right up your street. Then, when he needed her, he found out she wasn't so enchanted with him: he'd gone for her sister instead of her; and he'd picked the sister up and let her down over and over like a yoyo. Better yet: the partner now had solid reason to hate him – don't matter how modern you think, no one can stand being cuckolded. I learned that in my last big case. I didn't believe Kat when she said Tony didn't mind.

'I didn't think about it, though, because I was looking at the wrong bits of the puzzle. Also, though I thought I recognized Matheson, at the Clairmount, I didn't bother to follow it up. I'd seen him before, chatting with Galucci at Cannons: people look different dressed for sport, you notice different bits of them.

'Putting it together with they've done a disappearing act, which Dowell asked me about today, I think what Dowell's interested in is illegal, external, racketeer influence in gambling. I think they've set it up so no one's going to believe Martin didn't know the deals they were conducting with his own uncle. Gimme a break, willya, tell me how I'm doing?'

'I'd say,' he choose his words carefully: 'You've said nothing about James Mather that is out of character.'

It was as good as I was going to get. I didn't bother spelling out about how Matheson had rung Beat or Tony to tell them what he'd told me about Andrew and Wainwright. One of them had rung James. He had reacted much as had Martin: he'd take care of it. I still didn't know how he'd arranged to get Wainwright to attend his own funeral, but I had an idea:

'This notion, this revenge, is there any reason why it should be confined to Martin?'

'Not that I'm aware of,' he said dryly, sensing my direction.

'I'm told he's not active any longer, pretty much like you said. But, oh, say ten years ago, would it be an astonishing proposition he could have dictated whether supplies of a certain illegal substance saw their way into certain hands?'

He held up his:

'I've never known anything about that, and I never want to. I couldn't say it was impossible, or to use the same expression, out of character, but I refuse to comment further. I'm sure you understand.'

'Oh, yeah, I understand. I'm not sure I respect it a whole bunch. But I understand. You said: it's part of your job to keep him in touch. . . Yeah?'

'I, or that of my understrappers,' he had an affection for obsolete English words too close to my own for comfort: 'I never met Wainwright, Mr Woolf.' So it didn't matter he had set him up by passing the message from James back to Randolph. There could be no suspicion attached to such a call, from a businessman to his lawyer.

'Tell me something else, then: if you're so frightened of him, why are you telling me so much now?'

'I'm not telling you anything. I'm electing not to deny things you think you've worked out for yourself. That could be,' in a court of law, 'because I don't think they're worth denying.'

'And perhaps because?'

'Perhaps because. . . As you said, Mr Woolf: Mrs Pankhurst was a fine woman.' Sounding like: it's gone far enough.

'And perhaps because it suits for someone like me to come along and get rid of the monkey on your back for you?' I was doing what he was too scared to do for himself; James couldn't attribute any of it to him.

He asked me:

'How sure were you when you came in?'

'Not a hundred per cent; maybe ninety-nine. I knew there were connections. But I'm a lawyer, I know a case can seem unanswerable until you hear the other side. Then you confirmed it for me.' I went on without waiting for him to ask how: 'When you said that crap about not asking how you found something out, but working it out for myself. That's a James Mather line. He told it to Martin, years and years ago.'

He winced: more, I think, because I referred to the line as crap than at what it had given me.

'There's something you ought to think about, then, Mr Woolf. As you've astutely observed, none of this ill-suits me. But it ill-suits James. It's not his style to throw away money or power, not even for the sake of letting Ian find out what he's done to him.'

'What are you saying?'

'Someone lit the touch-paper, Mr Woolf. I have to ask: who?'

Before I could take him up on it, he glanced overtly at his watch:

'I have now spent three appointments with you, which has probably cost Latimer International more even than your weight in worth. . .'

Why does everybody find it necessary to point out I'm overweight? I got eyes; I look in the mirror. Occasionally. If I have to.

'I'll go, Mr Latimer, as soon as you answer my question,' I said without making a move to leave.

'Which question was that, Mr Woolf?' As if he didn't know.

'Who told you Katrina Pankhurst leaked the report?'

He hesitated before he told me, but probably he intended to all along:

'Randolph Mather. I told Gauldie I wanted the name. I told him I wanted a name within forty-eight hours. That was as long as James Mather gave me. Randolph rang me and that was who he told me. That was who I told James.' Randolph had given Latimer Kat's name, instead of the name Kat had given him – that of his sister. 'I'm sorry. I'm very, very sorry. I hope you believe that?'

As a matter of fact, I did. But looking at him, remembering just how rich he was and it wasn't kosher, remembering how many got hurt to help him make his start, even if he had nothing directly to do with it, I couldn't for the life of me think of one good reason to tell him so.

Chapter Twelve

Now I had everything, except a client to tell the story to. I felt like end of term jollies, but no one to share them with. There was, however, some unfinished business. Not on behalf of my client (which wouldn't stop me charging for it) but for myself.

I was still in the office before my normal hour of arrival. So was John Gauldie. Marion was waiting for me, to tell me he wanted to see me and to pour coffees down my throat. I checked that Ian had not re-appeared and when she confirmed it, I guessed how the interview would open:

'I want you out of this building, Woolf.'

'I work for Ian Mather; I'll leave when he tells me to. Unless, of course, you've got some reason for thinking he won't be coming back. . .'

'Where from? Do you know where he is?' I was pleased he didn't.

'Of course I do. Listen, you might walk out on a partner, a law-firm or a wife: but you don't walk out on Woolf.'

He sneered:

'Bravado, Woolf. You've no more idea than I have.'

'You a gambling man, Gauldie? Let's make a little bet: you write down your guess, and place it in an envelope with your cheque for, oh, let's say, five grand, and I'll write down mine and do the same. OK?'

This was real bravado. I've never gambled five pounds, and you could ride a car on my cheque for five thousand. I did not for a second believe he would take me seriously. To my astonishment, he licked his lips greedily. Through sheer stupidity, I'd named a sum of money large enough to excite him. It was a cold day: I was sweating like a sauna. It was more money than I'd earned on the case. If I lost, I'd have to drag it on for another month; the way things were going, that probably meant half the rest of the staff would get wasted.

He shook his head to clear it:

'I'm not playing with you, Woolf,' but he was a little reluctant: 'I want you out of here.'

I shook my head:

'You're the next senior partner; but you don't own that big a slice of the action. Andrew's out of it for the time being, but he's still a partner and I think I'd carry his vote for now; same for Martin. I know I'd carry Allison's. I don't know the exact figures, but my guess is that even if you can tell Randolph what price to sell at, you'd need to call a full partner's meeting to have a majority.'

'What do you mean? Tell Randolph what price to sell at?'

It was just an expression, like the price of eggs, or the time of day: I'd struck a nerve. Even if it was irrelevant, I couldn't have resisted putting pressure on it.

'You trying to say you don't know what Randolph and his prolific Prolistic prelates are up to?'

He absorbed the incidental reference to his Chapter of Improvement. If there was any evidence he ever went in for anything as mundane as breathing, he would have been breathing shallow. He was between the horns of a masonic symbol. I don't think he did know what I meant; but he didn't want to ask. I said, equally casual:

'You set a crooked example, kids are going to play crooked games too. Know what I mean?' I had finally found a use for Lewis' favourite phrase. All I needed now was to be able to distinguish between a phrase and a clause.

I told him anyway. I don't care if he knew beforehand or not; it's an idle detail. The important thing was that I knew. I prefaced it with the same assurance I had given Latimer: nothing I would tell him wasn't fully documented.

'The way I see it, there's two layers of activity through the Chapter. One is you, Uncle Jim, Sterling, let's work out the next rip-off, just like the good old days when you could deal face-to-face, before you got him out and your friends decided it wasn't in the public interest for the police to probe too closely how you did it.

'It's an odd thing, Gauldie, but lawyers rarely get as rich as people on the outside think: it's all income, not capital. The trouble is: they're arrogant. Since they think they're so much more clever, they think they ought to be that much richer too. But you, you're real rich: I wouldn't like to guess what you're worth, but a lot richer that Ian, who you've always been jealous of, and you did it without a rich daddy to help. You must be very proud: to have conned all those people to trust you with their privileged information and plans.

'The other layer is Randolph, who got a bit impatient to run his own show, and maybe he wanted to prove he could make his own money too, uninherited. What it makes me think of is that old legal maxim, when an employer is not responsible for the acts of his employee, 'cos he's said to be 'on a frolic of his own'. Fizzy drinks, fuzzy memories, funky sex and frankly indiscreet.

'You brought too many kids in, Gauldie: you thought they'd all serve willingly as foot-soldiers in your army,' like Orbach, I stole the line from the Hackney report: 'But some of them wanted a commission of their own. Secret money of their own. Secret power of their own. Maybe just secrets of their own. They wanted to make that old masonic black magic work for them, not you. They wanted to see if it could be applied to modern methods of turning a dishonest buck, not boring old back-scrubbing business deals. Deals the way my generation means the word; crooked deals the way your generation always did it. It's the only way to stay ahead of the money game nowadays.

'You know the irony of it all? I'll tell you: it's all so damned small, so petty. You wanna know how much coke they ran in from the Bahamas? You wanna know how much money they made out of it? They've jeopardized your cosy little set-up for less money than you've spend on medieval weaponry.'

There was one more thing I could've told him. I could have said that behind every – including this – scam skulked the omnipresent James Mather. I didn't think he'd dare do anything about it if I did so. I don't want to claim more credit than is due. I didn't know exactly how he'd react. But I only had to look at the horror on his face and in his eyes to realize it wasn't going to be fun for someone else. If the game was over for him, it was going to be over for everyone.

It wasn't going to be fun for me either. It was a bad day, the worst of all. Nothing happened. Nothing at all. You ever tried to wise-crack about nothing? What I had to do was to update and finish the report I'd started the day before, to give Ian on his return and to post safety copies off elsewhere.

Now that the case was coming to an end, the rest of my life started to come back into focus and a bit of it was missing. It was a long time since I'd seen or spoken to Sandy. If I'm honest, even now I can't claim that my loins were aching; or, if they were, it wasn't with passion for her, but a result of the excessive strain put upon them by unaccustomed antics with Ali. I punched the number I knew as well as my own, as indeed once it had been.

'Can I talk with Sandy?'

'Who's calling, please?'

'Dave. Dave Woolf.'

'What's it in connection with, Mr Woof,' as in dog.

It's great to feel well-remembered, loved:

'Uh, it's personal. She'll know who I am.'

'Oh. I see. Just a moment, please, I'll see if she's free.'

She sounded surprised Sandy should get a personal call. At what she does, Sandy's more thoroughly professional than the reputation the Mathers were about to lose.

'Hi,' she sounded brisk.

'Bad time?'

Pause.

'No.'

'Uh, well, you're obviously glad to hear from me.'

'Of course I'm glad to hear from you, Dave. I've been meaning to ring you. We ought to meet.'

'That was what I was thinking, kid.' She was four months older than I: 'I'm just about wrapped up here, at Mather's. 'Nother couple of days.'

'Yes.' Her enthusiasm and curiosity knew no bounds: they weren't even acquainted.

'Sandy, what's up?'

'What's up?' her voice raised: 'You let me walk out of a pub, on my own, in the middle of the day, without trying to stop me; you let me walk out of your life without even saying so long; you ignore me for weeks, then you ring up cheerful as a sand-boy, and you ask me – what's up already?'

I hadn't said 'already', had I?

'Look,' I said, calming and conciliatory: 'This hasn't been a lot of fun. . .' She hadn't even asked who done in our ex-employee.

'What's the matter? Weren't the high-class bimbos falling over themselves to hop into bed with you?'

Well, uh, yes, as a matter of fact.

'Oh, shit, we always argue on the 'phone. We'd better meet,' she conceded reluctantly: 'How about the twenty-third?'

If 'phones could see, I'd've boggled down the line:

'Sandy! That's nearly three weeks away!'

'Well,' she sulked: 'I'm pretty busy right now.'

You love someone in as many different ways and for as long as Sandy 'n' I've loved each other, there's some things don't need spelling out:

'You're seeing someone, aren't you, Sandy?'

Silence. Then:

'I don't want to talk about it on the 'phone, Dave. Maybe I could make next Thursday, later on in the evening. . .'

'Tell me, Sandy.' Tell me Sandy: I love you; I know I'm a jerk; I know I've been fucking around with someone else, but I always thought, you know, you understood the way I was, am; I always thought you, you loved me anyhow, at any price. That was what I wanted, Sandy; that's what I needed; someone to love me more than

218

life itself; someone to love me as much as Robin loves Mick.

She said flatly:

'I warned you. Dave.'

And so she had.

'You take care, Sandy. You take care, you hear? Doesn't matter how long; I'll still be here, well, there anyhow. Y'know: I'll still be around for you. You've only got to call: it'll always be true.'

I replaced the receiver gently before she could catch me start to cry. I'm ugly on a normal day; you don't want to see how ugly I get when I cry. It only happens once in a while: like when something sad happens on Hill Street, or Benny the lovable idiot is especially cute on L.A. Law, or every episode of Cosby and half the episodes of MASH You know: the really serious things. Or when I see someone's mother dying. Or when I forget I don't really give a damn about anything or anyone, and for a brief moment someone else seems to matter.

I was so depressed and lonely, I bought Marion a farewell lunch. In a desultory fashion, I tried calling Ali, but if she wasn't with Martin, she was catching up on clients. Someone had to keep the firm fruitful. I didn't mind: now she wasn't icing on another cake, I wasn't so sure how I felt about her. On the way to the restaurant, I popped into the post office, but I didn't let Marion see where I'd addressed my envelopes.

'Go on, have a drink, what the hell, there's no one left to complain.'

She laughed nervously, I was asking her to act entirely out of keeping:

'Alright, then, I'll have a glass of. . .' I waited for her to say white wine or a spritzer: 'Beer. A pint, I think,' she said firmly. If you gotta break a habit, break it good.

'That's my girl.'

'What's going to happen, Mr Woolf?' The greatest failure of the case to date was my inability to persuade her to call me Dave.

I shrugged. Cases aren't like a t.v. programme. You never see the detective poring over files, going home to his wife and children and fighting over who does the washing-up, making 'phone calls to people who just aren't there, or getting a constant busy signal. It all happens, crammed into an hour. I wonder how they ever charge enough to make a living. The big bucks come when the case takes several days longer then you see on screen.

'You're going to find out, though, aren't you, Mr Woolf?'

'Oh, yeah, I know most of it anyhow.'

It wasn't her place to ask, so she didn't. Not directly. She said:

'Everything that's happened, it's. . . It's frightening. Mr Andrew, Mr Martin. You see, well, I'm sorry,' we were now on our second drink: 'I'm frightened. . . I don't want to hear. . . Well, that Katrina. . .' I got her point: she didn't want to hear Kat had also been bad.

'Listen, Marion: don't you worry 'bout Kat; she's up there in heaven, jiving to jazz happy as a cloud.' Can you jive to jazz? 'Everyone else in this whole saga stinks like. . .' I was going to say 'shit', but I remembered who I was talking to: 'Well, just stinks. But she was good, Marion, and she didn't do nothing to hurt anyone. Whatever else comes out of this, it won't be nothing bad about Kat.'

She smiled wanly:

'I don't think I believe in heaven, Dave, but I want to believe she didn't do anything bad, and. . .that she's listening to jazz now.'

She'd called me Dave at last. I'd finally won.

We got so pissed at lunch neither of us could work during the afternoon. Nothing continued to happen, but it was easier to cope with than in the sober morning. I punched the digits for Dowell about twenty times, and half of the time got the right number, but he was never in, or not in to me.

I was about to quit and go home for the day when Ali burst frenetically in to my office. Remember Ali? Until a while ago, I'd've crossed mountains, walked through fire, swam an ocean for the privilege of laying down just once more to lick between her legs. Then I'd spoken to Sandy. She was about to fail to restore the gloss. She said, breathlessly:

'Dave, I've just had a 'phone call from Heathrow. My father's there. He's, well, he's in something of a state; they said he wasn't making a lot of sense. The thing is, I've got to see a client in ten minutes, it's really important, especially now. Could you? Andrew's gone out to Oxfordshire, and I can't find Randolph,' and Martin wasn't doing time as a chauffeur: 'Could you go and collect him, Dave? They won't put him in a taxi, I asked. They want someone to go and collect him.'

Last night, I'd lain on one side, resting on an elbow, and watched her drift off to sleep. It was warm in her flat, and we'd thrown off the duvet. I thought: I've never been this close to someone as beautiful before. I looked at every inch of her, parts of her I'd touched and that had touched me, and been filled with wonderment. I didn't know now what was different: what I was seeing, or the eyes I saw with.

I shrugged off my mood; I'd lost one girl-friend that day, I could scarcely afford to lose another. I said:

'Sure. I'll go. Where is he?'

I took the tube: I was still on expenses, but even four hundred a day couldn't compensate for an hour or more of inane prattle. I found Ian, as instructed, in British Airways' hospitality suite, attended by a ground-stewardess. She looked relieved to see me:

'You've come from the family?'

'Well, maybe. Or the firm.'

She looked almost as confused as he did, but I didn't elaborate:

'I'm a friend. I've come to take him home, OK? You want I should sign for him?'

So I led an old man, uneasy on his feet, his eyes vacant, to the taxi-rank. I sat him in the back, whispered to the driver that he was sick in order to shut him up, and put his baggage in the space next to the driver's seat. S'far as I could tell, he hadn't bought any souvenirs, nor even duty-free. I gave the Hampstead address; I didn't think it would do much for the firm's flagging morale to see him in this state, but he wasn't yet bad enough to take to the nursing home.

'What happened?' I asked gently.

He didn't answer.

'When you saw James,' I promoted: 'What happened?'

'James,' he said dully.

'Yes, James. You went to see James.' This wasn't only my educated guess; they'd confirmed where he'd come from at BA. I would have won my bet with Gauldie.

'James,' he repeated.

'You went to see your brother. Did you see him?'

'Yes. James.'

'You went to see him about your sons, didn't you?'

After a while, he said:

'I knew where he was. I've always known where he was. He was angry, but I was hurt.' I wasn't sure if he meant during the visit, or when they'd broken up all those years before. 'He didn't think of that. He didn't think about how hurt I was.'

'People don't, Mr Mather.'

I don't think he heard me.

'He's an old man; I'm an old man; we're all old, Mr, uh, Mr. . .'

'Woolf,' I supplied helpfully.

'Even John's old, now.'

I hoped he wouldn't get much older.

'Did you see him – James?'

'He wouldn't see me, Mr, uh. . .' I don't like it when people forget my name, but he wasn't people anymore. 'He sent men to me. They took me away. They took me to an airport. That's all.' There was probably a lot more, but it was all that mattered.

I waited with him in Hampstead until Ali appeared, around nine o'clock. The Italian woman made us a meal, but he wouldn't eat anything and I wasn't hungry either. Ali ate for us all and asked for a bottle of her father's wine which I helped her with. She gobbled her food, intermittently talking about an important new client she thought she could keep notwithstanding everything that had already begun to break; Martin was going to be alright – they didn't have nearly enough to convict on the murder charge, and criminal charges would probably not stick on the Clairmount either; she'd reached

Andrew – Marilyn was angry, but Andrew sanguine; Randolph was nowhere to be found.

This was an Ali I hadn't seen before. I'm not sure what I really felt. I didn't feel loving, or horny, but that was hardly surprising in the circumstances. I didn't feel sympathetic, either: she was too much in control – of him, of me, of the firm, of herself. I suppose it's sexist: I couldn't cope with her when she was so patently capable of coping with everything for herself. I must be sentimental: I expected her to be shaken by what had happened. I was; I resented that she wasn't.

I left around eleven o'clock. Initially, I planned just to go home. But in the minicab, I remembered I'd left in the office a copy of my final report. There were two reasons why it made me uncomfortable. For one thing, I wasn't sure yet who I wanted to read it; for another, I didn't know there was anyone who was going to pay my account. I told the driver to change route; he argued – I was booked to Earl's Court, and Holborn wasn't Earl's Court, he was sure of that; well, pretty sure. I told him I'd pay the full fare to Earl's Court anyway.

I stood outside Mather's, looking up at its floors all the way to mine own attic. It was a depressing sight. I pressed the night-bell: at least I'd wake up the watchman, that would be a positive achievement for the evening.

He answered quick enough to deprive me of even that gratification. I had met him before. He was not a reserve policeman. He was a rotund, unfit, elderly man appropriately entitled Ernest.

'Good evening, sir,' he touched his peaked cap, recognizing me and my right to enter at this ungodly hour, re-locking and bolting the door behind me.

As I signed in, he said:

'You're not alone, sir. Mr Randolph is in his office.'

'On his own?' I tried to sound casual but that wasn't what my heart-beat said.

'No, sir. He came in with a gentleman. He said it wasn't necessary for him to sign in,' Ernest added, pre-empting my next question. I had the impression he was glad there was someone with some sort of authority to whom he could confide his concern that the rules had not been obeyed.

'What did he look like?'

'I didn't see, sir. As I let Mr Randolph in, the other gentleman slipped past and went straight up the stairs. I didn't catch a look at him. I'm sorry, sir.'

'Not your fault. I'll go up and see him.'

I walked up the stairs, remembering the first thing they teach a policeman: don't run into trouble, walk. I was on the first floor, turning towards Randolph's office, when I saw the man. He was hooded. I had time to recognize it as a mason's hood and the weapon in his hand as Gauldie's much-prized medieval sword, now dripping with blood, before he charged me, roaring at the top of his lungs the way soldiers do to scare the enemy: he needn't've bothered; I was already scared shitless.

We went backwards together and almost toppled down the wide, main steps. Upside down, I saw Ernest's astonished expression, then heard him cry out in a classic of understatement:

'Oy, you, what do you think you're doing?'

It was distraction enough for me to fight back. I clung onto his sword-carrying arm. We reeled from side to side while Ernest clambered wheezily up to assist me. At the last moment, my assailant broke free and charged him in his turn, knocking him against, then over, the bannisters. He was at the main front door at the same moment as I rose too late to save Ernest from the fall.

He fumbled with the door, but couldn't get it open. He turned and waved the sword at me, daring me to come down the stairs. He didn't need to wave twice. He knelt down by Ernest to search him for the key. While he was distracted, I stepped backwards up the stairs until I reached the landing, and once out of his sight darted down it: if he wanted a part in the movie of the Wars Of The Roses, I did too. I grabbed from the wall opposite the vacant space where the sword had hung its sister spear. It was astonishingly heavy.

When I got back to the stairs, he was already at the

door. The key was in the lock, but he hadn't undone all the bolts. I howled:

'Stop. Stop.'

He swung angrily around, as I staggered down towards him hefting the spear in my hand. He swung the sword wildly about him, to keep me back, danced a couple of steps forward, a couple of steps back. We froze for what seemed an eternity, but was only ten or twenty seconds. He thrust at me again; I jumped back and, without thinking about it, without intending to do it, with all my strength, I flung the spear straight at him.

He screamed just the once as it drove through his chest and pinned him against the door. Blood gushed from the mouth-opening in his hood. I stared at him horrified. He stared back at me, still alive but only just. I said:

'Who? Who sent you?'

I could see his lips move but only just. He mumbled what sounded like:

'Hyram Abyss.'

Then every limb twitched the once, like a single sharp pull on a puppet, and he slumped dead, still affixed to the door.

I picked up the sword where it had fallen, and went to see how Ernest was doing:

'You alright, old chap?' I sounded more like a Mather or a mason than myself.

He didn't look alright. He couldn't speak. His eyes were yellow with pain. I muttered that I'd get help and was half-way to the telephone before I remembered Randolph. I hesitated, but I knew what I'd find and my methodical mind told me it would be preferable to be able to announce all in the one call.

The poor little bastard was still alive, though I daresay he'd rather already have died. He didn't have long to go. He'd been cut open from his throat to his waist; naked, bloody flesh hung off him like raw meat in a butcher's. His eyes, pleading, met mine, then moved slowly down to the sword in my hand, as if asking me to finish the job. I gagged back the rising vomit and clung to the side of the door, whimpering:

'Oh God, oh God, oh God.'

I couldn't stop it. Lunch, coffee, wine and what looked like a large chunk of my own guts poured out of me. From some point on the edge of life, Randolph, still conscious, watched, as incapable of speech as Ernest, but a lot closer to final relief; the last thing he would ever see was me throwing up.

I couldn't stay in the room with him. I couldn't touch him. I couldn't offer him comfort. I staggered into the next office and, for the first time in my life, rang the emergency service, gasping into the receiver that I needed police and ambulance, now now now now now.

I went back down to wait with Ernest. He had maybe a rib through a lung, one or two broken bones sticking out through his skin: nothing compared to Randolph. He was gradually achieving coherence. His hand reached out to grip mine. He wanted to say something. I leaned down so he could whisper in my ear, without breathing into his face: the state of my breath might have finished him off.

'I'm sorry, sir. I'm sorry. Tell Mr Mather, won't you?' Mr Mather meant Ian Mather.

I don't know how long we waited like that before the police arrived. Later, Dowell told me the time lapse between logged call and officer on scene was less than ten minutes. When I think about it, it still seems like it was most of my life. The officers had to ring at the bell and bang and bash at the door before I heard them.

I couldn't open it properly. I got it open maybe about an inch, but then the man's body jammed it. I was pulling and sobbing and screaming in frustration. A voice was saying:

'Take it easy, sir, take it easy.'

'There's a body, on the door. I killed him,' I whispered.

I tried extracting the spear but it wouldn't come out. In the end, the police had to ram the floor to get it to open another few inches, enough for them to squeeze through. I fell into the arms of the first one in and he half-carried me back inside, leaning me against the

226

reception desk and not letting go until he realised I wasn't actually wounded.

He was followed by other officers and an ambulance crew. I pointed to Ernest, holding onto the police officer's arm with my other hand:

'Take him first. He's alive.'

The police officer took one look around him and had already switched on his radio to call for more back-up. I said:

'First floor. Office off to the right. Another. He's probably not alive anymore. He's been cut open. I warn you. He's been cut right open. He did it,' I gestured at the body on the door.

'Take it easy now, sir. Sit down here.'

He jerked his head to one of his mates to go upstairs. The pounding in my head and chest that had begun when I arrived was beginning to slow down. I was beginning to breathe fairly normally again. I said:

'Ring the Yard. Get D.I. Dowell's home number. Get him here. It's his case. Tell him I'm here. Tell him Randolph Mather is the body upstairs.'

For once, a police officer didn't give me back-chat. He just asked:

'What's your name, sir?'

I told him, then leaned back in the chair and closed my eyes as they carried Ernest out on a stretcher. I think they had given him a shot of something, because he was completely unconscious. I envied him. As I sat there with my eyes shut, I thought: I'm going to have to tell Ali. Then I thought: I'm going to have to tell Ian. I didn't know which prospect caused me more pain.

I half expected Dowell to be angry. I don't know why: I suppose I felt guilty, responsible. I'd kept the pressure on and the pimple had popped. He wasn't angry. He ignored me when he came in and went straight upstairs to see the body. As I'd expected, Randolph had been dead before the first policeman found him. Dowell came back down, his face ashen. He went out to his car, and returned with a hip-flask. I remembered it from before, during Disraeli Chambers. He took a slug from it first, before he handed it to me:

'Go on. Deep now, Dave. Go on.'

I didn't need telling twice. It was the straight stuff. There must have been a quarter pint. I drank it all. It burned its way down insides raw from puking, but it stayed down. I grit my teeth to stop them chattering as I thrust his hip-flask back at him:

'Have you got any more?'

He nodded and threw his keys to one of the many policeman now milling about Mather's main hall:

'Car. Boot. Bottle.'

He looked at me wryly:

'I don't normally keep it in the car. But Sheila was still up when I got home.'

I smiled weakly. Sheila was his wife. Dowell was scared of her disapproval. I thought: what a wonderful life; to be able to enjoy the disapproval of a loving and loyal partner. It was the sort of sublime fantasy I needed to bring me back to reality.

'Tell me,' he ordered.

'There's a Chapter – a freemasonic Chapter. . .'

'Lodge,' he corrected wrongly.

'No, Chapter. This isn't about craft freemasonry, Tim. It's Gauldie's. It's about as old as freemasonry itself, and it's completely, utterly bent. D'you remember Jack the Ripper was supposed to be a freemason?'

'I've heard the tale,' he said dryly, not particularly eager to extend his enquiries that far back in history.

'It's the Chapter he was supposed to be a member of. They're the ones with the international links. I've been doing a lot of reading, Tim. You wanna know how many books there are on freemasonry? It doesn't matter. Ian got me the information from the freemasons. That's when it all came together.'

He pulled up a chair as the police officer arrived back with our bottle. He took a swig, then passed it to me, muttering I shouldn't finish it all too, then said:

'Go on.'

'Not much more to tell, really.' I told him where he'd find the envelope containing the final report I'd come back to collect. I outlined what he would read.

Dowell whistled:

'Gauldie? That dry old stick?'

His eyes met mine.

'You already knew, didn't you?' I accused.

'Not as much as you told me. But some of it, maybe.'

'Who's Hyram Abyss, Tim?'

He smiled thinly:

'It's possible, just possible, mind you, he said "Hiram Abiff". He was an an ancient master of the freemasons who was said to have suffered terrible tortures to try and get masonic secrets out of him, but who died rather than reveal them.'

'Oh, yeah, you really did know all along.'

He said:

'I'm going to have to take you down to the station, Dave. You understand that, don't you?'

'What about Gauldie? You've got to arrest him.'

'What for? I've no evidence yet; maybe after we've identified the door handle.'

'Ali. Ian. Who's going to tell them?'

'Sorry, Dave. I've got to take you in now.'

I was at Holborn Police Station for the rest of the night and much of the day. I wasn't charged; just assisting the police with their enquiries. A doctor examined me, and gave me a pill. They fed me: Martin was right; it was pig-swill. In the afternoon, I asked if I could see him. Dowell said:

'I don't think so, Dave. He's still got a murder charge to answer.' He'd let me the day before, though; or was it two days ago?

'Haven't you read my report, for God's sake?'

'It's not up to me; most of what it contains is guesswork or opinion.'

'What about Kelly and Galucci? Did you pick them up?'

'Ah,' he sighed: 'It seems they flew away. To Switzerland.'

'Extradite 'em,' I protested. He could bring them back on the Clairmount charge, but what I wanted them for was to give the evidence that indicted James Mather on Wainwright, and cleared Martin.

'Sorry, Dave, can't do it.'

'Why not? They'll talk.'

'I don't think they will, sunshine,' he said sardonically. I got the message. 'Car crash, as they left the airport. That fast, mate, that quick. These people have got – what shall we call them? – branch offices? – all over the world.'

'Which people,' I asked bitterly: 'Masons or James Mather?'

'Your version is Mather did Pankhurst and Wainwright. . .'

'But not Randolph. Randolph's his nephew. Can't you see, especially now, he only hits the ones around the family, not the family themselves? Have you identified. . .?' I couldn't bring myself to say who I meant, but he knew.

He coughed apologetically:

'Wainwright, Stephen Wainwright.'

'He's a mason, he was wearing a mason's hood, he said Hiram Abiff,' I said urgently, trying to reinforce my case at the same time as I realized how stupid it sounded: 'That proves it.'

'He's the brother of the second dead man; Randolph was potentially in the frame, and anyway the brother of the man we'd arrested for it. Revenge. That's all. What does it prove if he dressed in a bit of masonic regalia at the end; what does it prove if he mentioned – if, mind you, I'm not saying he did, – if he mentioned a famous old mason at the last moment of his life? He would have been deranged by then.'

'What was your commission, Tim? Keep the masons out of it?'

He didn't deny it. He said:

'I told you if you brought me proof, I'd follow it down. But the proof's lying in the morgue, isn't it? Where you put it.'

I licked my lips. He poked his head out of the door and asked someone to bring me some more tea. I said:

'Are you going to proceed against Martin on the Clairmount?'

'No, not with the other two dead. Matheson will lose his licence. We can't prove complicity by Martin. It would've been a bit more difficult for him if the others were still alive to deny it, but now they're dead, he can lay it off on them too easily to be worth the trouble. It wouldn't've been that serious a charge, anyway.'

'But you want to go ahead on the murder?'

'Want to? No. But we've already charged him for it, there's no new evidence and that means it's got to be left up to the courts now.'

On the table between us lay a pad, onto which my formal statement had been recorded. I said:

'I've got something to add, Tim.'

'What?'

'Randolph was still alive when I saw him. I asked him, he told me he'd set Wainwright up.'

'You're lying, Dave. You would've told me before.'

'I had a shock, Tim; and these drugs they've given me, know what I mean?'

'You really gonna do it, Dave? You gonna stick by it?'

I nodded.

'What else did Randolph tell you? Did he tell you he did it for the freemasons, maybe? Or for his uncle? Did he tell you what he'd like for dinner when he arrives at the Pearly Gate?'

I thought about my answer. If I said freemasons, it was too easy to undermine; a lot of pain for no great gain. If I said James, he'd hit me before I hit the street. I said:

'That was all; just that.'

Pratt brought in a paper cup of tea. Dowell took it from the tray. Without any warning, he flung it in my face. It wasn't hot enough to burn, just enough to hurt and humiliate. The tranquiliser helped. I wiped some of it off my face with my fingers, and licked them dry, wetting my lips. Dowell said:

'Bring him a towel, for God's sake, Pratt. Can't you see the man's wet? Then take his further statement and let him go.' I wasn't going to be charged: I never was; the last thing that would have suited to keep the masons out of it was to give me a public platform to tell my tale from.

When he was at the door, I said to Dowell:

'You played me for a fool, Tim. It won't be easy to forget.'

He shrugged:

'We're all fools someone else is playing, Dave. I tried to warn you, enough so's you'd understand, not so much you wouldn't do what you were supposed to. We're just there to sweep up after the party's over, Dave. We can't either of us control what happens. Haven't you learned anything, Dave?'

'Sometimes you can try, Tim, sometimes you got to try.'

'Right,' he mocked: 'A man's got to do what a man's got to do. Shove it, sunshine. Grow up, Dave.' Just like Sandy had said.

I went straight from the police station to Central Towers. The security men wouldn't let me go up at first, but after I'd made enough of a fuss they called someone to tell himself himself I was there. I was escorted upstairs and given a more thorough frisk than the last time. I was shown in. He already had his overcoat on. He said:

'I have to leave in one minute, Mr Woolf.'

'Going abroad? Business?'

'Right.'

I said in a monotone:

'So I'll say what I have to say.' I paused one last time to get the words into the right order: 'He'll want to know who to blame. He'll want a name. You'll give him a name. If you don't, I'll whistle every tune I know about you until I find someone you don't own who's prepared to broadcast the whole damned opera.'

'What name?' He asked in a tone as flat as my own.

'John Gauldie. I'll know whether you've done as I asked, won't I?'

'I should think so.'

My last place of call was Mather's, where I expected to find Allison, as I did, settling into her father's old office. He wouldn't be back.

'Does it feel good, Ali?'

She had the grace to blush:

'Someone has to carry on, Dave.'

'I should think you'll be a bit busy for a while, won't you, Ali? Probably won't have time for – er – an old friend?'

'I could use a good solicitor, though,' she tacitly confirmed she had no other use for me.

'Forget it. You've got Martin. I should think he'll be grateful enough still to have a career to come to work for his little sister. Tell me something, though?'

'Go on,' she said tersely.

I was only going to get the one shot: 'How much of it did you know in advance? Just how bad did you expect it to be? How much damage were you prepared to do so you could get your hands on the firm? How much of it did you actually plan when you cracked the surface by leaking the LCP report, the way everyone else was leaking to serve their own interests? That was clever, taking me to see your mother: I really bought it, didn't I?'

I didn't expect an answer. And that's the one I got. I walked out before I was asked to leave. I didn't ask if she'd enjoyed playing me too for a patsy, or how much of our love-making had been acting. I didn't ask if she'd've sneaked out of my bed while I was asleep, to read my notes, if Dowell hadn't conveniently summoned me into the office the night Wainwright died and let her read them at her leisure. I didn't even ask if she was going to pay my bill.

I took one last taxi home. The driver said:

'You look tired, mate. Been hard at work?'

'You might say.'

'What do you do, then?'

This was advanced cab psychology. Most people pay more for the pleasure of talking about themselves. I said:

'I look into things for people with problems.' Not very well, of course; sometimes, they had more problems at the end than they started with. I rephrased it: 'I'm the one they call in to iron out all the loose ends.' At least that was something I wasn't bad at; that and mixed metaphors.

SOURCES

Among the sources I have used in this book are:

Darkness Visible, Walton Hannah, Britons (1970 ed.).
The Brotherhood, Stephen Knight, Panther (1985 ed.).
The Craft, John Hamill, Crucible (1986).*
Report to London Borough of Hackney, Andrew Arden, L.B.Hackney (1987).**

*John Hamill is the Librarian and Curator of the United Grand Lodge of England.
**Andrew Arden is an English barrister who was commissioned by Hackney Council to enquire into freemasonry within the authority. The account on pp.179–181 is a fair adaptation of how I acquired my copy of his report; in acknowledgement of the Chief Executive's courtesy and assistance, I ought to emphasize that copies are usually only made available by post.

Bernard Bannerman. August 1988.